Boys Like Kevin

A Coming-of-Age Novel

D.J. Ciccarello

BOYS LIKE KEVIN: A Coming-of-Age Novel

Copyright © 2025 by D.J. Ciccarello

Revised Version © 2025

Disclaimer: This edition contains revisions to the original text published in 2024. Changes include reordering chapters, minor textual updates, or editorial adjustments. While the core story remains unchanged, these revisions aim to enhance the reader's experience.

ISBN: 979-8-9898435-0-3 (E-Book)

ISBN: 979-8-9898435-1-0 (Paperback)

ISBN: 979-8-9898435-5-8 (Hardcover)

Library of Congress Control Number: 2024900725

For more information contact: https://www.djciccarello.com

Editing by Kristin McTiernan
Cover design by Bookcoversonline.com
Formatting by The Nonsense-Free Editor

Published by D.J. Ciccarello
Atlanta, GA 30328

Also by D.J. Ciccarello

Boys Like Kevin

The Lucky Chip

No Time for Duplicity

CONTENT WARNING

Boys Like Kevin is a coming-of-age story that includes realistic, consensual sexual encounters as part of the character's development. It also contains one brief depiction of nonconsensual sexual assault in Chapter 23. While the scene is not graphic and avoids explicit language, it may be distressing for some readers. Sensitive readers may wish to use discretion around Chapter 23.

To my mother, for her self-sacrifices and life-long encouragement.

"There is always one moment in childhood when the door opens and lets the future in."

— *Graham Green*

PROLOGUE

The 1960s was a turbulent and transformative decade where tradition and progress collided. It was a time when rockets pierced the sky, and societal boundaries were tested. The Space Race, the Civil Rights Movement, and the war in Vietnam unfolded against a backdrop of countercultural revolutions and iconic music that played like an anthem to change.

In 1961, as John F. Kennedy called for a man on the moon and the Berlin Wall rose to divide Europe, Kevin Summers was born into a Florida suburb that mirrored the era's paradox of stability and upheaval. At first glance, his world was one of polished terrazzo floors reflecting the glow of the family's black-and-white television and the shine of the aluminum Christmas tree. But beneath the surface of that suburban calm, the seeds of Kevin's own story—one marked by internal rebellions and a search for authenticity—were already being planted.

As the decade unfolded, Kevin's early years were marked by the shadow of monumental events: the Cuban Missile Crisis, Martin Luther King Jr.'s dream at the Lincoln Memorial, and man's first steps on the moon. Like most boys of his generation, he imagined himself as a hero—whether as an astronaut exploring the stars or a cowboy taming the wild frontier.

While the world outside rumbled with civil rights marches and anti-war protests, Kevin found solace beneath the sprawling branches of the Ear Tree. He fashioned spaceships from cardboard and imagined himself floating weightless among the stars, charting a course through galaxies far from the unrest of Selma and the tragedy of Kent State.

But childhood innocence could not last forever. The Hippie movement, anti-war protests, and the dawning of the Age of Aquarius signaled a world shedding its old skin. As the 1960s closed with Woodstock's muddy fields and Neil Armstrong's footprints on the moon, the 1970s ushered in a new era of self-discovery and individualism. It was a decade where Kevin's childhood dreams gave way to the complexities of adolescence, where the world around him shifted from the idealism of protest songs to the introspective beat of the "Me Decade" that would define Kevin's path in his coming-of-age years.

The story that follows is not just about a boy growing up in a world on fire but about the quiet ways in which the flames left their mark. It is a story of finding identity in the smoke of expectation and embers of doubt. It is a story about boys like Kevin.

1

Racing Toward the Past

(Fall, 1982)

Pulling the driver's door closed, echoes of other doors resounded in Kevin's mind, slamming shut one after another in rapid succession. He turned the key, and the car idled, a low hum beneath the chaos of his thoughts. It patiently awaited his decision as he considered the dire consequences of moving forward. He had already come so far and lost so much in such a short time. Kevin's young life teetered on the edge of ruin or renewal—only his courage now would determine which.

He stared through the windshield, past the manicured lawn of his childhood home, to the spot where the Ear Tree once stood. The absence of its familiar silhouette against the sky was as haunting as the past choices he couldn't take back. He could almost hear the whispers of his younger self beneath its branches, his memory of it clear and comforting.

The car remained in its steady idle. Kevin could see his parents, Bert and Carol Summers, still sitting on the sofa in the living room where he had delivered the news just minutes earlier—frozen in that moment of surprise seeing him back in town. It wasn't his intent to break the news without warning or without staying to discuss it, but better now, before they heard it from someone else.

There would be time to go into details later. Kevin was too tired and unsettled to discuss the particulars now—he needed time to transition from escape to refuge mode.

Just seconds passed, though they felt like hours. Kevin recalled the anguish of last night's fight with Maritza and the clarity that bloomed from panic when he decided this morning. Once he knew what to do, there had been no turning back—it was go-time. The small car had little room, so his time there was brief. It took just thirty minutes to pack a few belongings. There was an urgency in his moving quickly while everyone was at work and the house was empty. Maritza was also gone, which suited him fine—the last thing Kevin needed was another scene with her, especially if it allowed time for the others to return home to derail his getaway.

The drive back to his hometown had taken precisely five hours, including a ten-minute stop for gas and another twenty minutes spent on the shoulder of the road—breathing through the ache in his chest—reexamining what had happened and what he was about to do. Twenty minutes is a long time to be punched in the gut by a gang of emotions. After the cross-state drive, Kevin spent another thirty minutes parked a few blocks from his boyhood home, searching for the exact words to explain to his parents what had happened. It had been almost six hours between his decision and his flight to freedom. Six hours is an eternity when blowing one's entire world apart.

He drew a deep breath, the kind that reached down into the empty spaces inside him, shifting the car into reverse suddenly and deliberately. As he backed out of his parent's driveway, he cast one last glance toward the ghost of the Ear Tree. As a boy, it represented perfection and freedom. From its void now, all Kevin sensed was failure and fear. It was just a reminder that some things, once lost, can never be found again.

2

COFFEE AND CLICHÉS

Kevin knocked on the door, the sound dull against the thick wood. He saw his aunt Alice pacing the small living room through the window as she waved him in.

"It's unlocked," she yelled as he stepped inside. "Okay, talk later. Bye," she said into the phone, her voice sharpening as she hung up. "That was your mother, jeez Christ."

"I was just there two minutes ago," Kevin replied. "She's on the phone to you already?"

"You know how she is. Come here and hug your auntie." She approached with outstretched arms and a lit cigarette between her index and middle finger.

Alice was only ten years older than Kevin, and he viewed her more as an older sister than his aunt. She was the first and only phone call he made that morning, hoping she would give him refuge without question or judgment. "Come on, honey, I got a place for you here," she told him without hesitation when they spoke.

In Kevin's mind, moving back under his parents' roof, even if temporary, was not an option. The little cash in his pocket left him with few other choices. Although Alice and his parents lived only ten blocks from one another, it was worlds away, and he felt he could breathe and retain what little dignity was left if he stayed with her.

"What's going on with you? You want some coffee?" she asked. Turning toward the kitchen without waiting for his response, she added, "Come in here and sit down while I make a fresh pot. You look like crap."

"Well, it's nice to see you, too."

For as long as Kevin remembered, Alice had a cigarette burning and a half-cup of coffee getting cold somewhere in the house. The caffeine never bothered her, though. She was usually asleep on the sofa by 9:30 PM, the television's volume turned up and its glow illuminating the otherwise dark living room. The woman could sleep through an earthquake if Florida had any.

"So quit stalling and tell me what happened. Remember, I've been married twice, so don't piss on my leg and tell me it's raining." Alice's voice bellowed around the kitchen wall as the Mr. Coffee machine spit and spewed hot caffeinated water into the carafe.

Kevin surveyed the living room furnishings to see what was new or changed and found nothing. Everything was as he remembered from his last visit two years ago. The lack of change was comforting.

"Come in here and make your coffee. There's half-and-half and sugar, but don't expect any of that sweetener crap."

Oh, the irony, he thought, avoiding cancer from Sweet'n'Low but still smoking.

"So, how long is this going to last?"

"I don't know. How long are you going to keep smoking?" Kevin replied.

"Hey, screw you, buddy," she retorted, pointing her cigarette-holding fingers toward his face. "You're in the door two seconds and already trying to change me," she chuckled. "I need a man telling me what to do like a fish needs a bicycle."

Alice loved her clichés. She had more of them than the best screenwriters and playwrights in Hollywood. Kevin had no idea where she got them all or how she summoned them so quickly to use during conversations. Those clichés, along with cigarettes and coffee, were the foundation of any meaningful discussion for his aunt.

"So, what did your mother have to say?" she asked, taking her seat as he took his across from her at the small dinette table pushed against the wall, separating the kitchen from the living room.

"Not much," he replied. "I gave them the headlines and told them I was coming here. That's it."

"Them? So, your father was home? What did he have to say?"

"Not much," Kevin replied. "He was sorry to hear about it and was sure everything would work out."

Alice inhaled deeply before pursing her lips, sending a stream of smoke upward through the corner of her mouth and away from his face. "Well, that's as useful as tits on a bull," she replied. "And your mother? Tell me again what she said?"

"She started to ask questions and wanted to go into details, but I cut it short. I told them I wanted to get here before dark to get settled and that I was tired."

Kevin wondered if his aunt would now take the role of interrogator instead of his mother. He speculated on how much detail he would need to go into. He hoped his hints would show he was not up to discussing particulars, at least not right now. All Kevin wanted to do was hide somewhere and lick his wounds.

Still, the owner of the inn providing refuge from the storm deserves to have some questions answered by the wet and weary traveler.

"That's alright," she said. "I'm sure she'll call tomorrow, trying to squeeze the story out of me. I'll let you jump that fence when you get to it."

"That's fine," Kevin replied. "She's just worried; she worries about everything."

Alice twisted and crushed the remains of her cigarette in the ashtray while exhaling the smoke. "Well, it's good that you didn't get her pregnant. Or did you?"

"Hell no!" he snapped back. "If Maritza is, it's not by me." Kevin couldn't remember the last time they had real sex, at least with one another.

"Well, call me shocked then because I figured it was a shotgun wedding. It surprised the hell out of me when there was no bun popping out of the oven six months after the wedding."

Kevin cupped the warm coffee mug between his palms, letting the heat seep into his fingers. His foot tapped rhythmically against the linoleum floor, a soft, uneven beat beneath the drone of the coffee maker. The bitterness of the coffee matched the tightness in his throat—each sip a distraction from the words piling up inside him.

"Why would you say that?" he asked, his leg shaking faster and harder as the caffeine kicked in and the interrogation continued.

"Are you kidding me?" she said. "Well, let's see. You meet the girl, and suddenly, your head is all up her ass. Don't get me wrong, she's pretty, but honey, the lights are on, but there's no one home." Without a cigarette, Alice was using her fingers to count her list of answers to Kevin's previous question. "Then you quit school, up and move down there, and the next thing we know, you want to marry her. You hardly knew her. And we sure didn't."

Five fingers, by his count.

"Give me a F'ing break," she continued. Alice often used 'F'ing,' emphasizing the capital 'F' instead of saying the word outright, as everyone else did.

Kevin stared at her like a dog smacked between the eyes with a rolled-up newspaper, expecting another whack but hoping it didn't come. "I moved because I got promoted, okay? And yes, I admit I was lonely there, but we got married because we—."

"Oh, come on, don't blow smoke up my ass," she interrupted. "You were barely eighteen, for Pete's sake, and what was she, seventeen, if that? What do you know about love? You were just tired of driving back and forth every time your dick got hard. You got married too young, that's all. You made a mistake, no big deal." The truth usually stings, and Alice was never one to hold back opinions on any subject. Her courage and freedom to live as she pleased and with no one's permission or endorsement were traits he admired and envied about her.

Kevin corrected her. "She had turned eighteen the month before. She wasn't seventeen."

"Seventeen. Eighteen. Who gives a shit? It's all the same. Both still babies."

"Okay, sure. You're right, hindsight being perfect and all," Kevin replied. His surrendered voice sounded like the rolled-up newspaper landing smack number two.

Alice stood and walked around the table, hugging him from behind the chair. "Don't get your panties in a wad, okay?" She told him in a consoling tone. "I'm only yanking your chain."

Walking back to Mr. Coffee and pouring herself another cup, she added, "You've always been too serious. You need to loosen up and relax, or you'll end up like your mother, squeezing diamonds out of your ass from the internal pressure. Life isn't perfect. It's a bitch, okay? So get over it, figure yourself out, and move on. Get real!"

'Get real,' repeating the words in his head. So easy to say. While Alice poured her coffee, Kevin moved from the dinette table to the living room, asking, "Which side do you normally sit on?"

"The left is my side to watch TV. You can have the right. So, what happened?" she asked again.

Kevin paused, staring straight ahead at the silent and dark gray screen. It surprised him that the television was not on and playing in the background. The cushion was soft and comforting when he leaned back into it, staring up to study the ceiling while searching for the right words and appropriate level of detail. He pondered whether to start at the beginning and work his way forward or tell her what happened last night and work his way to the start of their issues.

"Here's the abridged version," Kevin finally said, fully acknowledging that he hated abridgments and lived wholly in the details. He told her about the car, the employment issues and debt, and finally, about Miritza's parents following them down to South Florida to live. Kevin rearranged himself in the sofa's corner, settling into a more comfortable position to face her. He explained how they finally had to move in with them.

"Yeah. Your mother told me they followed you guys down and that you all lived together."

"Well, here's the best part," Kevin continued. "Her sister Gabriela moves down with them and brings her new boyfriend Jimmy along for their fresh new start, too."

"Are you shitting me?" Alice asked, leaning forward to reach for a new cigarette and her lighter on the coffee table. "So now three couples are living together in the same house? Well, that's a recipe for disaster."

"Right," he replied. The floodgates opened, and there was no stopping now, so Kevin continued.

"Can you believe it?" she added in long, drawn-out pronunciation of each word. "I mean, you can't make this crap up!"

Alice just shook her head from side to side. "So, what happened yesterday to make you leave?"

It was time for the final can-you-believe-it round. Kevin felt his blinking become rapid as he crossed his arms. He drew a deep breath, then a few more, steadying himself, trying to keep his emotions under control while pondering what, and what not, to say next.

"So…," he said, his lips beginning to quiver. *Hold steady. Control it.* He drew another deep breath. The tears swelled as his vision blurred—he thought the words themselves might choke him as they piled up in his throat like a high-speed automobile accident on the rain-soaked interstate during a sudden summer deluge.

"It just came to a head last night when we fought about it all," Kevin finally replied. He couldn't tell her everything that happened or the real reason he knew this morning there was no choice but to leave. The emotional and physical pain of the rest of the story was still too fresh to divulge and discuss. Perhaps if he told her everything, it would make more sense. He couldn't, however, not now.

Alice's newly lit cigarette burned in an ash column between her fingers as she shook her head from side to side in disbelief. She felt his pain and waited for him, reserving comment or judgment, letting him know she was there to listen.

"So," he continued, drawing strength from another deep breath of humility and weakness. "If it's okay with you, I need a place to stay until I figure out what to do next." His voice quivered. "I sure as hell am not returning to that dysfunctional family." Kevin was unaccustomed to asking other people for anything or relying on anyone for help. It was a tough swallow of pride when he had so little of it left.

"So, you're choosing your family's dysfunction over theirs? Good luck with that!" Alice replied, adding a little levity to the moment's seriousness. They glanced at one another with a half-grin-half-frown and a 'what now' expression. While relieved to get that off his chest, he had not told her everything.

"You know you can stay as long as you want. I need some help around here, anyway."

Kevin looked around the room and over his shoulders, replying, "Well, that's obvious."

"Yeah, well, screw you too, buddy. You can have this room," tapping her knuckles on the wall directly behind the sofa where they sat. "You have to fix the toilet in there first, though. The water runs all the time."

"Great. I'm in the door thirty minutes and already have chores. I thought you said you didn't need a man around here?"

"I said I didn't need a man telling me what to do, asshole. A man's home may be his castle, but honey, you're living in my castle now, so just fix the damn toilet. I'm going to bed. You should, too."

"Yes, mam," he answered with a salute. Kevin was grateful for his aunt's generosity and looked forward to his first peaceful night of sleep in a week.

Alice always was Kevin's Auntie Mame—or at least the 1958 Rosalind Russell movie version of her. While not the Manhattan socialite or as flamboyant as Mame in the movie, Alice had as much spunk, determination, and influence on him as Mame had on her orphaned nephew, Patrick. He was now her unofficial ward, and Alice was his inspiration for freedom. Although they were sisters by the same mother, Alice was as carefree as his mother was anxious. Alice worked and relaxed at her own pace, without regard for or being influenced by the opinions of others. Like Auntie Mame, she projected fearlessness and independence.

It didn't take long for Kevin to unpack his car and get settled. The room had a small closet to hang the few clothes he had brought and some space for his sleeping bag on the floor in one corner. He had grabbed an odd mix of items for his flight to freedom: a self-assembled half-wall bookshelf, a few books and sketch pads from high school, a radio, a soccer ball, a fishing pole and tackle box, a diver's knife, and a few boxes of personal effects. They were trinkets and other items his parents and grandparents gifted him that carried special meaning. He collected them in haste that morning and was sure he had forgotten as many or more items of significance during the getaway. Kevin would have time to reconcile the gains and losses during the terms of surrender with Maritza in the days and weeks to come. For now, though, these few possessions were all he needed.

Kevin felt relieved to be back in the land of his boyhood once he put his things away and laid his head on the borrowed pillow in the stillness of the room's calm and darkness. The smell of the house and the pressure in the air were familiar, and he stared at the ceiling as if it were a movie screen projecting flashes and images from his childhood. Kevin recalled bits of happy suburban boyhood in the 1960s, blessed with love and security. He remembered riding his bicycle, climbing trees with his friends, and playing ball in the front yard with blades of lush green grass cushioning his bare feet. Those childhood recollections flowed into the awkwardness and curiosity of adolescence, where the seeds of authenticity failed to take root. Adolescence is seldom ideal. Failure quickly stripped away the façade of who he thought he was supposed to be and exposed the vulnerabilities he had worked so hard to conceal over the years. His secret was a hungry beast. The more he fed it, the larger and more powerful it grew.

The quiet in the room was deafening, with the sounds of his heartbeat racing faster in conjunction with the memories as they advanced. The images on the ceiling were now just one day old. Kevin had not slept since that panicked and painful incident before returning home from work—before his final confrontation with Maritza. Its physical and emotional marks were still fresh, deep, and painful.

The images on the ceiling eventually slowed as exhaustion set in. Kevin was safe for now, but he knew he would need to confront the beast before it consumed him completely. He would have to tell the truth, but he would first need to determine what that truth was. The rest of his life depended on it.

Once the images slowed and Kevin's heartbeat calmed, he fell into a long and deep sleep, and that was when he revisited the beginning.

3

THE BEE HUNTS

(Summer, 1968)

Th   he tree was a giant, its canopy spanning above half of
        Kevin's house on one side and into the neighbor's yard
        on the other. His parents called it an Ear Tree, named
after the brown and ebony ear-shaped seed pods it began
dropping each summer. A native of tropical regions and the
national tree of Costa Rica, it had an expansive and spherical
crown, valued for its ability to grow quickly in Florida's sandy soil
and hot temperatures.

The Ear Tree's seed pods were as hard as stones and durable.
By grasping the fallen pods with a thumb on top, index finger
along the edge, and remaining three fingers underneath, they
became formidable airborne weapons when thrown sidearmed.
Those hard spinning projectiles filled the suburban sky,
silhouetted against the setting sun in the evenings, as they flew
opposite directions across enemy lines during the skirmishes the
neighborhood boys waged in their great pod wars.

The Ear Tree was more than a source of ammunition,
however. Its massive trunk split in two directions about five feet
off the ground, providing Kevin with a saddle and a sturdy horse's
neck. With an old rope he found in Bert's shed to use as reins,

Kevin rode the imaginary steed for hours, chasing and being chased by Indians on the open plains of the wild West.

Spanning upward, his companion was a tree climber's delight. Its thick green foliage gave him a camouflaged perch, a vantage point high above the rest of the world where Kevin pretended to be a ship's lookout or a neighborhood sniper fighting in the war. The tree's leaves also transformed into billowing sails, powering the dreaded pirate ship Kevin captained when playing on the ground under the tree's cool shade. When turned upside down, Kevin's bicycle became the ship's helm as he captained and steered the mighty vessel with the front tire. The chain-driven back wheel served as extra motor power, aided by a playing card clicking against each spoke as he hand-cranked the pedals faster and faster and faster until the bike bucked upward in revolt.

"We're hit!" Kevin would announce to his imaginary crew. "Damage report!" he commanded. Sometimes, Kevin had to grab the wheel to turn the ship hard to port to avoid the rocky jetty ahead. At other times, the maneuver was hard to starboard to turn the ship into the wind to position themselves advantageously for the next round of broadside barrages against their attacking enemies. As the breeze shifted and filled their sails, the vessel gained speed until it either caught their adversaries and destroyed them or outran the blockade placed at the harbor's mouth to entrap them. Either way, Kevin's mighty tree ship and crew were always victorious. The Ear Tree was Kevin's best friend as a child. He could do anything within and beneath its protection.

When Kevin was not chasing Indians on the open plains or captaining his mighty sailing ship, he caught bees in the front yard. God, how Kevin loved the bee hunts. When the days were long, and the grass was tall, clover patches assaulted his front yard each summer. The clover's white rounded flowers shot up from their leafed base, balanced atop their two-inch solid stems. They looked like small dandelions or miniature bursts of white fireworks above a forest of green grass, and they were a magnet to the bees collecting the clover's nurturing pollen.

Bee hunting was its best during the late afternoon when the sun was large and dark orange sitting low on the horizon. Kevin moved from one patch of clover to another, systematically combing the front yard with a washed and de-labeled mayonnaise jar in one hand and its lid in the other, catching the bees by slowly bringing the jar and lid together. As the bee sat atop the clover's flower, the lid severed the clover's stem in half, with bees and flowers falling into the glass container. The jar had air holes, of course, which he had punched through the metal lid with a screwdriver he borrowed from his father's toolbox without permission.

Occasionally, one of his prey would fly off of the clover as the two hands of entrapment closed, resulting in the angry bee landing on the back of Kevin's hand and stinging him. When it happened, Kevin would shake his wounded hand wildly, like a rodeo bull trying to throw his rider, the jar falling to the ground, allowing the other captured bees to escape. Kevin would have let them all go eventually, but it was principle and not the sting that frustrated him. He had caught them—therefore, he should have control over their release. Kevin liked to be in control, even at this young age. But he was still a small boy and had not yet learned the complete meaning of control or the peril in its pursuit.

4

THE CHANGING WORLD

(Summer, 1969)

Kevin sat inches from the television, his breath fogging the glass as the grainy image of the lunar module appeared. The darkened room seemed to hold its breath along with him, the only light the flickering glow of the screen. When Neil Armstrong's boot met the moon's dusty surface, Kevin's fingers dug into the long green fibers of the living room's area rug. The shag carpet anchored him to the earth while his imagination soared into space.

Nothing grabbed Kevin's attention more than the U.S. space program. His interest grew with each mission as he became obsessed with space and space travel, consuming anything related to astronomy, spacecraft, space-themed books, television shows, and movies. He built model kits of actual and fictitious spacecraft. After completing the available model kits on the market, he built and launched rocket designs of his own.

Kevin's bicycle and the family automobile were transformed into an Apollo capsule, the Starship Enterprise, or Jupiter 2 spacecraft, whisking him through space and time. Outside, the swing set in his backyard became a launchpad. He and his friends tied ropes around their waists, hanging from the great Ear Tree to sway like astronauts in zero gravity. Cardboard boxes became command modules, scrawled with NASA logos in crayons and black magic markers. His backyard became the moon's surface, the worn path between the swing set and the Ear Tree a makeshift launch pad.

The Apollo 11 mission wasn't just a broadcast but a doorway to another world. Kevin watched in awe as Buzz Aldrin piloted the lunar module Eagle to its landing in the Sea of Tranquility. Less than five hours later, Neil Armstrong jumped off the Eagle's ladder and became the first human to step on the lunar surface. His words echoed through the room: "One small step for man, one giant leap for mankind." Kevin repeated the phrase under his breath, committing it to memory as if it were a secret code.

The astronauts spent just twenty-one hours on the surface. They took photographs and collected rocks and soil samples before lifting off and rejoining the command module Columbia for their trip back to Earth. The event declared U.S. victory in the space race and fulfilled John F. Kennedy's national goal, set one month after Kevin's birth, to put a man on the moon and return him safely to Earth before the decade was out. Astronauts were the greatest heroes of that time—Kevin and his neighborhood friends built entire worlds from cardboard and clouds to emulate them.

Kevin's fascination was not just play—it was purpose. He saw himself as a future astronaut, mapping out constellations on his bedroom ceiling with glow-in-the-dark stars. He read all the library books he could find, every page a stepping stone to a distant planet. His dreams stretched as wide as the Milky Way, a constellation of hopes against the dark unknown.

That summer, however, wasn't just about astronauts and moon dust. The television also showed scenes from a very different gathering—a sea of muddy, dancing bodies at Woodstock. On a rain-soaked and muddy dairy farm in New York, a music festival promoted as "three days of peace & music" became a pivotal moment in popular culture. Almost half a million people attended, and the images of the festival were as foreign to him as the moon's dark side: faces painted, hair wild, bodies swaying to music that Kevin's parents didn't play at home.

His father would sit back, arms crossed, shaking his head at the television. "What kind of future is this?" Bert would mutter while Carol remained quiet, her expression unreadable. The screen flickered with scenes of tie-dye shirts and muddy feet, of musicians lost in their own world, strumming guitars as if the world outside didn't exist.

The country was transitioning from the Swinging Sixties into the Me Generation of the 1970s. The world around Kevin was shifting between the structured order of a space mission and the chaotic freedom of Woodstock. As a young boy, he couldn't yet appreciate the full weight of those changes, yet he felt the pull of two worlds—the promise of the stars and the tangled reality of Earth below. While his father saw the chaos of Woodstock as a warning, Kevin saw it as a mystery—a puzzle of a world he wasn't ready to understand but couldn't help but watch.

~

Just days after his birthday, Kevin joined the world to watch the launch of Apollo 13, the third mission to the moon. Two days after launch and nearly halfway to the moon, an oxygen tank exploded, depleting most of the spacecraft's oxygen and causing a loss of water, electricity, and propulsion. The crew had to abandon the command module *Odyssey* and reconfigure the lunar module *Aquarius* as a lifeboat. They rationed supplies and power.

After careful manual calculations, they changed their flight plan for a swing around the moon and return to Earth.

Kevin and his classmates gathered in the school's cafeteria each day to watch news coverage of the event as it unfolded. The world stopped and watched along with them, praying for the crew.

"Do you think they'll make it back?" a boy beside him whispered, the broadcast showing the drifting module against the black void of space.

"They have to," Kevin replied, his eyes never leaving the screen.

The cafeteria erupted in cheers five days later when the white capsule finally splashed into the Pacific. Kevin felt a swell of pride, a lightness in his chest like he was the one returning home safely. The mission would later be called NASA's most successful failure, a lesson in finding victory among wreckage—one he would understand all too well in the years ahead.

But the pride and relief of Apollo 13 soon gave way to something darker. Three weeks later, Kevin played on the living room floor with his plastic soldiers strewn around him in mid-battle. The television flickered with news footage of Kent State—gray smoke curling through the campus, students running, bodies crumpled on the ground.

His father sat stiffly in his chair, knuckles white against the armrests. "That's what happens when you cross the line," Bert commented, his voice low and tight. "Maybe they'll think twice before throwing rocks at soldiers."

Kevin glanced up to the screen, where a young woman knelt over a body, her mouth open in a scream that the speakers could not catch. "Why are they fighting, Dad?" he asked.

"Because they don't know their place, son," he answered.

"They think they can change the world by shouting. But the world doesn't work that way."

Kevin nodded, but his chest felt heavy. He looked down at his soldiers, their plastic rifles aimed everywhere. In his games, the good guys always won. The astronauts always made it home. But the images on the screen told a different story—one where smoke and bullets filled the air, and not everyone got to walk away.

Outside, the wind rustled through the branches of the Ear Tree. Kevin closed his eyes, wishing he could climb into its cool shade, where the world was make-believe, and the only battles he fought ended with his mother calling him in for dinner.

Kevin was a boy of rules and order, a Cub Scout with a perfectly pressed uniform, the son of a military veteran and firefighter who lived by discipline and duty. His world was neatly divided into good guys and bad guys—heroes wore badges or space suits, and villains hid in jungles or behind protest signs. Under the cool shade of the Ear Tree, he practiced being the cowboy lawman, delivering swift justice to imaginary outlaws. On his hard terrazzo floor, his plastic army men stood at attention, ready to defend their little world from threats he couldn't quite understand. How could he ever side with the wild-eyed students on the television, the ones who threw rocks at soldiers or burned their own country's flag? In his young mind, chaos had no place in the universe—not in the disciplined halls of his Catholic school, not on the moon, and certainly not in his own backyard.

~

Kevin sat cross-legged on the terrazzo floor where he had been setting up his army men, but now his eyes were fixed on the television screen. The images flashed in bursts—crowds of people marching down city streets, signs waving above their heads, and chants that echoed even through the tiny speakers of the old Zenith set. His young fingers twisted the edge of his T-shirt with a mix of curiosity and confusion.

"Mom, why are those people protesting?" Kevin asked, glancing over his shoulder at his mother, who sat on the sofa behind him.

Carol leaned forward, resting her elbows on her knees. "They're marching for their rights, honey. They want to be treated fairly, like everyone else."

"What kind of rights?" he pressed, his voice small but insistent.

"They want the same rights as everyone else—to work, to live where they want, to love who they want," she explained gently, choosing her words carefully.

Bert, who sat in his recliner with a newspaper spread across his lap, grunted softly. "Kevin, go play outside. You don't need to watch this."

"But, Dad—"

"No buts. This isn't for kids." Bert rustled the newspaper, a not-so-subtle hint that the conversation was over.

Kevin hesitated, his eyes darting between the screen and his parents. The TV showed a man in a feathered boa, his hips swaying to a beat that Kevin couldn't hear. The crowd around him cheered with a mix of joy and defiance.

"Why is he dressed like that?" Kevin asked, his voice barely above a whisper.

Carol reached over, brushing her hand gently against his back. "Some people express themselves differently, sweetheart. It's part of who they are."

Bert's paper snapped shut. "Kevin, go outside and play. Now."

Kevin shifted his weight, reluctant to move. "But why are they showing it on the news?"

"Because it's important," Carol said softly. "The Stonewall Riots in New York started all this. People were tired of being mistreated. They stood up for themselves, and now they're marching to make sure the world hears them."

"What kind of marches are they?" Kevin asked.

"They're called Gay Liberation marches," Carol explained.

Kevin's brow furrowed. "What does 'gay' mean?"

"It means when two people, like a man and another man, want to be with one another," she answered.

Bert sighed, folding his newspaper tightly. "I'm going to the garage. You want to come with me, son?"

Kevin shook his head, already reaching for his toy soldiers. "Na, I want to keep playing."

The footage on the television screen cut to a different scene—rows of police in uniforms, batons at the ready, as marchers held their ground. Kevin's fingers gripped the handful of army men, the hard plastic digging into his skin. "Are they going to hurt them?"

Carol hesitated, a shadow crossing her face. "I hope not, baby."

The living room fell into silence, save for the hum of the television. Bert stood, dropping his newspaper onto the chair. "I'll be in the garage."

As the door closed behind her husband, Carol pulled her son into a soft hug, her arms warm against his shoulders. "You have a good heart, Kevin. It's okay to question things."

Kevin nodded, but his mind still spun with images of feather boas, the flamboyant sissy-sashays with exaggerated movements of hips and shoulders, the police with horses and batons drawn, and mobs of people chanting and shouting. He didn't understand everything he saw but couldn't shake the feeling that it mattered. Kevin could sympathize with people who want equality, but at the same time, the topic made him uncomfortable. As a first-born, pro-establishment, Catholic-schooled future astronaut, Kevin wanted no affiliation with the behavior portrayed by the marchers on those newscasts.

5

New Battlefields

(Four years later)

K evin's first day at West Bayview Junior High felt like venturing into an unfamiliar galaxy, a place far larger, louder, and more chaotic than the Catholic school halls he had known. Everything seemed magnified—the sheer number of students, the towering lockers, the echo of hurried footsteps in wide hallways that smelled of industrial cleaner and cafeteria pizza. His Catholic school had been strict, structured, and predictable. Here, in public school, it felt like being stranded in Apollo 13— adrift, disoriented, and caught in something bigger than himself.

Even before stepping foot inside, Kevin learned that the school bus stop was its own kind of battlefield. The stop sat just four houses away and one street over. Still, Kevin timed his departure carefully, arriving at the last moment before the bus pulled up. Arriving too early meant exposure to teasing, shoving matches, or worse. Waiting for the bus was an idle time among restless teenagers, and someone usually paid for it. Some days, it was just harmless mockery. A kid might be left with a torn book or ripped homework on other days. At its worst, some delinquent with a can of lighter fluid would set an abandoned tire on fire, sending a column of thick black smoke curling into the sky.

When the bus arrived, Kevin headed straight for the back row. It was easier to see trouble coming when it was in front of you rather than lurking behind your head, where a sudden smack or a spitball attack could catch you off guard. Be Prepared. The Scout motto wasn't just for the outdoors but for daily survival.

West Bayview was an old, converted high school, which meant everything about it felt oversized with its high ceilings, heavy doors, and wide hallways. The vastness of it made Kevin feel small and insignificant. The students also looked different. Unlike the neatly pressed Catholic uniforms, kids at West Bayview wore denim and sneakers, some with band logos or graffiti-like designs on their shirts. He walked the halls quietly, head down, trying to blend in. If he could avoid standing out, he might stay under the radar, untouched by the chaos and change.

Nothing unnerved Kevin more than physical education class. P.E. at West Bayview was unlike his old school's tame recess period. Here, the students changed their clothes for P.E., dressing in short blue shorts and plain white tees stamped with the WBJH logo. The class rotated sports every two weeks—basketball, football, archery, baseball, kickball, tennis. It was old-school P.E. with mandatory participation and mandatory sweat. And at the end of every class, mandatory showers.

Kevin dreaded this from the first day—group showers. The very phrase made his stomach knot. There was no experience like being a thirteen-year-old in a group shower with dozens of peers for the first time—exposed, vulnerable, and curious.

The locker room was loud, humid, and smelled of sweat and chlorine. Towels snapped through the air as boys joked and shoved each other toward the showers, where rows of metal spigots jutted from tiled walls with no stalls or curtains and nowhere to hide. Kevin moved carefully as if each step required calculated precision—an inappropriate or involuntary reaction could set off a silent alarm, attracting unwanted attention.

Jose was the one everyone noticed. At thirteen, most boys looked like boys. Jose didn't. He was at least a year older than the others, possibly two. His body had already broadened, defined in a way that set him apart—muscles taut, legs dusted with dark hair, his chest sculpted in ways Kevin had never seen on anyone his age. He moved effortlessly, his towel draped around his neck, the water streaking down his back as if he belonged there, entirely at ease in his own skin.

Kevin's eyes lingered a second too long. His stomach twisted, heat rising up his neck. He turned sharply, blinking hard, forcing himself to stare at the blank tile wall—just water—a normal shower. *Boys didn't look at other boys*, he reminded himself. That's not how it worked.

It wasn't attraction, not in the way he would later come to understand it. He didn't want to be *with* Jose—he just wondered what it would be like to *be* Jose. Perhaps he was just impressed. Or maybe it was something else entirely, something unnameable.

But in that moment, Kevin was hyperaware of everything. The way the water dripped from Jose's chin. The way his shoulders shifted—the sound of boys laughing and roughhousing, utterly oblivious to the storm in Kevin's head. He forced himself to stand still under the lukewarm stream, eyes locked on the tile wall before him. The shower felt longer than it was, a test of endurance, a place where every movement had consequences.

The group shower wasn't just a locker room. It was a minefield. Kevin kept his eyes forward, counting down the seconds in his head, waiting for the signal that it was over, escaping back into his clothes, into the world where he didn't have to think about any of this.

6

BOYS IN THE CLOSET

J ose was not the only Latin boy Kevin met that year. While trying to avoid becoming the daily target of rowdy kids on school bus rides, Kevin met Miguel, a round-faced, pudgy kid doing the same thing. The two sat together in the back of the bus when they could, seeking obscurity during those long rides to and from West Bayview.

Kevin and Miguel's friendship deepened over the summer, usually at Miguel's house, where he had the place to himself while his parents worked. Unlike Kevin and the other neighborhood kids, Miguel had no interest in playing ball in the street or riding bikes under the sweltering Florida sun. He preferred the crisp, artificial chill of the air conditioning, where he could comfortably lounge. He made up for his lack of athleticism with humor—his sharp wit and effortless charm masking an instinct for self-preservation. Miguel had a way of pushing boundaries, throwing bold suggestions into the air, only to reel them back with a grin if met with hesitation. It was impossible to tell when he was serious or just testing the waters, which was precisely how he liked it.

Keith, who was their age and lived a few blocks away in the same neighborhood, often joined Kevin and Miguel. He, too, was sometimes tormented by the tough kids in their suburban hood, probably because of his slight stature. He was a welcome addition, making the three an unlikely band of brothers that summer.

After making baloney and cheese sandwiches on soft white bread with mayonnaise, a staple at Miguel's house, they settled in to listen to the latest 45s Miguel had picked up. When Kevin was alone in his room, he tuned in to the radio, waiting for Redbone's "Come and Get Your Love," Elton John's "Bennie and the Jets," or David Essex's "Rock On" to play. But Miguel had the good stuff—the different stuff. Miguel had music that moved. He had "Dancing Machine" by The Jackson 5 and Kool & The Gang's "Jungle Boogie" and "Hollywood Swinging." It was music you could feel and dance to, and dance Miguel did.

When the music ended, and Miguel finished dancing, he spun toward Kevin and Keith with a grin. "Alright, boys, time for some fun," he announced, wiping his forehead dramatically.

Kevin groaned. "What now?"

"I've got a surprise for you."

Keith smirked. "Last time you said that—"

"This is better," Miguel interrupted, waving a dismissive hand. "Just trust me. Hide in the closet. Stay quiet."

Kevin hesitated, his pulse kicking up at the word "surprise," knowing Miguel's idea of entertainment always had a twist.

Miguel held up his hands in mock innocence. "Just watch through the slats."

Keith shot Kevin a look, then shrugged. "Might as well see what he's up to."

Still wary, they stepped toward the closet, inspecting the bifold doors, testing the hinges, and checking for hidden locks. Satisfied that Miguel could not trap them inside, they squeezed in, maneuvering around old shoes and shifting hangers aside, jockeying for the best viewing position.

Miguel gave them a quick thumbs-up before heading toward the hallway. The moment he disappeared, Kevin swallowed hard.

The two boys fell silent as soon as they heard the front door open and close, followed by two muffled voices traveling down the hallway headed for the bedroom in the rear of the house where they were hiding.

Kevin tensed, his body going rigid in the cramped space. The voices grew closer, muffled but unmistakably headed straight for the bedroom.

Then Miguel's voice, light and casual: "Go ahead. Get ready."

Kevin's breath came slow and steady, but his heart raced as he pressed his eye to the wooden slats of the closet door. The air inside the cramped space was warm, stale, and thick with the scent of old shoes and mothballs. Keith was frozen beside him, barely breathing, his hand slapping the back of Kevin's leg, silently instructing him to "Look! Look! Look!"

A slow realization crept over Kevin. Whatever this was, it wasn't just a prank. He should look away—he wanted to look away—but his body ignored him. He wasn't sure if it was shock, curiosity, or something worse.

Beyond the door, the boy sat on the edge of the bed, his shorts around his ankles, his erection stiff and unwavering, pointing toward the ceiling. Miguel stood just outside their view, his voice light and teasing.

Kevin recognized the figure on the bed. It was Dennis, Miguel's next-door neighbor. Dennis was around their age and a big boy, not fat, but not muscular. He was a big-boned, midwestern farm boy type of husky. They had never seen Dennis in school and didn't know if he was even in the same grade as they were. Kevin only knew what Miguel told him in the past—that Dennis was 'slow' and 'simple.'

Kevin's eyes widened as he leaned slightly closer to the slats in the door, adjusting his head for the best possible view. Keith's hand was now firmly gripping the side of Kevin's shorts as if he was teetering on the edge of a cliff, clutching a rope for balance.

Dennis patiently sat and waited for Miguel, sporting the hugest hard-on Kevin had ever seen in person. Before now, he had only seen pictures of them in dirty magazines that boys had passed around in the back of the school bus once or twice.

"Do you still want me to suck you off?" Miguel asked.

"Yeah," Dennis replied. "You said you would."

The air in the closet felt thicker, pressing against Kevin's skin. His pulse hammered at his temples, his fingers tightening into fists at his sides. *Step back. Move. Look away.* But his body refused. Instead, he stood there, trapped—not by the closet, but by the surprise of what he saw, by the sickening mix of shame and curiosity swirling deep in his gut.

Why would anyone want to suck someone's dick in their mouth? Kevin wondered. *Why would Miguel do that?* Kevin was still quite naïve when it came to matters of sex. He had no idea what oral sex was, let alone understand how anyone found it desirable or pleasurable. He sensed it was wrong or immoral. Still, he was curious and wanted to see what was about to happen. Kevin was also beginning to feel embarrassed that two of his best friends seemed to know more about these matters than he did.

Miguel let the silence stretch. Kevin could hear Dennis's breathing shift, the slight sound of shifting fabric. Still, Miguel said nothing. And then, finally, his voice casual and detached—he spoke.

"Yeah, nah… let's not today."

Dennis hesitated, hands gripping his shorts. Confused. Dejected. Then he nodded once, mutely, and started to dress. Miguel was already walking out of the room as if none of it had mattered at all.

The boys remained quiet in the darkness, watching Dennis dress, his hands fumbling over his pants and belt.

Miguel turned away before Dennis pulled his shorts up, laughing under his breath. 'Damn, that was too easy,' he muttered, shaking his head as he walked past, glancing at the wooden slats of the bifold doors. His grin was wide, like he'd just pulled off some great magic trick.

The front door clicked shut a few moments later, and then Miguel laughed.

Keith let out the breath he had been holding, shouting, "Holy shit!" Miguel turned toward the closet, swinging the doors open, grinning like a magician after a successful trick.

"I told you it'd be worth it."

Keith burst out laughing, but Kevin didn't. Something about it felt wrong, but he didn't have the words for it.

"You think Dennis wanted you to do that?" Kevin asked, keeping his voice light and careful.

Miguel rolled his eyes. "Dennis is a faggot. He wants to suck me off all the time. I just wanted to show you." Miguel claimed to have never let him do it, though.

Kevin played along, careful not to say too much or divulge the depth of his innocence. He feared he might become the next target of Miguel and Keith's ridicule if he had.

Keith snorted, shaking his head. "Man, that was crazy."

Kevin forced himself to laugh, though it felt strange in his throat, like something stuck there. Miguel and Keith's laughter filled the room. Still, Kevin felt off-balance, unsteady, as if the floor had shifted beneath him. He went through the motions, grinning, nodding, playing along—but the unease stuck with him. It clung to his skin, followed him home, and curled beside him in bed that night. And even when he shut his eyes, Dennis's quiet disappointment stayed with him. 'It was just a prank. No harm done.' That's what Miguel would say.

But Kevin had felt something watching through those wooden slats hidden in the closet—a mix of curiosity and shame, like seeing something he shouldn't want to see.

Kevin forced himself to forget, erase it, and shove it into some dark corner of his mind. No harm done. But the feeling stayed—not that night, not the next day, not even weeks later. Every time he shut his bedroom door and caught himself lost in thought, the moment in the closet returned to him in pieces. Not just what he saw but how he felt watching it: the way his heart had pounded, the way his breath had slowed, the way his stomach had tightened—not in disgust, but something else.

Kevin kept telling himself it was just shock. Shock at Miguel's trick to amuse his friends by embarrassing Dennis. Shock at Dennis's eagerness and shock that people did things like that. Most of all, Kevin was shocked at his eager anticipation, curiosity, and guilt for hiding in the closet and voyeuristically watching Dennis stroke his penis while waiting for Miguel to return. It was all a complex combination of emotions he had not yet mastered.

He was sure of one thing, however. If Dennis was a 'faggot', as Miguel had labeled him, Kevin was nothing like Dennis.

Yet something about it wouldn't settle. The memory crept in at the edges of Kevin's thoughts—at school, at home, in the quiet before sleep. It wasn't just what he saw. It was how it made him feel—how it made his breath slow, his pulse quicken, his stomach tighten in a way he didn't understand. And that was the part he couldn't shake. The part that scared him the most. Why couldn't he stop thinking about it?

7

Truth or Dare

Kevin hadn't thought about Dennis in weeks. Or at least, he told himself that. He was good at pushing things aside, stuffing them into dark corners of his mind where they wouldn't resurface. The moment in Miguel's closet had been just that—a moment. A prank. No harm done. He repeated Miguel's words until he finally convinced himself of them. It was easier that way. But there was something different about tonight—this wasn't Miguel's game— it was his.

The Summers family owned a travel trailer they frequently used on camping trips and vacations. The Starcraft was the ultimate in camping comfort with its full kitchen, bathroom, and shower. To the right was a dining table that seated six and converted into a spacious bed comfortably sleeping two adults. Past the kitchen on the left was the rear sleeping compartment with four bunk beds and various storage areas. Bert routinely pulled the Starcraft into the driveway to clean and supply it for their next planned trip. When parked in this position, the camper became Kevin's retreat to read, dream, and escape.

Occasionally, Bert and Carol allowed Kevin to invite a friend for driveway campouts. Kevin was growing past the stage for friend sleepovers, so this was likely the last time he would ask. Naturally, he invited Michael, the neighborhood boy who lived down the street.

Kevin sat on the edge of the lower bunk, his back pressed against the cool interior wall of the camper. The Starcraft creaked with every move, the slight sway of its frame reminding him of being on a ship, adrift but anchored in his parent's driveway. The air inside was a mix of old canvas, sugary pop-tarts, and the tang of summer sweat. Across from him, Michael sprawled on the opposite bunk, his legs stretched out and his arms folded behind his head, the picture of bad-boy confidence.

Kevin considered telling Michael about what he had seen from Miguel's closet but didn't. The three boys had sworn an oath to keep the event a secret. Besides, Kevin didn't want to risk Michael ridiculing him for what he had witnessed, even if he had not actively participated. The last thing Kevin wanted was for Michael to bully him or call him a faggot.

They told jokes, made fun of kids they knew, and giggled the way boys do when left unsupervised. The night was a slow build of laughter and bravado, an energy that eventually led to Kevin bragging about streaking one night with Keith and Miguel. He told it offhandedly, but his words were careful, measured—just enough to test the air, to see if Michael might take the bait. A smirk, a shrug, anything that might hint he was willing to play along.

Michael shrugged it off. "That's nothing."

Kevin raised an eyebrow. "Oh yeah? You wouldn't have done it."

Michael stretched, folding his arms behind his head, his confidence unwavering. "Hell yeah, I would've. I'd have smoked you in a race, with or without clothes. You wouldn't have stood a chance."

Kevin smirked. "You weren't there. I doubt you would have."

And so it began.

"Truth or dare?" Michael asked. The words hung in the air between them. His lips curled in a smirk, a challenge Kevin felt more than heard.

Kevin swallowed, his fingers twisting into the hem of his T-shirt. "Dare." His voice sounded steadier than he felt, the syllable sharp and clear between them.

Michael pushed himself up, his shadow stretching long in the dim light of the camper's single overhead bulb. "I dare you to show me yours."

Heat rushed to Kevin's face. His skin felt tight, his pulse quick and loud in his ears. He shifted—the rough cushion beneath him scratching against his legs. "Only if you show me yours first." His words mirrored Michael's, but his tone was softer, testing the edge of the dare.

Most teen males spend excessive time inspecting their penis, covertly or overtly comparing themselves to other boys. Without a doubt, the overwhelming obsession or concern is always with size. Kevin was oblivious to both the science and the societal norms as he pushed the game forward, cautious about leaving himself room for an out should Michael abruptly become upset or take offense at the nature of the game.

For a moment, neither of them moved. The camper held its breath, the walls closing in around them. Outside, a car rumbled down the street, its headlights flashing through the small window, painting their faces in stripes of light and shadow. Michael shrugged, his movements loose, almost lazy. "Fine, but at the same time."

He sat up, his hands moving to the waistband of his shorts.

Kevin mirrored him, his body taut, the air between them thin as paper. Each movement felt magnified—the rustle of fabric, the shift of knees, the soft thud of a sneaker kicked off to the floor. They moved in tandem, neither rushing nor hesitating, a dance of nerves and unspoken rules.

Michael's expression remained neutral, his face a mask of practiced indifference. Kevin tried to match it, to mirror that cool detachment, but his hands trembled as he lifted his T-shirt, exposing a sliver of pale skin. The bulb above them cast shadows that moved with them until they switched it off.

When the dare unfolded, it was slow, almost clinical. Michael's gaze was steady, his breathing even, and Kevin felt a strange mix of pride and vulnerability. There was no laughter, no jeering, only the soft rhythm of their breaths in the confined space. The moment stretched, pulled tight and thin until Michael finally leaned back, his expression unchanged.

"Not bad," Michael said, his voice low, laced with something Kevin couldn't quite place—disappointment, dismissal, or something else entirely. A dare met, a challenge answered. They dressed in silence. The weight of the moment lingered between them, unspoken and unshaken. Kevin couldn't shake the feeling that something had shifted between them, though neither would ever say it aloud.

They lay back on their bunks, the hum of a passing plane overhead filling the silence. Kevin's skin still tingled, not with fear or shame, but with something else—a quiet victory, a slight shift in the balance of power.

"Guess I'm not as big as I thought," Michael muttered, his voice a thin thread in the dark.

Kevin didn't respond. He didn't need to. The shift between them was as palpable. His chest felt full, his thoughts both sharp and clouded, a mix of triumph and something unnamed. It was not about size, not really. It was about how Michael's voice had softened and how his shoulders dropped—how he saw Kevin differently—if only for a moment.

In the weeks that followed, Michael's demeanor changed. Instead of teasing Kevin, he acknowledged him with a subtle nod—an unspoken truce, a quiet shift in their balance. And then, one afternoon, without a word, the baseball glove Michael had stolen years ago reappeared on Kevin's front porch, placed there like a peace offering.

The camper remained parked, its windows reflecting the summer sun, a capsule of secrets and small victories. Kevin returned to it often, hiding away with his books and dreams, the space between truth and dare a refuge where he could be whoever he wanted—astronaut, cowboy, or just a boy on the edge of becoming something more.

Michael never mentioned it again. Neither did Kevin. But sometimes, in the quiet moments, Kevin replayed it—not the game itself, not the moment of comparison, but the way Michael had looked at him afterward. The way something had passed between them, unspoken. He told himself it meant nothing, just another childhood game. But some nights, lying awake in his bed, he wasn't sure if he believed that.

8

THE HALLWAY OF KNOWLEDGE

Hiding in closets and driveway sleepovers aside, Kevin took full advantage of summer break's freedom by riding his bike around the neighborhood and playing catch in the front yard. He designed, built, and flew kites outside. When it was too hot or raining, Kevin watched old movies broadcasted on local television stations. Hitchcock's *The Birds* was a favorite and was telecast regularly every few weeks.

He played chess by and against himself, reading books to study and memorize the classic opening, mid-game, and late-game moves of great grandmasters like Boris Spassky and Bobby Fisher. His father taught him how to play, but Kevin took the board game to an obsessive level. He preferred to play white to give himself an opening-move advantage and took his time without opponents to object to long delays in his moves. He agonizingly planned and strategized each move and occasionally took one back in a do-over after recognizing a better move to make. Kevin was assured of victory in each match, giving him a false sense of confidence while promoting his internal struggles—the black and the white pieces, the right and the wrong choices, and the indecision in the pursuit of perfection. It was easy to win when he controlled the game.

Kevin also spent a lot of time reading the gold-bound annual editions of the *World Topics Yearbook* or the *Illustrated How It Works Science and Invention* encyclopedias that Bert and Carol purchased. These were his informational sources of reference for homework assignments, and it may have been odd that Kevin read encyclopedias during summer vacation out of want rather than out of requirement. Still, they were a great source of illustrations and pictures for him to practice sketching, and they fueled his interest in science and the mechanics of how things worked. The encyclopedias were not the only books Kevin read, however.

When Kevin had the house to himself, he frequented the bookshelf at the end of the long hallway where Bert and Carol kept their books shelved. Amongst the various *Better Homes and Gardens* cookbooks and novels like *The Godfather* and *Love Story*, right below the weight loss and just above the self-help bestsellers, set the one book Kevin returned to repeatedly.

After ensuring he was alone, Kevin sat on the cool terrazzo floor with his back against the hallway wall. He carefully removed the object of his curiosity from its assigned place on the shelf. Then, after finding the page last read without the aid of a bookmark, he picked up where he last left off, consuming the material with the interest that only a young male teenager can consume. When his reading sessions were complete, always conscious never to read too much material at once for fear of being caught, Kevin carefully placed his parents' copy of *Everything You Always Wanted to Know About Sex* (*But Were Afraid to Ask)* back in its sacred place on the shelf. The book opened a world Kevin didn't know existed, answering some basic questions about a subject no one had explained or discussed.

It was a revolutionary bestseller, but much of what it claimed was outdated, exaggerated, or wildly inaccurate. Kevin read about dubious contraceptive methods and bizarre assertions about sexuality that seemed more like cautionary folklore than fact.

The section on homosexuality was particularly unsettling, filled with descriptions that painted gay men as dangerous, compulsive, and incapable of love. It portrayed them as lurking in public restrooms, exchanging secret notes on toilet paper, and engaging in anonymous encounters without sentiment. The book described a world of depravity and secrecy, insisting that those who indulged in such behaviors were broken, unworthy of real connection, and, in the most extreme cases, among the cruelest individuals in history.

Kevin's fingers tightened around the book's spine as he reread one particular section, his stomach twisting in a slow, sickening turn. He didn't know much about homosexuality—no one talked about it, not in school, not at home. The only images he had seen were the exaggerated caricatures on television or the flamboyant marchers in parades that reporters covered with a mixture of fascination and contempt. If what this book said was true, then this was dangerous ground—something best avoided at all costs. And yet, he still read on.

He skimmed through passages that claimed gay men sought pleasure through degrading acts, inserting foreign objects into themselves—pens, pencils, tennis balls, and enough fruit to stock a small grocery store. But the book also offered a solution, a glimmer of redemption: homosexuality, it assured, could be cured through psychiatric treatment. Kevin was unaware that medical professionals had already begun discrediting such claims by the time the book was published. But it remained on his parents' shelf, its pages unchallenged, its words carrying an air of authority.

Kevin shut the book and placed it back on the shelf as carefully as he had removed it, ensuring it went into its correct spot. The book gave him answers, but they weren't what he expected. It confirmed something he already feared—something unnamed but undeniable, something that made his throat lump and his hands tremble as he pressed them against the floor.

The nervousness in the group showers after P.E.. The sharp thrill of watching Dennis from Miguel's closet. The quiet charge of playing truth or dare with Michael. These moments clung to him, circling the edges of his mind like shadows cast by the slatted closet door—things he wasn't ready to see but couldn't seem to unsee.

Yet, if the book was to be believed, these feelings led to something dark, something grotesque. Kevin couldn't be what it described. He wasn't. But if that were true, why did he keep returning to these moments? Why did he keep feeling them?

The encyclopedias in the hallway taught Kevin about the stars, the mechanics of machines, and the laws of physics. The sex book was supposed to teach him about this too—about people, about himself. But instead, it only left him with more anxiety, questions, and answers he was afraid to believe.

9

GREAT EXPECTATIONS

(Fall, 1975)

Although John Pierce Middle School was just two blocks from his home and across the street from Miguel's house, Kevin shared no classes and rarely saw Miguel or Keith once their ninth school year began. Their little band of merry men had unofficially disbanded as each found new friends and joined different cliques, separate from one another.

Middle school years can be difficult for most boys as they enter their hormone-stupid years, and Kevin was no exception. Body hair and acne took root, while braces on his teeth elevated his self-consciousness to a new level. Kevin's braces were the old-fashioned, heavy metal type, not the smooth and transparent braces available in later years. As a practice, he tried to avoid any altercations or fights when he could. However, when the unavoidable happened, he quickly learned that smiling was the most important thing to do in a scuffle. It was far better for opponents to cut their knuckles on his fighting smile than to have the inside of his mouth ripped apart on sharp metal edges. His first hormone-stupid fight taught him that.

Kevin had once been taller and larger than most boys his age. His growth spurt came early in life, making him a first pick in sports. His size commanded respect, but that changed at John Pierce. The student body was larger, and the students were suddenly stronger. The hierarchy had shifted, and Kevin found himself outmatched on the basketball court, the ball swatted from his hands with a dismissive laugh. "Damn, Summers, what happened to you?" someone called, their voice laced with amusement. He wasn't the tallest, strongest, or fastest anymore. Somewhere between hiding in Miguel's closet and driveway camping with Michael, the world had caught up and passed him.

Kevin also found himself in classes where he was no longer the most intelligent student. The educational head start from Catholic school had worn its worth, rendering Kevin only average now, on par with most other students.

Size and intellect were not the only self-deficiencies Kevin struggled with. There were boys he deemed better looking or had better haircuts than he did. Some boys were more fashionably dressed or more sociable than he was. Suddenly, and without warning, Kevin had become the proverbial smaller fish in a larger pond and felt inadequate. True to a Dicken's tale, his great expectations for popularity were rapidly waning. Until his semester in Mr. Nelson's shop class, that is.

The new classmate introduced himself as Steve, turning away from the noise and power of the drill press long enough to shake Kevin's hand with zest before returning his attention to his woodworking project. His full name was Steven James Mason. He was an inch taller than Kevin, with straight black hair parted from the side and a white smile any dentist would be proud of. Kevin watched his new shop partner drill holes into the triangle peg game that was the class project. As Steve drilled, he involuntarily held the tip of his tongue exposed between his lips, in total concentration as he focused through his plastic safety goggles on the precision of his work.

Kevin followed his movement between machines, picking up pieces of wood and discarding others as they chatted and got to know one another. Steve's lean length and movements, his carefree attitude, and frequent chuckles at everything and nothing gave him the initial impression of nerd-goofy yet adorable. It took Kevin less than one class period that day to learn the definition of smitten.

"Hey, you play chess?" Steve asked, setting his project aside and wiping the sawdust from his hands.

Kevin nodded, "Yeah. My Dad taught me. I play against myself a lot."

Steve smirked. "That's a little weird."

"No, it's good practice," Kevin replied.

"Well, I don't play with myself," Steve said, grinning. "But I do play. Think you can beat me?"

Kevin stood up straighter. "I don't lose much."

"Good,' Steve said. "Then it'll be fun proving you wrong."

They played their first match on a board with pieces made in Mr. Nelson's shop class. Steve played aggressively, taking risks that made Kevin's careful planning unravel faster than he liked. The match ended in a draw.

"Damn," Steve muttered, staring at the board. "We're actually pretty even."

Kevin smiled. "Guess we have to play again." And they did. Again and again, every chance they got over the following weeks. Soon, their conversations stretched beyond chess, drifting into science, tennis, and the odd jokes Steve tossed into every discussion.

Kevin realized, mid-conversation, that Steve had never once talked about girls in all their time together. Or boys. It just never came up, and he never asked. Maybe that meant something. Perhaps it didn't. Either way, something about it gnawed at him.

Kevin and Steve's friendship became effortless. They spent hours building the rockets Mr. Nelson taught them how to make, launching them in an open field near Steve's house on a canal by the bay. Occasionally, one of the rockets, gently floating back toward the earth under its parachute and guided by the wind, made a watery splashdown in the canal, just as the Apollo capsules carrying the astronauts did when they returned to Earth. When an unplanned watery landing occurred, the teenagers ran toward the site, waiting on one of the two opposing canal walls until the current floated the rocket and parachute to them for retrieval.

They loved tennis and often hit together at the school's courts near Kevin's home or the public courts near Steve's house, where they launched rockets. Their tennis skills improved during that school year, so they entered small city tournaments at the community college but were not good enough to win any.

The first time Kevin visited Steve's house, he marveled at the deep, screened-in pool and the manicured St. Augustine lawn. Steve laughed when Kevin stared too long. "It's just a pool. Come on." Kevin's home also had a pool, just as many Florida homes did, but it was not as deep or screened-in as Steve's was.

Kevin started watching Steve more closely—how he moved effortlessly through the world, never hesitated before speaking, just fitting into everything. If Kevin could learn how Steve did it, maybe he wouldn't feel like an outsider.

That summer between junior high and high school, when they weren't playing tennis, they spent hours swimming. The boys held contests: racing one another, practicing flip turns, holding their breaths underwater, and racing to see who could retrieve objects from the bottom of the pool the fastest. Steve was the better swimmer. His long limbs sliced through the water to give him the reach and speed that Kevin couldn't match. All that time spent in the water under the Florida sun gave both their bodies a healthy and golden hue, with stark tan lines where their speedos covered them.

After the two dried off and changed following a long afternoon in the pool, sprawled across his bedroom floor, Steve pulled out a stack of comedy albums. He dropped the needle onto the record, grinning. "Ever listened to Prior?"

Kevin shook his head.

"You're missing out. Listen."

Steve played the bit about two guys walking across the Golden Gate Bridge, stopping to pee over the edge as they reached the bridge's center. One turned to the other to say, "Goddamn, this water is cold!" His friend responded, "Yeah, and it's deep, too!"

Steve played other albums by Prior, as well as by Bill Cosby and George Carlin. They laughed so hard their sides hurt, their bodies occasionally knocking together as they rolled on the floor.

Kevin caught himself staring—at how Steve's face lit up when he laughed and how his confidence never wavered. Kevin suspected that those comedy albums were, to some degree, responsible for Steve's relaxed sense of humor. Kevin took his cues from Steve, laughing when Steve laughed at the bits that Steve thought were funny. Steve wasn't just fun. He was magnetic.

Then the thought crept in, unwanted, but Kevin quickly shoved it down. That wasn't him. He wasn't like Dennis. He wasn't like the men on TV in parades, the ones people whispered about. *I'm not*, Kevin thought, swallowing hard. He wanted to be better—like Steve. For a second, just a flicker of one, Kevin wondered if this was normal—if other boys felt this way about their friends. Then the thought vanished, replaced with something heavier. No, it wasn't that. It couldn't be.

The longer Kevin watched Steve's smile and listened to his laugh that day, laying on his carpeted bedroom floor as they innocently brushed against one another, reaching for albums and thrashing around on the floor in amusement and laughter, the more Kevin realized it wasn't enough to be Steve's friend. He wanted to *be* Steve.

Kevin understood his idolization of Steve's upscale house with its deep pool and perfectly manicured lawn of thick St. Augustine grass. He was also aware of his envy of Steve's tennis racket, bedroom record player, and his family's apparent wealth. But in the blur of Pryor's jokes and Steve's laughter, Kevin subconsciously measured his friend's good looks, natural athleticism, carefree demeanor, intelligence, and a seemingly endless supply of confidence. Kevin watched and wondered how everything came so effortlessly to someone his age. For the first time, Kevin wanted to be someone else and live their life. He wanted to be Steven James Mason.

Steve was the blueprint. Everything would be fine if Kevin could mirror and become more like him. Moving forward, Kevin would make better choices. He'd focus on sports, school, and his future. Kevin would push out the thoughts that didn't belong. He'd fix himself before there was anything to fix.

The two friends would meet again, years later and for one brief hour, when Kevin's night was near its darkest. When they did, Kevin would again measure himself up against Steve—only this time, the truth would be impossible to ignore.

10

DRIVER'S EDUCATION

(The following year)

Kevin held one of the rockets he designed and built a moment longer than the others. Its paint chipped, the fins slightly bent, but he remembered the rush of lighting the fuse, the way his heart jumped as it shot into the sky. That was a different Kevin—a kid who dreamed about flying—but now he needed to be someone who kept both feet on the ground.

Holding onto them felt foolish now, a reminder of a version of himself he no longer wanted to be. He exhaled and let go, giving them all to a younger kid he barely knew in the neighborhood. He did the same with the model airplanes that hung by fishing lines from his bedroom ceiling. It was time to focus on high school, time to trade dreams of flying for something real. Kevin was turning sixteen soon, which meant getting his learner's permit to drive. With Steve as his new blueprint, it was time to be an adult and plan for future success.

Kevin was changing in other ways, too. The hours of playing tennis and swimming with Steve after school and during the summer paid off for him physically. While busy comparing other boys his age against one another, Kevin failed to notice how quickly his own body was changing. Tennis gave him large calf and thigh muscles, which Carol pointed out one evening in the kitchen as he stood in lighting that flattered his growing muscularity. She also pointed out how full and firm his buttocks muscles had become.

Kevin's shoulders broadened, and he developed a strong, V-shaped back from all the swimming. His proudest accomplishment, however, and sole point of self-focus was his chest. It was larger and much better defined now. A muscular chest was something Kevin had desired since childhood—he gleaned its importance from his faithful watching of Tarzan reruns and wrestling matches on television each Saturday and Sunday morning. He knew a muscular chest was a requirement of manhood and of being respected by males and desired by females.

To be admired was to have control. To be envied was to have power. It meant never being the one left in the background, never being invisible. Kevin had spent too long watching from the sidelines, and it was his turn to be the one others watched. He wanted others to admire and envy him like he admired and envied the more athletic boys with better genetics than his own. While his muscles grew, all the running and biking toned the rest of his body. Those miles finally removed the last of his baby fat and sculpted him into a real teenager with an athletic frame he could be proud of.

Kevin caught himself in the mirror one evening, flexing absently. The reflection was better now—stronger, leaner. He should feel different. He should feel like one of them. But sometimes, in the quiet moments, he still felt like the kid hiding in Miguel's closet, watching someone else be fearless.

In the weeks preceding his first day as a sophomore, as if planned perfectly on the calendar, Kevin's braces were removed to reveal a mouth full of straight teeth. He could now smile without being self-conscious, and that new smile and maturing body gave Kevin the confidence he needed. He would be more sociable and outgoing—like Steve. He had to be. High school would be different. He would make sure of it.

~

Lakewood High School conducted double sessions because of the large student body. Sophomores and Juniors attended the afternoon session from 11:30 a.m. until 6:00 p.m.. Seniors attended the morning session from 6:30 a.m. until Noon each day. Despite his newfound confidence, with twelve hundred students in his graduating class, Kevin sometimes felt like baitfish in a vast ocean of older and larger predators.

There were guys two and three years older than he was with deeper voices, larger muscles, and hairy chests or mustaches and beards. Many owned muscle cars, driving them to school and taking dates out in them. The girls were just as mature, often smirking at or ignoring the smaller, younger sophomores entering the large school for the first time. They could make teenagers feel like little boys. It was intimidating and often overwhelming when Kevin allowed himself to feel insecure. The environment could also be a sea of opportunity when he felt confident. Unfortunately, Kevin couldn't yet control his insecurities or confidence at will.

As a sophomore, Driver's Education was a required course. The class was in a small portable building, or educational trailer, near the practice driving course and student parking lot. Kevin sat in the front row of the class, an unusual and uncomfortable place for him. He preferred the obscurity and safety of the back row, just as he had on the school bus rides in seventh grade. From the back of the class, he could watch his classmates and observe their behaviors, trying to assess their personalities and guess their stories. Kevin also enjoyed sitting with his back to the wall, vigilantly watching for signs of potential trouble from misbehaving students or being able to duck the view of the teachers surveying the class to solicit student answers. When Kevin had to sit in the middle or front of the class, he often sensed eyes on the back of his neck and could feel the judgment those stares might contain. Unfortunately, the seats in that class were assigned based on who claimed them on the first day of that semester. Kevin had a long trek from his English class at the front of the school to the Driver's Ed trailer in the back, so he had to settle on one of the few vacant seats that first day.

Before the end of that first week in his new school, Kevin felt a light tap on his side as the girl sitting behind him covertly passed a tightly folded piece of paper to him. His fingers hovered over the fold, his pulse quickening. A note could mean anything. A joke. A trap. A public humiliation waiting to happen.

Kevin hesitated before unfolding the note. He glanced back, expecting to see mocking grins, but found only the girl in the last row watching him with a knowing smirk. Not cruel, not shy, just waiting. She wanted him to read it. And she wanted him to know it.

Carefully unfolding the note under his desk, Kevin glanced down at it. "*Let's meet. Jennifer.*" He read it once. Then again. Three words were impossibly clear, yet his mind twisted around them like a riddle. Was she serious? Was she watching him now? He had heard her name called during roll call earlier in the week. He had caught her grin once or twice, but was she now trying to say she wanted to meet him?

A reply note? No way. If the instructor caught it, he'd be a laughingstock for the rest of the year. Should the wrong student get hold of it, the same result—just louder.

Kevin decided to wait until the end of class—it meant sitting with his heart and brain racing and palms sweating while considering what he might say and how this might play out. He turned a simple hello into a mental chess match. Every move had consequences. Every word had weight. And now, he had an entire class period to sweat over it.

Kevin tried to recall what Jenny looked like without turning around again to look at her. She had long and straight dark hair. Yes, he remembered that. She wore glasses. Yes, he remembered that, too. She also had a few freckles around her nose and cheeks. They were cute and flattering, not overbearing or distracting. That was an odd observance to remember from a glance or two in her direction over that first week. Still, Kevin had a particular affection for a light sprinkling of freckles on a young model's face in magazine advertisements—or on Steve's wet shoulders and upper back when his tan deepened from hours of swimming.

But was he interested? He wasn't sure. It didn't matter—this was how things worked—how normal boys got girlfriends. Maybe she had already decided for him, and all he had to do was play along.

Kevin developed a list of possible greetings but was interrupted by the chime over the intercom, signaling class change. It left him surprised and panicked. The other students in his row quickly rose and filed past him. After they passed, Kevin turned to see Jenny slowly collecting her books under her arm, apparently stalling as the classroom cleared.

"Hello, Kevin," she said, smiling as she approached.

"Hi, Jenny."

"Jennifer," she corrected.

"Oh, I'm so sorry," he replied, trying to ignore the heat of flushness creeping across his cheeks. *Great job, Kevin*, he thought. *You've already blown it.*

"Jennifer. Got it," he added.

"Oh, no, that's okay," she said, smiling as though trying to ease his discomfort.

"Thanks for the note. I've wanted to meet you." The words felt strange in his mouth, like trying on someone else's voice. The words were also a lie—Kevin wanted her seat in the back of the classroom.

She chuckled, probably seeing right through him with the glasses she wore. There was something familiar about her, but it was not until he looked into her eyes through those large glasses that it hit him. She looked like Ali MacGraw in the 1970 film *Love Story*—right down to the name. Jennifer Cavalleri. The resemblance was uncanny. It wasn't just the name or the looks. It was how she carried herself—the same quiet confidence and unshakable certainty. Like she already knew how this would go. Kevin blinked, realizing he was still standing there, staring like an idiot while his brain ran through movie trivia. He needed to say something—anything.

"Took you long enough," she teased. "I was starting to think you'd never say anything."

After chatting for a few minutes, they exchanged numbers and began speaking on the phone nightly. Driver's Ed was the only class they had together, so they started meeting before and after school to talk or to pass notes to one another, complimenting their now nightly phone conversations.

Kevin wasn't sure when it happened exactly—between the late-night phone calls and the between-class conversations,

Jennifer decided they were a couple and officially dating. And Kevin didn't argue.

Maybe this was it. Perhaps this was the part of himself that had been missing. A girlfriend. A normal relationship. Proof that he wasn't like Dennis.

He let the thought settle in, waiting for the relief, the certainty. But if he was just like everyone else, why did it feel like he was holding his breath, waiting for something to fall apart?

~

Jennifer was Kevin's first real girlfriend, though he was not her first. And she wasn't the only one passing him notes.

Allen was in Kevin's geometry class. He was also Jennifer's ex-boyfriend. He wasn't thrilled that she had moved on and didn't waste time telling Kevin. As the classroom emptied one afternoon, Allen stepped in front of Kevin, too close, his breath sharp with resentment.

"You're dead," he muttered through clenched teeth, his eyes locked on Kevin's, unblinking. Then, with a hard shoulder check, he was gone.

The threats didn't stop there. Occasionally, a note landed on Kevin's desk—folded tight, scrawled in rushed handwriting. *"I'm going to kill you,"* or *"See you after school."*

Allen looked tough but wore braces like Kevin had worn in junior high. Kevin figured he might use that to his advantage if Allen's threats ever resulted in a fight. A well-placed punch to the mouth could do some real damage.

Jennifer dismissed it all. "He's just mad," she told Kevin, rolling her eyes. "He won't do anything." She was confident, but Kevin wasn't so sure.

So Kevin did what he always did—he stayed out of the way. He did his best to avoid Allen while trying not to appear to be cowering away or giving in to his intimidation. In the end, she was right. Allen's threats stopped within weeks, his notes disappearing, his glares turning lazy. He had moved on.

Jennifer was a giver—the first girl to openly vie for Kevin's attention. Other girls had sent him notes or had their friends deliver messages, but with Jennifer, it was different. She was direct, confident, and unapologetic. For the first time, Kevin felt pursued. And he liked it.

One girl, Kelly, was particularly persistent. Every day, a new note landed in Kevin's hands—long confessions, original poetry, or song lyrics carefully copied in neat handwriting. She never delivered them to him herself. Instead, classmates did that for her. When he looked up, he often found Kelly lingering outside the classroom or a few lockers down the hallway, waiting, watching, and hoping to catch his reaction.

Kelly was kind and intelligent but painfully awkward. Her infatuation with Kevin made him feel wanted yet a little uncomfortable. He collected a shoebox full of her letters over the first two years of high school, many tucked away unread for weeks. He never told her outright that he wasn't interested. He just let the notes and her hopes pile up unanswered. His regret for leading her on stuck with him longer than the attention ever did.

Jennifer was different. More mature. She didn't cling to a pack of giggling girls or rely on whispered messages between friends. She moved with quiet confidence, unafraid to walk up to Kevin and introduce herself—no hesitation, no games. Like Ali

MacGraw in Love Story, she was her own woman. She knew what she wanted and didn't wait for permission to take it. Kevin admired that about her. The same way he admired Alice. The same way he wished he could be.

That summer between his sophomore and junior years, Kevin began riding his ten-speed bike to Jennifer's house. She lived about five miles away—an easy ride through back roads and quiet neighborhood streets. Jennifer lived alone with her father, with no siblings and no interruptions. In the air-conditioned refuge of her home, with her father at work and the Florida heat pressing against the windows, Jennifer taught Kevin about sex.

She was a good kisser—slow, deliberate, and unafraid. Kevin had kissed girls before, but Jennifer was the first to pull him in deep, to teach him how to move with her, how to part his lips and match her rhythm. Kevin had pecked girls on the lips before, but Jennifer was the first to probe deep into his mouth with her tongue, teaching him how to French kiss. Long, lingering sessions turned into exploring hands, fingers tracing new territory, hesitation melting into curiosity.

Weeks passed, and Kevin grew bolder while Jennifer grew impatient. Unzipped shorts. Unhooked bras. The first press of bare skin, soft and electric. She didn't hold back, sighing as his hands moved over her, guiding him, showing him what she liked.

Kevin rode to her house every day that summer, legs pumping, heart racing—not just from the effort but from the hunger that built inside him. It wasn't romance or love. It was something urgent—something he couldn't resist. Kevin was like an addict chasing a fix.

It happened during one of those heavy petting sessions. As Kevin lay on top of her on the carpeted floor of her father's living room, she stroked him with her hand through the elastic band of his soccer shorts. She was topless, and the more passionately Kevin kissed her, the more rapid his breathing became. Jennifer moaned and sighed as her chest brushed against his, their bare skin acting as the conduit for the teenage energy building between them.

Her hand moved in slow, steady strokes, sending a tight heat coiling in his stomach. His breath hitched. A pressure built, deep and insistent, rolling through his body with an intensity that made his muscles tense. He clenched his jaw, willing it to stop, to slow down—but it only grew stronger, an unfamiliar wave surging up as he tried to control it. Then it snapped—a release he didn't understand, flooding through him in hot, pulsing bursts, leaving him gasping and shaking.

Kevin abruptly excused himself and ran to the bathroom, but as hard as he tried, he couldn't hold back the pulses of urination as he ran down the hallway. He locked the door and slid his shorts down as fast as he could, but it was too late.

He slammed the bathroom door shut, his breath ragged. He yanked his shorts down, heart hammering as he stared at the milky mess across his leg and fabric. White. Sticky. Not urine. Not sweat. His stomach flipped. *What the hell just happened?* He paced the bathroom floor, franticly wiping as much fluid out of his shorts as possible. He was panicked and out of breath, trying to think of a way to get out of the house as he heard her voice after a soft knock on the door.

"Kevin?" she whispered, laced with concern. Another knock. "Are you okay?"

His pulse kicked harder. He wiped at his leg, at his shorts, his mind racing. How the hell was he supposed to walk back out there?

Kevin didn't remember what excuse he gave her for leaving so abruptly. It was all a blur. He pedaled home in a daze, every shift of his body making him hyper-aware of the drying, humiliating evidence clinging to his skin. He barely made it through the door before bolting to the bathroom, stripping off his shorts like they were contaminated. He scrubbed his skin raw under scalding water, but the confusion and shame clung to him deeper than sweat and anything he could wash away. When he finished showering, he buried the ruined clothes at the bottom of the garbage can outside, pressing them under coffee grounds and paper towels like that would erase what happened.

For the rest of that afternoon, Kevin spent hours combing over his only source of sexual information in the house, the familiar book from the hallway bookshelf. Kevin had just experienced his first orgasm, and it nearly killed him. He wouldn't let that happen again. Next time, Kevin would be ready. He had something to prove to both her and himself.

A few days later, Kevin was back at Jennifer's house, determined. He had spent hours absorbing every word from the book in the hallway, dissecting its lessons like a student cramming for a test. This time would be different. This time, he'd prove— to her, to himself—that he could be the boyfriend she expected.

That summer, Jennifer taught Kevin things he never imagined. The first time she took him in her mouth, he tensed, his breath catching in his throat. It was overwhelming—too much and not enough all at once. He barely had time to process the flood of sensation before it unraveled him completely. With her guidance, he learned how to please her, too.

Now, he understood. The rush, the loss of control, the way it drowned out everything else. The way it made the rest of the world disappear. It clicked in ways it hadn't before—why Miguel had toyed with Dennis, why Dennis had been so willing. Why Miguel had laughed it off but never indeed denied it.

With Jennifer, everything was how it was supposed to be. He told himself that often, let the thought settle in his mind like a mantra. He liked kissing her. He liked the way her body fit against his. He liked the way she wanted him. And that meant he was normal. Didn't it?

Kevin never had intercourse with Jennifer. He was sure she would have let him, probably even waited for him to try—but he never did. They came close once, in her bedroom, the last time Kevin rode his bike to her house. It wasn't that he wasn't attracted to her—he was. Kevin felt it in the heat between them, how she pulled him closer and how his body responded without hesitation. But sometimes, in the quiet moments after, when her fingers traced lazy circles on his chest, he felt a strange distance, as if watching himself from the outside—going through the motions, waiting to feel what he was supposed to feel.

Throughout that summer with Jennifer, Kevin convinced himself he was where he was supposed to be. He buried thoughts of Jose in the showers, Dennis on Miguel's bed, Steve in his swimsuit—pushed them so deep they barely flickered in the back of his mind. He had a girlfriend. A normal relationship. Wasn't that enough?

One evening, as they lay on her couch, Jennifer ran a finger down his arm and smiled lazily. "You like me, right?" she asked, almost teasing. Then, softer, "You'd tell me if you didn't?"

Kevin blinked at her, caught off guard. "Yeah. Of course."

She held his gaze for a moment, then let it go. "Good," she murmured, but the air between them felt thinner, stretched at the edges.

But when the school year started, the space between them widened. They had no classes together and barely ran into each other between periods. Jennifer had given him more than he ever asked for, bent backward to please him, but Kevin had stopped wanting it somewhere along the way. He had everything he was supposed to like, yet it wasn't enough.

Kevin started spacing out during their phone calls. He gave shorter answers and dodged her attempts to make plans.

Jennifer sighed, shifting the phone against her shoulder. "You've been weird lately."

"No, I haven't," he replied.

"You barely talk. You dodge plans. I feel like I'm dating an echo." She paused. "Are you even into this anymore?" Her voice wasn't angry. It wasn't even sad. Just steady and sure, like she already knew the answer.

Kevin hesitated too long before answering, and that was enough. "I've just been busy," he mumbled, knowing she didn't believe him.

His telephone calls to her tapered off, and a short time later, he wouldn't take hers.

He wanted what she gave him—the rush, the proof, the certainty. But somewhere along the way, the wanting faded, and all that was left was its shape—empty and weightless. Like chasing something in a dream, only to wake up and wonder why you ran after it in the first place.

11

Brave New World

(Two years later)

Kevin had once cared about tennis—back when Steve was around, back when the game still felt like part of something bigger. But now, he watched from a distance, more interested in working extra shifts than hitting with the high school team. Maybe it was because Steve wasn't there anymore. Perhaps tennis had just been another thing he needed to outgrow.

Answering a help-wanted ad, Kevin got a part-time job at Grand Union, a grocery store chain expanding into the South. It was his first step into the real world, earning his own money, something tangible that made him feel like he was moving forward. He earned $3.00 an hour, and that first week's earnings of $176.99 made him feel like a millionaire.

He stacked shelves for two weeks, ensuring every label faced forward, every row lined up just right. Precision mattered. At least, he thought it did. But on his last day of employment, the manager shook his head, telling Kevin he was too slow. He wasn't lazy. He wasn't sloppy. But that didn't matter. He was out.

It only took a few weeks to find his next job—this time at Selman's Merchandise, a catalog showroom a half-mile from home. It paid ten cents less than Grand Union, but the real value wasn't in the paycheck.

Selman's had two separate worlds. The showroom—bright, air-conditioned, with soft music piped through the speakers—was where the salesgirls smiled and helped customers pick out jewelry, electronics, and sporting goods. That was called the Light Side, but it wasn't where Kevin worked.

He was a Darksider, part of the warehouse crew—a world of towering shelves, dusty cardboard boxes, heat, and sweat. The Darksiders were lumpers, runners, and pullers. Lumpers unloaded trucks, stacking boxes high, muscles burning in the humid Florida heat. Runners raced down the warehouse aisles, balancing towering loads, dodging obstacles, and skidding around corners on the smooth concrete floors to stock shelves. Every trip became a competition, and Kevin threw himself into it. Pullers grabbed merchandise for customers, tossing it onto the belt that sent it through a portal to the showroom, the connection between the two worlds.

Kevin loved it. The physical labor. The competition. The unspoken hierarchy of who worked fastest, who lifted the heaviest loads, who could keep up. It felt like a test—a real test. He and the other warehouse teens turned every shift into a game of endurance, pushing themselves harder, sweating through their shirts. It was a rush. It felt like something he could win.

While his classmates worried about homework and prom dates, Kevin bought his first car—a 1969 Ford Bronco, deep Caribbean blue, the same one his father had owned for years.

"$300," his dad said. "It's yours if you want it."

Kevin handed over everything he'd saved from those two weeks at Grand Union. His father dropped the keys into his palm, metal cool against his skin. The first time he slid into the driver's seat, he ran his fingers over the grooves of the leather steering wheel, inhaling the familiar mix of sun-warmed vinyl and old engine oil.

This wasn't just a car. It was his ticket out—out of school, out of dependence on others for rides, out of waiting for something to begin.

Kevin's new car and the new friendships he formed at work left him entirely uninterested in the final six months of his senior school year. Mentally, he checked out well before graduation. He went through the motions of class, but when the dismissal bell rang for seniors at noon each day, he headed to work or to spend the rest of the afternoon at the beach with friends. He put himself on the schedule for as many hours and shifts as possible. Kevin couldn't wait to leave the mundanity of high school and most of the people in it behind. He preferred earning money to studying. Money meant success. Success brought respect. Both success and respect produced admiration from others.

~

January in Florida could be unpredictable—some years, cold fronts sent temperatures plunging, but it felt like summer this year with highs in the upper 70s and low 80s. Perfect beach weather. When senior classes let out at noon, Kevin and Ricky didn't need to discuss their plans. If not scheduled to work at Selman's, they'd be on the white sand beaches of Clearwater or Sand Key within forty-five minutes—two seventeen-year-olds scouting for girls who were there doing the same.

"Hey, Ricky!" Kevin called to get his attention as he punched his time clock card. "You want to hit the beach tomorrow?"

"Yeah, if you're driving. Let me check the schedule."

"I already looked," Kevin replied. "We're both off."

"Cool, yeah, for sure. What time?"

"Meet me in the parking lot after the bell," he told Ricky.

Ricky smirked, flipping his feathered hair back with a practiced ease—like he knew exactly how to catch the light. "Give me a ride home tonight?"

"Yeah, that's right. You're too lazy to walk."

Ricky laughed. "Gotta conserve my energy for the ladies tomorrow, man."

Kevin rolled his eyes but didn't argue. He knew the drill. Ricky didn't have a car, but he did have the looks, the confidence, the easy way with girls. Kevin didn't mind playing the wingman—at least, most of the time. But there were moments when he wondered what it would be like to be the one catching someone's attention first.

Ricky Esposito lived with his mom in a rented house less than a half-mile away. Kevin had been to their previous apartment in junior high, though he had never met his mom. Ricky never mentioned his father, and with no siblings and a mother who was absent most of the time, he raised himself and was free to do whatever he wanted. Kevin had known him since seventh grade when their friendship mainly involved putt-putt golf and arcade games. But it wasn't until they worked at Selman's that they started spending real time together again.

They crossed the bridge toward the beach with the windows down and the salty breeze rushing in. Ricky rifled through Kevin's cassette collection.

"Let's see what we have," Ricky said as he ran his index finger down the neat rows of cassette tapes Kevin kept in the car. "Fleetwood Mac. The Cars. Billy Joel. Earth, Wind, and Fire. Aja by Steely Dan. A little Donna Summer here. James Taylor. "Oh, Teddy Pendergrass, too," Ricky teased, rubbing the case like a love letter while rocking his shoulders in a slow and rhythmic motion. "Is this your 'I'm-a-gonna-do-you-slow' tape?"

"Hey, don't rip on Teddy," Kevin replied, keeping his eyes on the road as they crossed the second bridge over the intercoastal. "Or Barry White," he added. "Stay away from Barry, too."

"Queen. More Cars. The Police. More Billy Joel," Ricky continued, taking 52nd Street out of the case and inserting it into the radio. "You've got quite the range, don't you?"

"Anything but country," Kevin replied. "I don't do sad cowboys and dead horses."

The beach was quiet, the way it usually was on weekday afternoons. The real crowds didn't roll in until the weekend. A few retirees walked the shore, collecting shells while seagulls stalked the sand for scraps. North of the pier, the unofficial gathering spot for students, a scattered mix of high schoolers sprawled across towels soaking up the winter sun.

Kevin and Ricky kicked a soccer ball around, aiming strategically near groups of girls—a wayward pass, a quick apology—an easy conversation starter. Ricky handled the rest.

Kevin let him take the lead, watching Ricky charm a blonde in a bright orange bikini that complimented her year-round tan. She laughed, touching his arm and leaning into him. Ricky was good. Too good. Watching him was like watching a magician—you knew it was a trick, but it still worked every time. And Kevin? He was just the guy holding the props.

Kevin could've joined in and tried to strike up his own

conversation. A few of her friends were sitting nearby, glancing over. But the thought of forcing it—of fumbling through small talk that never came naturally—felt exhausting.

The sky darkened over the Gulf, thick clouds swallowing the horizon as afternoon thunderstorms formed over the warm Gulf waters. Kevin suggested leaving soon to beat the traffic and rain home, while Ricky suggested the girl in the orange bikini give him her phone number.

Kevin watched as Ricky flashed his easy grin, already securing her number like it was inevitable. He kicked at the sand, smirking to himself. Ricky always knew what to say while Kevin was still figuring out the script.

~

Joni's Pub wasn't much from the outside—just another small neighborhood bar wedged between a laundromat and a barber shop, the kind of place you could drive past a hundred times without noticing. Inside, though, it was its own world and smelled of cigarette smoke, old wood, and stale beer. Neon signs buzzed softly above the bar, casting a dim glow over the young and old regulars hunched over their drinks. Dartboards thudded against the far wall, and the jukebox hummed with a rotation of old rock and country, its songs cutting through the low babble of conversation of faithful patrons.

Most of the boys were still seventeen, but Joni let them drink anyway. Jeff Hayward's mom owned the place, and she figured it was better for them to drink under her watchful eye than out doing God-knows-what somewhere else. She only allowed it when she was there herself, though, which was all the time.

"You guys go fishing today?" Jeff asked as he poured them a draft pitcher from behind the bar. Jeff was another Darksider who worked in the warehouse with Kevin. He had a six-foot-three slumped-forward frame and lumbering walk. Jeff wore squarish, wire-framed glasses, which he claimed made him look like John Lennon but didn't. John Lennon always wore round spectacles. Jeff's square glasses only made him look like a Yeti with poor eyesight.

Kevin smirked. "We tried."

Ricky scoffed, shaking his head. "More like I caught three, and Kevin caught a tangle of seaweed." He filled both their glasses before leaning back with a grin. "I'm telling you, man. You gotta work on your form."

Kevin shrugged. "I caught the cooler. That counts."

Ricky laughed, shaking his head. "You just wanted an excuse to drive that Bronco somewhere."

Kevin didn't argue. That was partly true.

Across the bar, a couple of older regulars leaned into their drinks while a few young women hovered near the billiard tables, eyeing them between shots. Ricky noticed. He always noticed.

Unlike Kevin and the other Darksiders, who spent their shifts sweating in the warehouse, Ricky was a Lightsider, working on the showroom floor, staying clean, and smelling like cologne instead of cardboard dust. He was among a few guys on the sales floor, giving him the first pick of customers, coworkers, and anyone passing through his department. He had a gift—one none of the other boys could quite figure out. Ricky could talk any girl, even older women, out of their clothes in minutes. It wasn't just confidence. It was something else. Something unteachable.

The Darksiders tested him constantly, singling out girls in a crowd to challenge his abilities. Chachi, the nickname they gave him, rarely disappointed. Ricky hated the nickname, claiming he looked nothing like Scott Baio's character on *Happy Days*. Still, the resemblance was undeniable—the dark feathered hair, the cocky smirk, the way girls gravitated toward him. Kevin thought that resemblance alone probably accounted for half of Ricky's success.

Kevin didn't have much in common with Ricky regarding girls, so he settled for playing the wingman—at the beach, the mall, or high school football games. It usually meant standing around and conversing with the girl's friend while Ricky was already making out with her behind a department store rack or in the back seat of the Bronco. Kevin wished some of Ricky's technique would rub off on him, but it never did. He figured it was one of those things you were born with or not, like height or eye color.

Across the table, Ricky took a sip of his beer and exhaled, shaking his head. "We come here nearly every damn night, you realize that?"

Kevin took a sip of his beer. "So?"

Ricky exhaled, shaking his head. "I dunno, man. Maybe I'm just sick of sitting in the same place, doing the same thing." He tapped the rim of his glass, then looked up. "Let's do something different tomorrow."

Kevin arched a brow. "Like what?"

"Fishing. Real fishing. Not just standing on the shore of a lake. Let's go saltwater fishing."

Kevin smirked. "Yeah? You gonna teach me how to 'really' fish?"

Ricky grinned. "Hell yeah. I'll even let you borrow a lucky lure."

Kevin rolled his eyes, but the idea wasn't bad. They hadn't been out in a while.

"Fine," he said. "Tomorrow night."

~

The Gandy Bridge stretched low and long across the bay, the water on either side dark and restless under the moonlight. Kevin pulled the Bronco into a gravel spot near the bridge, the tires crunching over crushed shells as he killed the engine. The tide was moving out, pulling the shallows back into deeper channels, leaving behind the briny scent of seaweed and salt. Ricky popped the cap off his beer with a practiced flick of his thumb, taking a slow sip before turning to Kevin.

"So, you think we're gonna catch anything?"

Kevin smirked, dragging the gear from the back of the Bronco. "I think you're gonna run your mouth the whole time, and I'll be the one who catches something."

Ricky took a slow sip, watching Kevin drag the gear out of the Bronco. "You wanna put money on that?"

Kevin didn't look up. "You already owe me five bucks from the last time we were out here."

Ricky waved a hand dismissively. "Allegedly."

After walking a few hundred feet down the long boardwalk that hung below the bridge, they picked their spot and settled in. The boys baited their hooks with fresh shrimp and cast their lines over the railing, the weights plunking into the dark water below. The bridge above hummed with passing cars, their headlights streaking across the bay before disappearing into the night.

For a while, neither of them spoke. The only sounds were the quiet lap of water against the pilings and the occasional splash of a mullet breaking the surface.

Ricky spoke first. "You ever think about just… taking off?"

Kevin reeled in his line slightly. "Like leaving town?"

Ricky shrugged, his gaze fixed on the horizon. "Yeah. Just getting in a car and going. No plan. No looking back."

Kevin thought about it. "Where would you even go?"

Ricky smirked. "California. Or maybe New York. Somewhere where there's action, and people have actual adventures, you know?"

Kevin shook his head, casting his line out again. "You wouldn't last a week."

Ricky laughed. "Bullshit. I'd be fine." He leaned against the railing, watching the car lights move across the causeway, flickering in the distance across the dark waters of the bay. "I just don't wanna wake up one day and realize I wasted my life in this place."

Ricky exhaled, smoke curling from the cigarette pinched between his fingers. "You ever notice how guys like us get stuck here? They say they're gonna leave, but next thing you know, they got a wife, a kid, and a job at some furniture store, and that's it. Game over."

Kevin opened his mouth, then shut it. What was he supposed to say? That he wondered the same thing sometimes? That maybe Ricky was right, and Bayview was nothing more than a waiting room? He cast his line again instead. He understood the feeling—restlessness, the nagging sense that something else was waiting just beyond the edges of their world.

Ricky suddenly jerked his rod, reeling fast. "Oh, hell yeah! Told you!"

Kevin turned just as Ricky pulled up a small, wriggling fish. Ricky held it up triumphantly, grinning like he'd just won the lottery.

Kevin deadpanned. "That's just a whiting. It's practically bait."

Ricky cackled, tossing it back into the water. "Still counts."

They fished for a few hours, using all the shrimp and finishing the six beers they brought. The conversation drifted between work, girls, and Ricky's latest theories on why some guys had it and others didn't. He swore it wasn't about looks. "It's about energy, man. You walk in like you own the place, and they notice. Every time."

Kevin only half-believed him.

"So, what now?" Ricky asked as they packed up.

Kevin checked his watch. "Drop you off and home for me."

Ricky reluctantly agreed. "Let's go."

The Bronco rumbled to life. Kevin watched the headlights flicker across the bridge, disappearing into the darkness ahead. Some cars kept going, fading into the distance. Others looped back toward the city like they were doing. He wondered which kind he and Ricky would be.

As they crossed the bridge, Ricky rolled down the window, letting the wind rush through his hair. "California, man," he muttered, half to himself. "Maybe sooner than later." Kevin didn't answer. He just kept driving.

12

THE GREEN FLASH

Joni's Pub felt like home on Friday nights—the hum of conversation, the clatter of pool balls, the jukebox humming out classic rock. It was familiar. Predictable. But Ricky wasn't. He shifted constantly—tapping his fingers against the table, glancing toward the door, cracking his knuckles like he was waiting for an escape hatch to appear.

It was a slow night, even for a Friday, with sparse attendance by the usual crowd. When the two boys finished playing darts and shooting pool, Ricky asked if he could crash at Kevin's house for the night. Without asking why, Kevin agreed, offering to drive him home in the morning. Each took a couch in the living room, but after about twenty minutes, Kevin heard Ricky whisper.

"You still awake?"

"Yeah," Kevin replied.

"Let's go to Daytona," Ricky said, sprawled out on the sofa like the idea was as natural as getting up for a glass of water.

Kevin blinked. "Now?"

"Yeah. Why not?" Ricky sat up, already energized. "We'll be there before sunrise. Spend the day on the beach, pick up some college girls, and drive back. Easy."

Kevin ran a hand through his hair. "Dude, that's a three-hour drive."

"So? We've got all night."

Kevin exhaled, rubbing his hands over his face. Every instinct screamed no. He should tell Ricky to sleep, that they'd go another time, that this was ridiculous. But Ricky's gaze sparkled, daring him to say yes, and Kevin never wanted to be the guy who said no.

"Man, this is stupid," Kevin muttered, shaking his head, but Ricky just grinned, waiting.

Kevin let the silence stretch between them, hoping Ricky would drop it, but he didn't. Ricky just raised an eyebrow— amused, patient, like he already knew the answer.

Kevin sighed, already knowing it, too. "Alright, I'm in. Let's fucking go."

Kevin might have been taller, stronger, the better student, the one with a car. But Ricky? Ricky knew how to take what he wanted. He never had to beg. He never had to worry. People— Kevin included—just went along with him. Kevin wondered if the girls Ricky seduced felt the same way—a little used but never quite able to say no.

While Carol slept in the back bedroom and Bert was on duty at the fire station, Kevin needed to think of something to tell her. He was a planner, and the impulsiveness of Ricky's suggestion tripped every internal safety fuse he had. Kevin's intuition didn't matter, though. He didn't want to be labeled scared, not by Ricky, and especially not by the other Darksiders at work. He might as well make the adventure sound like mutual agreement.

Already wearing shorts to sleep in, the boys put their shirts and sneakers back on and were ready to go.

Kevin scrawled a note on the counter: "Up early, heading to the beach to take pictures of the sunrise. Back a little later." It wasn't a lie. Not really. He left the note on the kitchen counter where Carol would see it when she made the morning coffee. She would never have been comfortable had she known he was driving three hours and 150 miles away to the opposite side of the state. But that was not relevant right now. Kevin would call her later in the morning to let her know he was okay, was with friends, and would be home later than planned that afternoon. Telling the truth while not divulging every little detail was not a lie. If he didn't lie, he was telling the truth.

Kevin let the clutch out and allowed the Bronco to roll backward down the driveway and into the street. They pushed it past a few houses with some effort before starting it. It was a stealth getaway intended not to wake his mother. Carol was a light sleeper whenever Kevin was out at night, especially when Bert was on duty. This trip would be the farthest from home he had ever driven and the first time out of town, besides frequent trips to the Clearwater and St. Pete beaches.

Without traffic, the drive was easy in the middle of the night. Daytona was a straight shot along I-4 and through Orlando. Once off the interstate, the main beach area was a quick jog up Hwy-1 and across the intercoastal waterway to A1A.

The Bronco's tires hummed against the pavement, the faint glow of the dashboard clock marking the passage of time in slow increments. The night felt endless, the dark stretching in all directions, swallowing the world outside their headlights.

Ricky drummed his fingers against the dashboard, humming along to the radio as relaxed as if they were cruising the beach on a Saturday afternoon. Gripping the wheel too tight, Kevin kept glancing at the gas gauge, the mile markers, and the empty road stretching far ahead.

The farther Kevin drove from his sleeping and unaware mother, the darker it got between cities on the interstate. If something unexpected were to happen, no one knew where they were or where they were going. More importantly, Kevin didn't know where they were, who they might meet, or what would happen that day. How would two seventeen-year-olds protect themselves in the event of trouble? Fatigue was sure to set in since they had not slept that night. Kevin's mind raced with apprehension while Ricky spoke about how great their day ahead would be. Kevin took deep breaths once he realized how shallow his breathing had become.

Ricky talked about college girls, hookups, and everything that made this trip worth it. Kevin thought about crashing, about his mother waking up in an empty house, about dying a virgin before his eighteenth birthday.

The boys arrived well before sunrise, giving them time to drive along the main strip to look for entrances to the beach. Cars were not allowed on the beach before dawn, so they found a parking spot near an old stone archway leading onto the beach and parked there to wait.

As they sat on the stone wall facing the ocean, the breeze from the Atlantic was cool and refreshing, especially after the overnight drive. They listened to the surf roll in, its repeated rhythm, waves higher and mightier than on the Gulf side of the state. It was soothing until Kevin suddenly had a horrific realization. His camera was safe in its case in his bedroom back home. He had forgotten to bring his alibi with him. He knew his mother wouldn't go into his bedroom, and even if she did, she wouldn't have known where he kept it or noticed it missing. Still, Kevin would have no pictures of the sunrise, no documentation of their adventure, and no photos of the girls they would meet. There would be no proof for the Darksiders back at work. It didn't matter now—it was too late. Kevin would have to think of what to say to his parents if they asked to see the sunrise pictures.

"Let's see if we can catch the green flash," Kevin suggested.

"The green flash? What's that?"

"You know, the green flash at sunrise and sunset," he replied, having to think for a second about whether it occurred only at sunrise or sunset. Maybe it was both. "It's a split-second flash of green light that appears on the horizon where the sun rises and sets."

"Really?" Ricky asked, questioning whether it was true or Kevin was pulling his leg, which would have been unusual.

"Yeah, it's real. I saw it once at sunset off Clearwater Beach."

"Why's it green?"

"It's an optical illusion. The sun's light gets bent through the atmosphere just below the horizon. It's the same reason the sun looks red or orange when it's low on the horizon instead of bright white when it's overhead."

Kevin continued to scientifically explain the phenomena as he watched Ricky take long, slow tokes from his cigarette.

Ricky had a peculiar way of holding his cigarette between his thumb and index finger with the lit end hidden in the palm of his hand, instead of between his index and middle finger with the lit end outward like most people held their cigarettes. Kevin had seen enough war movies to know this was how soldiers smoked in their foxholes. It helped prevent them from being spotted by enemy snipers who targeted the red glow. Maybe that was just Hollywood, though.

Kevin didn't let Ricky smoke in his car and didn't care for the smell himself, but he understood the tough-guy machismo it was supposed to symbolize. *Was that why Ricky smoked?* Maybe not. Kevin remembered reading an article some time ago regarding the psychology behind how people held cigarettes. Yet, he couldn't recall what the various methods were subconsciously supposed to have represented.

Ricky exhaled slowly, the cigarette tucked between his fingers, his face unreadable. Kevin watched him, searching for something—an answer, a reason why Ricky could move so freely while Kevin overthought every step.

Ricky didn't look away from the horizon. "You'll miss it if you keep staring at me."

Kevin blinked, heat creeping up his neck. He hadn't realized he was staring. Or maybe he had. Perhaps that was the problem.

Sitting there, watching Ricky smoke, watching the sky brighten, and the green flash fail to appear, Kevin wasn't sure if he had missed something real or had been looking in the wrong place for something that wasn't.

As the light of day replaced the darkness, the iron gates to the stoned arch entrance finally opened, and they were allowed to drive onto the beach. Kevin had never seen such a vast expanse of compact sand and was amazed that they let the public drive and park on it wherever they wished. Then he thought again about forgetting to bring his camera and what he might say to his mother when he called to tell her he would be home later than expected.

The further they drove on the beach, the more bikes they saw. First, a few parked along the street. Then, dozens. Then, an entire stretch of beach lined with them—Harleys, choppers, bikes gleaming under the morning sun. Everywhere they looked, leather jackets, bandanas, tattooed arms gripping handlebars.

Ricky's grin faltered. "Uh… dude."

Kevin swallowed. "I think we're in the wrong place."

Ricky's head snapped to the side, eyes darting from biker to biker, from the revving engines to the girls clinging to the backs of bikes instead of frat boys with beer cups. A group of men in leather vests walked past, one of them shooting them a look that made Kevin's stomach tighten.

Ricky exhaled sharply. "Oh, shit. It's Bike Week."

By noon, the truth was undeniable. Spring Break wasn't for another two weeks. They were surrounded by leather-clad bikers revving Harleys in every direction, not college girls looking for hookups with high schoolers. They had driven half the night to land in the middle of Daytona's annual Bike Week, along with a half-million bikers from around the country that also descended the beach town. Daytona's theme weeks were well known by its citizens, the hotel and hospitality trade, and fans of various interests who subscribed to magazines about those interests. The theme week schedule was not so well known by naïve seventeen-year-olds who lived on the other side of the state.

Besides Kevin leaving his camera at home and driving to Daytona on the wrong week, their third significant error was having a total of five dollars in their combined pockets. Ricky assumed Kevin had some money with him, which he usually did. But this time, Kevin had spent most of his cash at Joni's the night before, paying for the rounds of beer like he regularly did. Neither owned an ATM card yet, so they stretched the folded Lincoln as far as they could throughout the day. A little over $4.00 of it bought them a chilled six-pack. Ricky finagled two hot dogs from a promotional event hosted by Coppertone suntan lotion on the beach that afternoon.

When they decided it was time to call it a day, and after Ricky resigned himself to the fact that he wouldn't score without a Hog to cruise around on, they headed home. The two were exhausted, grimy from the day's sweat, hungry and thirsty, and had a floorboard full of sand. With some quarters left in his pocket, Kevin was concerned they might not make it home without running out of gas, so he insisted they drive home with the windows rolled up to maximize fuel efficiency.

By the time they reached the outskirts of Bayview, the Bronco was running on fumes. Kevin stopped and pumped those seventy-five cents into the beast to get Ricky to his house and him to his. It was the briefest gas stop and the most precise squeeze-control of a gas pump handle in Kevin's short driving history, but it did the trick.

The house was empty when he arrived. By the time Bert and Carol returned from dinner, Kevin was showered and had fallen asleep on the sofa watching television. Although a bit sunburned, he told them what a great day he had had with Ricky at the beach while they told him what they had just eaten at their favorite Chinese restaurant. Kevin apologized to his mother for being gone all day without calling to check in, and she told him there were leftovers in the kitchen if he was hungry. After taking her up on the offer, Kevin spent a comfortable Saturday evening at home quietly contemplating the adventures of the past twenty-four hours and what he would tell the Darksiders at work on Monday.

Kevin was tired and glad to be at home safely. The day had been an adventure of many firsts, but he felt guilty for having lied to his parents. Kevin was also relieved they did not meet any college girls and didn't hook up. He couldn't imagine how that might have worked with so many people around them.

Kevin thought about the green flash—how it happens in an instant. Blink, and it's gone. Maybe that's how life worked, too. Perhaps that's why Ricky never stopped chasing the next thrill before the last one even faded.

But if Ricky ever caught something—if he got what he wanted—would he know what to do with it? Or would he always be looking past the horizon for something better?

And Kevin—what was he chasing?

13

Feels Like the First Time

Two weeks after their day trip to Daytona Beach, on a Friday night like most other Friday nights at Joni's Pub, Kevin and Ricky were still talking to coworkers about their adventure. They agreed to go again next spring, with a few other Darksiders eagerly volunteering to join them. They were also careful not to discuss the trip around Rachael, who was often there at Joni's. She was the receptionist behind the plate-glass window overlooking the dock area where they all worked. Bringing her along next year would be awkward.

Rachael smoked like Ricky but held her cigarette between her fingers with a bent wrist like a girl was supposed to. She smoked with her right hand and made wide, arching motions through the air between puffs. After each puff and arching motion, she would prop her smoking hand in a resting position high in the air and plant her elbow into her hip for support. Rachael was a straight shooter, both at the pool table and with her words, and her smoking and directness reminded Kevin a little of his aunt Alice.

Once Ricky and Kevin lost their game and gave up their run on the table, Kevin announced, "That's it, boys, I'm done. I work in the morning." It was still early, but Kevin didn't want to make it a long night.

"Ready to go?" Kevin asked, turning to Ricky, who had ridden with him from work.

"I'm good. I'll catch a ride home later."

"Cool," Kevin replied as he reached around Rachael to place his empty mug on the counter. She sat at the bar watching them play, just as she studied them toil on the dock at work from her office. As Kevin reached around her, his face came close to hers, and he shifted his focus from his empty mug to her gaze.

"Give me a ride home?" she asked. It almost sounded like a statement.

"Yeah, sure," Kevin replied tentatively. He was not objecting but instead caught off guard by the unexpected request. "Ricky's staying. You didn't drive?"

"No, I rode with Jeff from work."

"Gotcha. Where do you live?"

"Not far. You'll see," Rachael answered, lifting herself from the barstool. She put her clutch purse under her arm and headed for the front door. She didn't stop to say goodbye to the others, and as Kevin followed behind her, he motioned a peace sign to his friends at the pool table. The gesture was his signature greeting and farewell, a relic from the counterculture sixties that he had adopted and still used, even though there was nothing counterculture about him.

Rachael and Kevin chatted as she directed him to turn here or to go straight there. It was just small talk, but he learned she had already been married and divorced and was twenty-four, six years older than him. She still lived with her parents, or more accurately, had moved back in with them after the divorce. She spoke openly and freely, though Kevin didn't want to probe for details. He was curious, however, and felt sorry for her having already divorced at such a young age and having to live at home with her parents. As he drove, they headed into a familiar neighborhood, recalling her saying 'not far' before leaving the pub.

Rachael cranked her window handle a turn or two and reached into her purse. Kevin considered whether to ask her not to smoke in his car or to allow it for the brief ride. Still, he couldn't help himself from saying, "If you don't mind. The smoke bothers me."

"It didn't bother you in the pub, did it?"

"Well, yeah, it did a little," he replied, "but that's a big space, and this is a small one." He glanced over to discern her expression at his response and to determine if he had offended her. Rachael continued to search the inside of her purse before pulling out a single house key and holding it upward between her fingers.

"How about this?" she asked, pursing her lips and cocking her head to one side. "Does this bother you?"

Kevin was embarrassed for assuming she would light a cigarette in his car without first asking. "No, of course not. Sorry, I just thought—"

"Turn right at the next street," she instructed, cutting him off mid-sentence.

"That's Ricky's street. You and Ricky live on the same block?"

"Of course not, dork-head," Rachael replied. Kevin couldn't tell if her words sounded more like humor or disbelief in his gullibility. "Park at Ricky's house," she directed, so he did.

Rachael was out of the Bronco and had turned the house key in the lock before Kevin unlocked his driver's door. He got out and followed, still trying to establish why they were there.

Kevin hesitated in the doorway, his hand gripping the open frame. He could ask—why here, why him, why now—but he didn't. Instead, he followed like he always did—like he was supposed to.

Once inside, she closed the door behind him and turned the deadbolt. Rachael took his hand and led Kevin across the room, pausing in the hallway of the modest house. She glanced first into the bedroom to the left and then to the one on the right.

For as many times as Kevin picked Ricky up and dropped him off there, he had never been inside the house. All the questions pulsing through his brain jammed up in his mouth. He couldn't correctly form or speak simple words for all the questions he wanted to ask. *Why did Rachael have a key? How did she know where Ricky lived? Where was his mother? And if Jeff had given her a lift from work to Joni's, how did she get to work earlier that afternoon? Where was her car? Where did she really live?*

Rachael looked and moved left, pulling Kevin behind her.

Kevin was beginning to feel a slight buzz from his last beer. He drank less than his friends, and beer sneaked up on him slowly and unexpectedly, unlike the few times he had tried liquor with its more immediate effect. In the dimly lit house and amongst the unfamiliar furnishings, time began moving slower. Suddenly and without warning, his mouth tasted like the cigarettes Rachael smoked. Kevin neither liked it nor was repulsed by it as she kissed him deeply and pulled his clothing toward hers.

He wanted to stop to catch his breath, but her lips wouldn't release him. His legs tingled as they did in the final hard sprint of a jog, weakened by the lack of oxygen. When her mouth finally released his, Rachael drew in a deep gasp of air for herself, and Kevin's lips instinctively fell to her breast that she had exposed to him. The room became hotter and continued to blur.

With all their clothing discarded, his need to bear down upon her intensified. His mouth moved back to hers, and with awkward lunges, he found her wetness as she drew him into it. Rachael wrapped her legs around Kevin's waist and dug her fingertips into his back, her breath hot against his neck.

She pulled him in, and with each deep thrust, his pace intensified until reaching a frenzy. Kevin couldn't stop—didn't want to—but his body moved ahead of him, desperate and unthinking.

Kevin broke his lock on her lips and arched his back, and as he did, his body trembled and shuddered uncontrollably. When it ended, it was like slamming into a wall. Sudden. Heavy. Final.

When Kevin's head fell onto the pillow beside hers, he felt her damp hair against his own. His body was too heavy to lift itself. Rachael's legs broke their lock around his waist and fell as well, sliding down his sweat-moistened hips and upper legs. Her fingertips and nails dug deeply into his back muscles, leaving impressions once she retracted them. Gliding down his spine, her hands stopped at his still-constricted butt muscles and held them tightly to prevent his withdrawal.

Kevin continued to press his chest into hers while she tried to contain him. His breathing slowed as his senses gradually returned. He could taste the saltiness of her sweat as he opened his eyes, focussing on the unfamiliar comforter pattern they lay upon. He could hear his heartbeat pounding in his eardrums as it slowed. Finally, Kevin could smell the staleness of the bedroom. He could smell her cigarettes and the remnants of their sex.

Rachael held him tighter when Kevin moved his arms and hands and began to press against the bed to pull away. He pushed away from her as she fought to retain him. Finally, the bond of sweat and semen that joined them together broke, and he withdrew himself from within her.

Kevin used his shirt to remove the event from himself and

quickly dressed his lower body. Rachael conceded and followed suit.

With the tossed shirt on the back seat floorboard, he drove Rachael back to Joni's. He saw her car in the parking lot where it had been all evening. Kevin couldn't escape the smells that lingered in the Bronco, accentuated by the lit cigarette she was now smoking. When they arrived, he sat in the driver's seat with the car idling and Rachael staring at him.

"You want to come in?" she finally asked, the first to break the silence.

Kevin gave her an uneasy grin and shrugged his shoulders. "No shirt, no service."

Rachael unlatched her seatbelt and turned toward him, putting her right hand on his bare chest, cupping his muscle as she lightly squeezed his nipple between her thumb and index finger. Rachael leaned in to kiss him, but as she did, Kevin instinctively turned his head slightly to the right, hitting her cheek with his lips instead to avoid the taste of her cigarette. Once pecked, she twisted her fingers before releasing his chest and moving her touch to the door handle instead.

"See you at work then," she stated.

As he drove away, Kevin watched Rachael walk toward the pub door and enter, presumably to return Ricky's key to him.

On the way home, Kevin rolled the windows down and let the incoming rush of night air cleanse the car's interior. It cooled his bare torso and helped dry the beads of sweat that still lingered on it. Then he reached behind his seat and grabbed his soiled shirt, tossing it out the passenger window on a stretch of road that was dark and isolated.

Home was close now—safe, quiet, familiar—a place where this

night wouldn't exist except in the sweat and sex still clinging to his skin. He would arrive home before his curfew—no longer a virgin—with his eighteenth birthday just two days away.

14

THE GRADUATE

The red cap sat awkwardly on Kevin's head, the stiff edges pressing against his temples. The tassel dangled in his peripheral vision, an irritating flicker of movement. Around him, classmates fidgeted with their gowns, whispered under their breath, or sat frozen with forced smiles as parents aimed cameras at the stage.

He rolled the program between his fingers, barely glancing at it, his name buried in a list of over eight hundred others. No distinctions, no honors. Just another graduate in a sea of identical red gowns.

When they called his name, Kevin moved automatically. He walked up the steps, shook the principal's hand, and took the ceremonial scroll representing a diploma. The lights overhead were blinding, hot against his skin. Somewhere in the crowd, Bert and Carol watched, maybe proud at their firstborn's achievement or perhaps disappointed his gown was not white and his academic accomplishments not more significant.

The moment was already fading when he reached his seat again. It was done—over—a milestone that felt more like a formality. Kevin sat down, adjusting the cap that still didn't fit right, and waited for the rest of the names over the loudspeakers.

Despite his growing perfectionism and judgment of non-achievers, Kevin never truly pushed himself academically—an irony he chose to ignore.

He applied to just two colleges under the pressure of teachers and his parents to start the application process. College was expected. Both Cornell and Stanford sent him conditional acceptance letters despite his mediocre GPA and because of his high SAT scores and well-written essays. He knew little about the schools—only that they were far away, expensive, and entirely outside the world he had only recently built for himself.

There was a time—brief, barely worth mentioning—when Kevin wondered what leaving might be like. To board a plane, unpack in some dorm room at Stanford, or walk across the manicured lawns of Cornell. But the thought flickered and died. Kevin had carved a place for himself here—his job, friends, and habits. The idea of trading it for something unknown felt less like an opportunity and more like a hassle.

Ricky would have jumped at the chance to go away for college had he the grades and financial means. Steve certainly was, though Kevin had not spoken to him since parting ways to attend different high schools.

On Monday, Kevin clocked in for his first full-time shift at work.

~

Selman's Merchandise offered Kevin a promotion, which he accepted without hesitation. He would be a full-time Receiver, spending most of his time unloading trucks and doing the counting and paperwork to receive the inbound merchandise. The promotion also meant he would spend time on the dock in front of Rachael's window, which he had mixed emotions about.

A large part of Kevin enjoyed being the object of Rachael's attention and affection, and they continued to have casual sex when it was convenient. Kevin enjoyed it, but he also knew she wanted much more than he was willing to give. He knew she wanted a serious and exclusive relationship; though she never stated it, it was implied. What they did both understand was that he had just turned eighteen and was only now beginning to experience his independence.

Kevin wouldn't commit more of himself—not to her. If he ever wanted something serious, it wouldn't be with a divorced receptionist still living with her parents. Kevin was self-aware and uneasy about that, especially under her steely gaze as he performed his new role on the dock in front of her window. Yet, despite that guilt, they continued to have sex while pretending to be content with the arrangement.

Sex aside, Rachael and Kevin rarely did the kind of things people usually do when dating. They didn't go to the movies. He never took her out to romantic dinners. They didn't have picnics in the park. He never invited her to join him or their group on their trips to the beach. The two never had those hours-long phone chats about nothing like young lovers tend to do. The nature of their relationship was precise, at least in Kevin's mind. Their relationship centered on sharing pitchers of beer at Joni's with the guys and occasional romps in the sack. If she was at the pub and the hour grew late, provided they had no other plans and were both in the mood, they borrowed Ricky's house key or had sex in the back of the Bronco.

Kevin rented a hotel room in advance a few times, knowing that he would take her there only after an evening out with friends. Those planned connections and hotel room use were over as soon as they completed the act. There were no afterglow chats, overnight sleepovers, or lazy late mornings under the covers. Kevin knew Rachael enjoyed being with him, especially as he became more experienced with the sexual practice that their rendezvous offered him. Still, he didn't consider or concern himself with feelings of what she wanted, what she enjoyed, or what she needed.

There were moments when Kevin wondered if he should end it—if he owed at least that honesty to Rachael. But the thought never lasted long. He liked her, sure, but he liked the arrangement more. It was clean and straightforward. No expectations. If Rachael was hoping for more or thought the relationship was going somewhere, that was on her. Kevin never promised anything. He never asked for anything. He just let things happen as they always did—effortless, uncomplicated, without the weight of expectations.

The more time he spent with Rachael, the less he wanted to. The excitement was gone, replaced by habit. And habit wasn't enough to keep him coming back.

He could have called her and ended it properly. Instead, he let weeks stretch into months, assuming she'd get the message. Assuming she already had. He was ready to dress and leave as soon as they finished.

On one such occasion, Kevin told her he was tired and was going home to turn in—he had to be at work early the next day.

Rachael walked into Joni's an hour later, her eyes locking onto Kevin from across the bar. He barely had time to register her presence before she stood at the edge of the table, her voice sharp and level.

"Early night, huh?" she said, crossing her arms.

Kevin felt Ricky's gaze flick between them, waiting for the show. He forced a casual shrug. "Changed my mind."

Rachael scoffed. "Right. That's what you do, isn't it?"

A few of their friends around them snickered. Kevin felt heat creep up his neck. She wasn't yelling or making a scene, but her words were heavy and sharp. He could have brushed it off, made a joke, or shifted the conversation. Instead, he sipped his beer and let the uncomfortable silence linger. Eventually, Rachael shook her head, gave him a look he hadn't seen from her before, and walked away.

Kevin exhaled. He wasn't sure if he was annoyed or relieved. Something unsettled him as he watched Rachael walk away— something sharp, barely there. It gnawed at him like the static hum of a TV left on in the background. But before it could take shape, Ricky clapped him on the back, cracking a joke, and Kevin let it slip away, just like everything else.

Rachael had been in control that first time before his eighteenth birthday. But that changed fast. Now, her affection and desire were his to abuse. He treated her feelings as dispensable and not his responsibility, and that was the last time they gave one another any of their time or affection.

Jennifer was his first kiss. His first girlfriend. His first blowjob. Rachael was his first fuck. Each one gave him something, taught him about women and sex, leaving their hearts behind in exchange for his building confidence in himself and evolving misunderstanding of intimacy. It was hardly a fair trade. He took what they offered and left the rest behind. Now, they were just names, just lessons. Pages in a book he had already closed.

Kevin was ready for what came next.

15

GIRL IN THE RED DRESS

The Darksider's ringleader was Mike Edwards. Mike was two years older than the others and already in college, studying to be a teacher. He specifically wanted to be a physical education teacher—he was not fond of academics but did enjoy sports. His favorite line was, 'Those who can't do, teach, and those who can't teach, teach P.E..' He was the most senior of the warehouse staff at Selmen's, training and mentoring each new employee hired.

Mike was the spitting image of Kurt Russell in Disney's 1975 film *The Strongest Man in the World*. He had the same facial features, blond hair, and body type. Like Ricky's uncanny resemblance to Scott Baio, Mike's likeness to Kurt Russell was astonishing. He loved having fun and played harmless practical jokes, cutting up over everything. He was a constant eruption of positive and unconstrained energy. There was an ease about him—he laughed louder, took up space, and owned every room he walked into. Kevin liked being around that energy; it complemented his seriousness and made him feel like he had a place as a piece of the group puzzle.

Kevin couldn't think of any movie or television star he resembled. The Darksiders never gave him a nickname, either. He was just Kevin—hard-working, well-liked, dependable Kevin.

Kevin split his time off from work between Ricky and Mike, but rarely together—two separate friendships and versions of himself. He developed both friendships in parallel but along very different paths.

With Mike, he played sports: tennis, soccer, and racquetball. They dressed in jeans, threw darts at neighborhood pubs, and shot pool at USF's student rec center. Mike loved classic rock—Pink Floyd, The Cars, Supertramp—and bands that Kevin also liked. Mike detested disco music. Every Friday night, the two were at the mall cinema for the midnight showing of *The Rocky Horror Picture Show* or sitting on the tailgate of the Bronco, drinking cheap beer as Mike talked about his girlfriend and the other girls he dated in secret.

With Ricky, it was different. Slacks, silk shirts, and seven-and-sevens at The Cypress Club. Flashing lights on the dance floor, overpriced cocktails, pretending they were older than they were. Disco anthems pulsed through the speakers—Michael Jackson, Sister Sledge, Earth, Wind & Fire—as Ricky effortlessly worked the room with Kevin hovering just outside the action.

Two lives, two identities. Kevin didn't quite fit in either.

Kevin spent his childhood watching the world from a screen, absorbing life through sitcoms, news broadcasts, and Saturday morning cartoons. But now, he was in it—living it, shaping it, navigating it in real time. His heroes weren't TV characters anymore; they were those around him. He studied them, looking for a reflection of himself, a blueprint for who he was supposed to be.

Music became Kevin's new language, filling the spaces in his moods and emotions that words couldn't. With Mike, it was rock anthems—guitars and rebellion. With Ricky, it was disco, rhythm, and seduction. But it was different when Kevin was alone, washing or waxing the Bronco under the Ear Tree, atop the green grass and white clover of his childhood bee hunting grounds. Something softer. "Sailing" or "Minstrel Gigolo" by Christopher Cross, "On and On" by Stephen Bishop, or Bobby Caldwell's "What You Won't Do for Love." Songs that felt like floating, like watching the world from a distance, like waiting for something to begin, even if he wasn't sure what.

~

Kevin and a few of the Darksiders kept their promise to go to Daytona as a group. After their return and a weekend of rest, they were back at work telling their Spring Break tales to others. That's when she walked through the employee entrance and made her way to the time clock.

Kevin and Mike worked to offload pallets from the trucks, cutting the shipping bands that held the merchandise onto the pallets securely. They then stacked the individual boxes into smaller stacks to be transported by hand-cart down the aisles to their storage locations in the warehouse.

That was when they saw her. She moved with quiet confidence, her dark hair swaying as she walked. She didn't rush, didn't hesitate. When she reached the time clock, her index finger glided over the punch cards like she had all the time in the world. She barely glanced at the dock workers watching her, as if she was aware of their attention but uninterested—a woman used to being looked at but rarely impressed by the ones doing the looking.

Mike and Kevin slowed their movements and remained partially concealed behind the stacks of boxes, trying to avoid blatantly staring at her. She was beautiful. Her silky dark hair flowed just past her waist to rest atop the upper curve of her hips. Her dress exposed long legs and shapely calves, and her olive skin glowed in the dimly lit chamber of the dock area. Her dress was cherry red, a shade lighter than scarlet but classier than candy apple, and it wrapped her figure like the fitted gown of an actress in a James Bond movie.

As a young adolescent, Kevin had discovered a rolled-up poster hidden in the back of his father's closet one dull summer afternoon when he had nothing better to do and felt unusually emboldened. It was an image of Cher, taken early in her career, wearing only tightly wrapped cellophane in a provocative pose. He was reminded of that poster as he watched the new girl punch the timecard. Behind the beauty in cherry red at the time clock, Rachael stood in her office, peering at him through that large plate-glass window sometimes serving as his conscience, her eyes cold in judgment.

"Who is that?" Kevin whispered to Mike.

"Don't even think about it," Jeff snorted, shifting his weight against his cart. "She's been here a week. Works Jewelry."

Naturally, Kevin thought. Where else would someone who dresses like that work?

"She won't speak to any of us," Jeff continued.

"What's her name?" Mike asked.

"Maritza."

"Why won't she talk to anyone?"

Jeff snickered and replied, "Are you stupid? Look at her. Rodney and Kenny have tried already, so forget it."

"Tried as in—"

Jeff cut Kevin off, "Hit on her. They both flamed—shot them right down, so good luck with that."

Wise woman, Kevin remarked to himself. *She saw right through those characters.* Rodney and Kenny were best friends and real players. They were Darksiders, too, but a couple of years older and in an arrogant clique duo. They were considered popular but dumb jocks. Rodney was more handsome than anyone deserved to be, with a muscular, ripped body from playing semi-pro soccer. He wasn't quite good enough to make the big league, but his skills kept his Adonis-like body in shape.

Kenny was not as good-looking and didn't have Rodney's naturally defined body, which made him Rodney's perfect wingman. They did, however, share the same machismo-like overconfidence and attitude, believing they were God's gift to women. Their Latin bravado was always on and dialed far past the point of annoyance. The two approached women for sport, and it didn't surprise Kevin that they had already tried to peacock their masculinity to the beautiful new employee. Kevin imagined what cheesy lines they likely used and how, even at a young age, Maritza had probably heard it all before. No doubt she found it easy to peg them as simply two more guys who wanted to undress and bang her, he figured.

"Does she have a boyfriend?" Mike asked.

"Dude, she just started last week. You think she's had long conversations with me?" Jeff replied.

Their eyes followed her as she walked down the long corridor through their dimly lit world, making her way to the brightness of the front showroom. Kevin tried to think of a movie star she resembled but couldn't think of one that did justice to the new girl in the red dress.

Kevin watched Maritza come and go many times over the next

few weeks, traversing the dock where they worked between the employee entrance door and the time clock. He sometimes couriered small packages to the Jewelry Department but, by policy, had to deliver them to the department manager. It would be too convenient if he were allowed to leave them with any of the sales associates.

Each time Kevin noticed her, he glanced her way—but quickly smiled and turned if she caught his glance. He wanted her to know he existed but didn't want her to think he would be the next fool to approach her. He didn't want her to think he was just another guy who thought she was sexy and wanted to sleep with her. Kevin wanted her to wonder when, if ever, he would walk up to her to say hello. He wanted her to anticipate his approach, although he was unsure if she would.

When Kevin discussed the new girl with Mike and Ricky, he asked if they intended to ask her out. Without hesitation, Mike was out. He had no intention of risking rejection and humiliation, especially after learning she had already turned Rodney down. Mike contended that if she were not interested in Rodney, she wouldn't be interested in them. Besides, Ricky had better odds of success working in the showroom and possessing the gift of effortless conversation with girls. Ricky's approach was never tacky—he possessed that envious combination of confidence and charm. Although younger, shorter, and not as athletic as Rodney, Kevin's money was on Ricky to be the first to find the right combination to open the cherry red safe.

Then Ricky confessed he had, in fact, already asked her out. It had happened three days earlier, and she politely turned him down. Kevin imagined Ricky himself must have been surprised, considering he kept the rejection quiet and had told none of them about his attempt. As Ricky explained his conversation with her, Kevin reevaluated his chance of success. It was slim, to be sure, yet the titillation of the challenge itself stirred within. He saw himself in the center of a Las Vegas casino, standing naked in front of the million-dollar payoff slot machine, holding a single quarter in his hand. Should he drop the coin and pull the lever— or cover his loin and run for cover? He concluded that a quarter has little value outside of the casino and that someone must eventually win the jackpot, so why not?

Kevin continued his eye-contact coyness with Maritza each time they were near one another, and he began noticing the same in return from her. She, too, began to glance back and then downward, smiling as if reciprocating in approval. *Was she signaling permission to approach her?* Kevin still wasn't sure and didn't want to seem like a creep, misreading something as simple as a glance or a smile from a distance for something it was not. She likely had a boyfriend or was interested in another guy, anyway.

Maybe Maritza was being polite and had no interest in any of them? She had already rejected the three boys with the best chance of attracting her attention.

Kevin knew that playing coy was an art that required a delicate balance between acting interested and behaving like you are not. Wait too long, and the moment would pass. Move too fast, and she'd dismiss him like the others. He wasn't just interested because she was beautiful. There was something else, something he couldn't name yet. But first, she had to notice him.

Kevin wasn't reckless like Rodney or smooth like Ricky. He didn't chase women like a sport. But something about Maritza made him want to try. Maybe it was the way she moved, or didn't seem impressed by any of them. Perhaps it was how she looked right through Kevin as if she were waiting to see if he had the nerve to speak first.

His approach had to be thoughtful, and neither Mike nor Ricky could lend advice or know his intentions. Kevin suspected Rodney had failed with arrogance and corny pickup lines. Kenny had undoubtedly failed with insincerity following Rodney. Ricky's failure was more challenging to decipher, given what a suave ladies' man he was. *Was he too short or not muscular enough for her?* Ultimately, Kevin speculated that Ricky's fault was probably in going straight for the date, but that was still pure conjecture. It was not an algebraic formula that had one true and sure answer.

Kevin's approach had to be different. He needed to begin an enjoyable conversation with her without trying to come on too strong or ask for anything she would have to commit to. As in soccer, he would play the long game by making short gains on the field when he could. He would avoid the mistake of trying to score too early. Keeping control of the ball was what mattered. Maritza had already noticed him, but now he needed to make a good first impression. Kevin needed to keep it casual and relaxed—it would suggest to her that he was comfortable in his skin. Unlike most adolescent males, he didn't want to appear needy, intense, or desperate. No chess or soccer match was ever won without strategy and planning. Kevin understood this.

16

American Gigolo

(1980)

K evin walked into the showroom an hour before closing on a day he knew Maritza would be on the schedule. There were fewer shoppers and employees then, along with minimum coverage by management. He let his gaze drift over the brightly lit cases as he worked toward the jewelry counter, stealing glances at her while idly browsing, watching as she finished a transaction with a customer.

He chose a Thursday because that was when Mr. Hanley was the manager on duty, and he knew Hanley would be in his office and inattentive until closing time. He also believed it was the day people most anticipated the weekend and began making their plans. It could be a conversational topic if his initial meeting with her went well.

Kevin was careful not to touch the glass with his fingers—instead using the metal edges of the case for balance—conscious not to leave fingerprints on the glass. He knew they would have to spray and clean the cases at closing and didn't want to create extra work for her. She might notice and appreciate his thoughtfulness.

As he completed his run down the length of the first row of

cases, Kevin glanced up just in time to see Maritza do the same. She was alone now, holding eye contact with him long enough to smile and look away. Kevin knew she was better at this game than he was, yet was admittedly encouraged by her smile.

Rounding the corner and strolling the center row of cases, Kevin continued studying the shiny items under the lighted glass until he heard the feminine voice.

"Hi, may I help you?"

He looked up, smiling to show her the straight white teeth he had earned with two painful years of braces. Kevin stood up straight, demonstrating a confident posture and his height.

"Hi, how are you? I'm Kevin. I work in the back," he said, gesturing to the back of the building with a half-turn of his shoulder and a slightly raised hand.

"I know. I've noticed you back there. You clean up well."

Kevin chuckled at her comment while his mind raced to process her body language and each word she spoke. Maritza said she had 'noticed' him in the back instead of saying she had 'seen' him there. He thought the word 'noticed' inferred that she was paying attention to him rather than simply observing him. She also told him he 'cleaned up well.' Did that mean she approved of what he was wearing? Part of his strategy for making a great first impression was to do it during his time off so he could dress nicely. She had already seen the dirty version of Kevin in jeans and a sweat-clad tee shirt. Tonight was the opportunity to meet the clean and smartly dressed version.

"I'm Maritza," she added, accepting his extended hand with a light touch and feminine half-shake.

"Well, it's very nice to meet you, Maritza. How are you enjoying your new job here?"

"I love it," she replied. "What's not to love surrounded by diamonds, gold, and pretty jewelry?"

"Fair point. It beats the dirty boxes and dusty shelves I'm around." Kevin continued to exude confidence through his smile and eye contact, however uncomfortable and unnatural it felt. He knew he had to stay focused on that critical element of conversation. *Eye contact, smile, exude confidence,* he repeated to himself. Her eyes were a deep and transparent green, like polished emerald jewels contrasted against her ruby lips and the satin sheen of her dark hair.

Maritza chuckled and replied, "That's very true, but at least it keeps you in great shape, right?"

Did she just give me another compliment? he wondered. "Now you're just trying to make me blush, and I can't hide that under these bright lights."

She giggled again and smiled as if pausing to see if he *would* blush.

Parsing his lips and grinning, Kevin lowered his head slightly and rolled his eyes as if embarrassed, which he was. The heat in his cheeks rose, as did his intrigue with her.

"Oh, stop it," she said lightheartedly, reaching across the glass countertop to land the light and playful tap across his bicep. "I know you're not embarrassed."

He glanced around and noticed no one was watching. There were no other customers in the jewelry department. Betty, an older lady and the only other sales associate on the floor, was preparing to close out the register on the far side of the department. She gave the two space to continue their chat. Kevin didn't want to interfere with other customers receiving proper service or overextend his initial meeting with Maritza.

"We're fine," she said intuitively, sensing his quick survey of their surroundings. "So, what are we looking for tonight?"

She said *'we,'* he noted. Was that just an expression, or was that intentional and designed to let him know she was joining him in his search for a gift? Perhaps it was a signal that she was ending their nice chat, and it was time to get on with business. Was he over-analyzing every word she uttered? Maybe the question had nothing to do with merchandise or shopping but was an invitation or suggestion for something more after the store closed. *Stay on script and stick to the plan,* Kevin reminded himself.

"A gift for your girlfriend, maybe?" Her head tilted, delicately tucking a few strands of flowing hair behind her ear as she softly spoke. Maritza looked at him with those emerald eyes and smirked, awaiting his reply.

"Oh, no. No girlfriend at the moment. I'm looking for a gift for my grandmother's birthday. She loves jewelry but already has so much of it, so I'm at a loss here." *Bravo,* he thought to himself.

Maritza smiled and told Kevin how sweet he was to want to give his grandmother a lovely jewelry gift. The thought touched her—it was as if he rescued a cute little puppy from the highway's center lane or donated his last dollar to help feed hungry families at the homeless shelter. How could that be viewed as anything but thoughtful and kind, winning her attention and admiration? Kevin spoke the truth, though. He loved his grandmother and enjoyed buying her small gifts he thought would bring her pleasure.

As they browsed the jewelry cases, Maritza showed Kevin a few items that might make an appropriate gift. She modeled a bracelet to show him how it looked on the wrist, extending it toward him so that he could get a closer look. She invited him to touch it, to feel the tiny pearls and gold charms as she explained its construction. Maritza held some earrings up to her ears, tucking strands of her silky hair behind them to give him ideas. They talked about their grandmothers as they moved to the necklaces and selected a few of them as potential purchases. She held each one up against the skin of her lower neck as if wearing them, showing him the difference between the shades of gold contrasted against the tone of her skin. Maritza showed Kevin a variety of gemstone pendants. He noticed how the ruby matched her lips, how the sapphire complemented her dress, how the amber flattered her golden skin, and how the emerald was an extension of her seductive eyes.

Kevin learned a great deal about jewelry and a fair amount about Maritza. Her parents fled Venezuela with her and her sister in the late 1960s, settling first in New Orleans and most recently in Bayview. She was seventeen and still a junior in high school, caught in an unusual lag in school grade by her move to Bayview and the date of her birthday. She attended the same Jackson High School that his friend Steve graduated from, and when asked if she knew him, she told him she didn't.

This sales position was her first job, and he let her know that. In his humble opinion, she was brilliant at it. The conversation flowed easily between the two, and Kevin forgot about his strategy and what he planned to say or how he planned to say it. They were both surprised when the announcement to make final purchases was broadcast over the intercom system, not realizing nearly an hour had passed.

"Oh my gosh, I'm so sorry," he said. "I didn't mean to monopolize your time. I hope I don't get you into trouble."

"Don't be silly," she replied. "You're one of the only customers we've seen in the past hour. I should be thanking you."

"Well then, you're welcome." Kevin smiled and suppressed all the other responses he wanted to say. He wanted to ask Maritza out or at least ask for her phone number. Kevin wanted to ask if she wanted to chat again. He even considered offering her a ride home since she revealed earlier that she didn't have a car or driver's license yet. But it would have been too forward of him to offer a ride so soon after their meeting. No, Kevin needed to stick to the plan and keep it light. He wanted Maritza to think about him, their meeting tonight, and their conversation. It was best to leave her wanting more—the same wanting she was leaving him.

"Seriously though," he added, "it was great to meet you finally, and I appreciate your help. You've given me a lot of wonderful ideas that I'm going to sleep on tonight." Kevin didn't realize how unscripted and unintentionally superb that statement was until after he uttered the words. As he made that long walk to the front door, he turned to look back, smiling just once as she watched him leave.

Kevin and Maritza ran into each other several times over the next two weeks. Sometimes, it was at the time clock when she came to or left work. At other times, it was upstairs in the breakroom when they happened to take breaks at the same time. Each time they ran into one another, they chatted and smiled, both sensing the coyness and flirtation between them. Kevin never planned or forced a moment to see her. When it happened, it happened by chance. He also never told the Darksiders about his meeting and conversation with her that Thursday evening, although he badly wanted to.

The Darksiders did, however, notice the glances and smiles that Maritza and Kevin exchanged. They witnessed the occasional undertone chats between the two. Mike and Ricky tried to convince Kevin that she was flirting with him. Rodney and Kenny wanted to convince him she was teasing him, making a fool of him. They all taunted him, alleging he had a crush on her, but he dismissed the implications. The last thing Kevin wanted was interference or unintended consequences of his friend's meddling. He encouraged nothing that might get back to her, thus negatively influencing her still forming perception of him. No, Kevin was playing the patient game and exercising restraint to let the tensions between him and Maritza build—partly by design and partly out of fear. Kevin had already made it farther than any of his coworkers, and he didn't want to join the list of the rejected.

After a few weeks, Kevin knew it was time to take the lead and ask Maritza out. He appreciated her not being as forward as Jennifer or Rachael had been in his past. Maritza was almost two years younger, and he wanted to court her like a masculine man should court a young lady. Kevin would be the hunter and protector this time. Maritza would be his treasure to hug, squeeze, and care for in his arms. He would make her feel special. They would fall in love. But first, Kevin needed to ask Maritza out. He seized the opportunity when he saw the new schedule posted, and they were alone in the breakroom.

"Would you like to see a movie next Saturday," he asked, "and maybe grab a pizza afterward?"

"Sure. Who with?"

Kevin grinned and courageously dove straight into her emerald eyes. "With me, of course."

"Oh." She playfully hesitated. "Oh," she repeated, as if surprised he would ask her to a movie and assume it was with him.

Kevin smiled and held steadfast, undeterred by her apparent hesitation. She had already said yes to a movie, and he knew she was off the schedule that day, so if she didn't want to go out with him, she would have to say the words.

"What would we see?"

"I was thinking of *The Empire Strikes Back*. It's got something

110

for everyone. There's science fiction, action, aliens, good guys, bad guys." A lesser man would have suggested they could see anything she wanted, but he was leading this dance and was determined to be decisive.

"Do you have to have seen *Star Wars* first?" she asked.

"It would likely help," he replied. "Have you seen Star Wars?"

"Yes, didn't you?"

"I did. Did you like it?"

"Oh yes," she answered. "I loved it! What about pizza?" she added.

Grinning, Kevin explained pizza was that round and doughy Italian food served warm with various toppings on top. He added that people bought pizza in a grocery store or ordered it at a restaurant. Sometimes, they even had it delivered to their homes.

"How would we get there?" she asked. Kevin was catching on to her game of stretching it out to see him sweat under pressure. He had no intention of faltering and answered every silly question she tossed his way with an even more clever answer.

"I thought I would pick you up in my X-wing Starfighter so we could fly to the theater."

"Oh, that sounds exciting!" she exclaimed. "Would I have to ride in the back with R2D2?"

"So, you know about R2D2?"

"Of course. Doesn't everyone?" Maritza replied.

"Well, no. You wouldn't need to ride in the back. That would be unsafe. You'd better ride in the cockpit with me."

"Oh," she responded, looking down and pausing again as in

deep contemplation. Kevin thought Maritza was either testing his playfulness or his patience. Still, he had no intention of wavering or asking her twice.

Maritza burst out laughing and reached across the table to grasp his forearm with both hands, saying, "I would love to go to the movies with you." She held her grip on Kevin's forearm after her laugh had subsided and gazed into his eyes before glancing downward. He could see her smile, and the delicate fragrance of her perfume was delicious. Kevin wanted to lean forward, gently lift her chin, and softly kiss her lips. But he resisted the temptation and let the opportunity pass. *Always leave them wanting more*, he remembered.

The two saw the movie that Saturday night and went for pizza afterward. They had a great time, and Kevin met her parents, Diego and Dolores, along with her older sister, Gabriela, when he picked her up. He allowed enough time before the movie to go to the front door and chat with them inside so they knew who their youngest daughter was going to the movies with. That was what a gentleman did.

~

Kevin and Maritza went to other movies over the next month. He took her to *Blue Lagoon,* and they discussed what it might be like to be shipwrecked on a deserted island together. They saw *Urban Cowboy* at the drive-in and decided the country scene was not for them, agreeing never to ride a mechanical bull in a country bar. Their next drive-in movie was *American Gigolo,* and they appreciated Richard Gere's wardrobe and his Mercedes Benz 450 SL convertible. Maritza confessed she thought his shirtless scenes were alluring. At the same time, Kevin failed to admit that

Richard's smoldering, enigmatic gaze held a seductive pull over him. Neither expected the full-frontal nudity scene in the movie.

As Richard Gere's character leaned against the window frame and gazed outside, the filtered sunlight cast seductive shadows around his toned, bare body. The scene showed him unconsciously caressing his chest and abdominal muscles as he spoke. Maritza sat beside Kevin and made the same slow, caressive motions with her fingertips across his knee. After a few minutes, Kevin gently took her hand and slowly guided it from his knee up his thigh. Her fingertips maintained their soft pressure as she continued the caressive motions, occasionally pausing to add a tiny squeeze before continuing.

Their eyes stayed affixed to the screen, and when Richard's seductive scene ended, her rubbing and caressing continued. Kevin released his guiding hand from hers and placed it on her seat's headrest. His stance was now open, allowing her to decide the path of her soft touch. She leaned in, her breath warm against his ear as her tongue traced its edge.

Kevin's body instinctively pushed deeper into the driver's seat. Her tender kisses and licks continued, alternating between his ears and neck. When she gently bit his earlobe, Kevin's feet pushed against the car's floorboard. He couldn't control his hips from impulsively rising upward as she unzipped his jeans, freeing the tension she had built with her touch. His body answered her without thought, a reflex, an inevitability.

With each stroke of Maritza's hand, Kevin's hips rocked faster within her firm grip. With his eyes closed and the fragrance of her perfume titillating his sense of smell, Maritza whispered into Kevin's ear to tell him what she wanted, and that's when Kevin surrendered, lost in her touch, in the warmth of her breath, in the way she took what she wanted from him.

It became evident to friends and family that the two were now dating. While they were careful not to display their affection at work, they didn't try to hide the courtship.

Maritza and Kevin dated into the summer, often seeing movies or visiting the beaches or parks. As a couple, they emulated the adults they saw in movies, picnicking with blankets and sweet Riesling wine with gouda cheese and crackers. They fed grapes to one another, pulling each ball of sweetness from its stem as the flavor of young love gushed into their mouths, softly kissing the fingers that fed them. It was all very romantic, and the more time Kevin spent with his new girlfriend, the less he had to spend with his other friends.

He now watched television at Maritza's house instead of drinking beer and shooting billiards at the pub. Friday nights became date night with her instead of midnight showings of *Rocky Horror Picture Show* with Mike. Kevin enjoyed the stability and certainty of it all, and their little band of Darksiders began to dissolve.

Jeff spent more time at Joni's Pub helping his mother. Mike continued his college courses and spent more time with his official girlfriend and less time with the secret ones. Daniel was the youngest of the Darksiders and the one who looked up to Kevin as a role model. His father forced him to quit his part-time job at Selmen's because of his poor sophomore-year grades and the need for him to focus on summer school. Ricky decided to focus on his future and get out of Bayview with a two-year enlistment in the Coast Guard. Kevin didn't know it yet, but change was coming for him too.

Selmen's built a second location on the northeast side of town. They asked Kevin to work there—a temporary assignment—to help establish the warehouse before the store's grand opening. Over five weeks, Kevin helped unload and set up warehouse racking, installed equipment, and received merchandise to stock shelves. During that time, they all worked twelve to fourteen hours per day for six and sometimes seven days a week, racing against the rapidly advancing deadline to ready the store. Like a trooper, Kevin devoted everything he had to the project to please his managers, with little time left for Maritza or his friends.

Just before the grand opening, the company's Director of Operations overseeing the store's buildout called Kevin into his office. It felt unnervingly similar to his first job experience at Grand Union a few years earlier. This time was different, though. Instead of firing him, they offered Kevin a promotion, asking him to be the Warehouse Manager of their newly acquired location in Ft. Lauderdale. Despite Kevin's youth, they were pleased with his work and were confident he could do the job. It was a salaried management role, no more punching a time clock, and their offer of sixteen thousand dollars per year sounded like a fortune to Kevin.

The offer was unexpected and more than he ever imagined— twice his current pay, a management position, a chance to prove himself. They also needed a response immediately. Kevin appreciated their confidence and did not want to disappoint. His hard work there paid off—he had progressed and was now important—he was a success. Still, the moment he shook hands and accepted, a quiet unease settled in his gut.

Kevin said yes without thinking, without talking to his parents or Maritza. Would she be proud of him? He wanted to believe she would—she would smile, call him ambitious, and tell him she always knew he was going places. But another thought gnawed at him. What if she didn't? What if she saw it as something else? What if she saw it as leaving her behind?

When the director told him he had two weeks to report to his new position, Kevin's gut wrenched for a second time. He was oblivious to the logistics of that timeframe. Still, he was overwhelmed with flattery over the offer. He was eager to inform everyone, confident they would be supportive—no, impressed— by his success.

But the adrenaline began to wear off as he pulled onto the highway to drive home. Kevin leaned back in his seat, gripping the wheel and letting the numbers sink in—sixteen thousand a year, no time clock, a management title. He should have been celebrating. But then the thought resurfaced. Maritza. He hadn't even considered what leaving Bayview might mean. How was he going to tell her? More importantly, what if she asked him to stay? What would he do?

Kevin told himself the answer was obvious—this was his future, his chance. But he could already picture the hurt in her eyes, the way her voice might falter when she asked him why he hadn't told her sooner. What if staying meant giving up everything he'd worked for? What if leaving meant losing her for good? And what if—just maybe—he couldn't have both?

17

WHAT A FOOL BELIEVES

The world outside was chaotic—riots in Miami, an erupting volcano in Washington State, and hostages in Tehran. But Kevin didn't notice. The chaos felt light-years away from his tightly sealed orbit. He had a girlfriend, a promotion, and a one-way ticket to South Florida's Gold Coast. The radical movements of the 1960s, the Vietnam War, Watergate, inflation, and the Cold War—all brushed past his childhood like distant storms. These weren't his burdens to carry. He was employed, physically fit, in love, and convinced he was on the right track.

Kevin didn't see himself as lucky or entitled—he'd worked hard, followed the rules, and made wise choices. He believed he'd earned his good fortune—and in many ways, he had. Kevin had been a good son, a decent student, and a loyal employee. He was deserving of everything now coming his way. But Kevin saw only the road ahead—clean, straight, and paved with promise. What he didn't yet see was how quickly the road could turn.

The news surprised Bert and Carol. As parents, they were anxious about their firstborn's plan to move away from home to a new city. They advised against it, concerned about postponing his college education once again. Still, they were supportive—they knew it would happen with or without their endorsement.

Kevin had already tried college three times, enrolling in courses and quitting more often than not. The first attempt in the fall was eye-opening. College required a new level of commitment and discipline—he could not drift through it effortlessly as he did in high school. Kevin was already working full-time at Selmen's and let work, pub life, friendships, and Spring Break interfere with his second semester. He fared no better with the summer semester, letting his courtship with Maritza take priority.

When Kevin enrolled in the fall semester again, he was serious. It was his fourth attempt at college, repeating previously failed classes. But this unexpected career move to Ft. Lauderdale would also require withdrawals from these classes.

"School could wait," he told his parents. This job, he told himself, couldn't. What he didn't say—what he didn't quite let himself think—was that he wasn't sure it would go any better the next time.

Informing Maritza of his promotion and all-to-soon move was more complicated than telling his parents had been.

"You already said yes?" she asked. Her smile held, but her eyes dropped for a beat. She was as surprised as Bert and Carol were but understood he needed to do it. He had no choice now. He had already accepted their offer.

The two were happy with how their new relationship was developing. There was no desire to break up, so they agreed to give a long-distance relationship a chance. Maritza had just begun her senior year at Jackson High. Kevin knew how busy he would be in the new job. The plan was simple—remain committed to one another and talk on the phone often. Kevin would make the 250-mile drive back to Bayview frequently on weekends. It was a tall order for teenagers six months into dating.

Kevin began his apartment hunt with one week remaining before starting his new role. He left Bayview early in the morning, drove the four hours down to Ft. Lauderdale, grabbed a newspaper, and circled listings in the classifieds.

He toured the first place he'd circled—a no-frills one-bedroom in a two-story walk-up overlooking a courtyard. It needed cleaning, but it was close to his new job. More importantly, it was cheap. It seemed good enough for someone with no furniture and plans to work long hours. Kevin handed over a cash deposit, signed his first lease, and returned to Bayview just in time to take Maritza to dinner.

The following weekend, Kevin headed south with a carload of clothes and a kitchen starter kit packed by his mother—cleaning supplies, basic utensils, and food. She was nervous about her first child leaving the nest. Kevin handed the manager the rest of the cash, received his key, and stepped into his first apartment—alone.

Kevin had been excited—ready to step into adulthood and prove his independence—but his first few days hit hard. No matter how thoroughly he scrubbed the kitchen or bathroom, it remained incredibly nasty. Grime clung to every corner like it had lived there longer than the walls. The apartment's only air conditioner, a rusty window unit in disrepair, lay useless on the bedroom floor. Its metal housing—a gaping hole in the wall—invited heat, humidity, and insects. The manager promised the unit's repair and reinstallation before he arrived, but it never got done.

At night, only an air mattress and sleeping bag separated Kevin from the stained carpet and the roaches that scurried freely across it. The building itself never seemed to sleep. The grassy courtyard, or what little grass was left, was filled with cars and rowdy tenants most evenings, their parties running into the early morning hours. The excitement of independence was fading fast.

Kevin learned quickly that Ft. Lauderdale wasn't what he'd expected. The city had few zoning laws, and neighborhoods blurred together—blocks of luxury homes sat beside warehouses, gas stations, and rundown apartment buildings with high crime. There was no clear deliniation between safe and unsafe, between polished and neglected. The hodgepodge layout and lack of planning felt chaotic compared to the world he'd known.

He also learned that apartment hunting on a weekday, during business hours, was a mistake. He should have returned at night, driven by more than once, or waited to talk to new coworkers about the city's neighborhoods. But he hadn't. He realized fortune might favor the bold—but it doesn't coddle the naïve.

Kevin barely slept between the courtyard parties and the wailing police and fire sirens that first night. The next night, he managed only a few hours. He was jolted awake more than once by car alarms—a few of those times from his own Bronco.

By the second week, Kevin knew he couldn't stay. The air conditioner still sat useless in the middle of the bedroom floor, the rectangular hole in the wall open to heat, rain, and bugs. He tried negotiating with the manager. He then pleaded. Ultimately, breaking the lease cost him his first month's rent and security deposit.

His mistake was the manager's windfall—a quick gain at a young tenant's expense. Kevin walked away, lighter in the wallet and heavier with the sting of his misjudgment and painful lesson.

Maritza's aunt and uncle lived in West Palm Beach, forty-five miles north of Kevin's new job in Ft. Lauderdale. The commute meant an hour on I-95 in heavy traffic, but it was a small price to pay. At Maritza's request, they let Kevin stay in their guestroom while he searched for a better apartment.

They were an older couple who spoke little English but were warm and welcoming. Kevin managed the basics through gestures, patience, and gratitude. The modest Spanish-style house had metal sunshades from the 1950s that jutted over the windows to help keep the house cool. It wasn't fancy, but after two weeks in that sweltering, bug-infested box, it felt like a five-star resort. Kevin slept in a real bed for the first time since arriving in South Florida. And he was thankful—deeply, silently grateful.

Kevin spent a month in the small stucco house, using the old wall phone in the kitchen to talk to Maritza each evening. Their calls stretched into hours, the long-distance charges adding up. Sometimes, when the words ran out, they sat in silence, listening to each other breathe, waiting for one to say again how much they missed the other.

As promised, Kevin made the four-hour drive back to Bayview every Friday evening, returning late Sunday night. Each weekend's goodbye came later than the last, until one Sunday night, fighting sleep, he drifted off behind the wheel. The Bronco veered onto the shoulder. The jolt woke him as he slammed on the brakes and pulled over. Breathless, his heart pounding, Kevin stared into the dark stillness of the highway. He hadn't just risked his life—he could've taken someone else's. The drive, the distance, and the exhaustion were all becoming unsustainable.

Something had to give. Like the filthy apartment Kevin had

already abandoned, the separation from Maritza and the long drives each weekend were becoming untenable.

Kevin's new job wasn't any easier.

Two older men who rarely left their offices ran the small, aging store. They spent more time checking their personal investments than managing anything on the floor. The warehouse was in disarray—its employees had taken control long ago and now supervised themselves. Their autonomist dysfunction had little use or patience for a teenage newcomer from the outside. They didn't just ignore Kevin. They resented him.

Kevin had no formal training, no real leadership experience—just a job offer he'd been too flattered to question.

Authority commanded respect—that's how Bert and Carol raised their son. In Catholic schools, disobedience had consequences. But no one cared about his title or how hard he worked here. They challenged, mocked, and laughed at his attempts to bring order, dismissing him. Kevin didn't yet understand the difference between managing and leading, and it showed. He was unprepared for defiance. Unfamiliar with insubordination. Respect wasn't automatic, and the rules he grew up with didn't apply.

After just a few weeks, the job that had lured him away from everything familiar was already unraveling. The apartment was gone, the commute grueling, and the work was unmanageable. Kevin had taken the leap—but the ground beneath him was crumbling.

Kevin had painted himself into a corner. Still, he needed to find a way to make it all work. In the evenings, he resumed his apartment search, shifting his focus to West Palm Beach—a quieter, greener place than Ft. Lauderdale. Maritza had family there. It felt safer. And if he had to quit his job, he'd rather start over in West Palm—or even return to Bayview—than be stuck in another lease under neon lights and noise.

He found a new complex in Palm Springs, a modest but growing suburb of West Palm. It was another one-bedroom, but larger, brighter, and brand new. Three-story buildings surrounded a grassy common area with a clubhouse and pool. Kevin signed the lease and looked forward to moving in at the beginning of the following month.

Even with a better place, Kevin was still desperately lonely. He had no friends in South Florida and dreaded going to work. Communication with Maritza's aunt and uncle was limited. The uncle drank heavily most nights, usually leading to an argument with his wife or passing out in front of the television. Kevin kept to himself, locking the guest room door and waiting for quiet before slipping into the kitchen to call Maritza. Their conversations were routine. She complained about school, and he complained about work. When they ran out of things to say, they sat in silence, listening to each other breathe, waiting for someone to say they missed the other first.

Kevin was not used to such isolation, surrounded by unrelatable strangers. He was not used to spending time alone. He had never even seen a movie at the theater by himself. Now, alone in a locked room, surrounded by people he couldn't understand, he lay in the dark and listened to the hum of silence. When the phone finally went silent, the dial tone lived on in his head— numb, constant, and steady. That was when the worst thought crept in. What if the loneliest person in his life wasn't someone else—but him?

~

Kevin sat on the kitchen floor, curled in the corner for privacy, the phone cord stretched taut across his chest. Outside the window, the hum of cicadas blended with distant traffic. On the other end of the line, Maritza's voice was soft, tired.

"I hate it here," she said. "My mom's on my back about school and grades. My dad won't let me go anywhere without Gabriela. I swear, they think I'm twelve."

Kevin smiled faintly. "I get it. I spent most of tonight pretending to watch a telenovela in the living room. I think your uncle offered me a beer, but it might've been motor oil. I'm not sure."

She laughed—quiet and strained. Then came a pause.

"I miss you," she said.

"Yeah." Kevin closed his eyes. "I miss you too. All the time."

Silence stretched between them—like a hallway with all the doors closed.

"So let's fix it."

"Fix what?"

"This. Us. Being apart." He exhaled slowly. "Come live with me."

"Kevin?"

"I'm serious." He gripped the phone tighter. "Let's get married." He hadn't planned to say it, but being without her had started to feel unbearable.

Silence stretched out on the line. Kevin could hear her breathing—slow, steady, then shaky.

"You're not joking?"

"No. I don't want to do this halfway thing anymore. I'm tired of missing you. I want you here, with me. Every day."

She didn't answer right away. Kevin imagined her curled up on her bed, hair spread across the pillow, eyes wide, and blinking into the dark.

"You want that?" she finally asked.

"More than anything."

There was a soft exhale through the receiver, then Maritza's voice. "Okay. Let's do it."

Yeah?" Kevin asked, his smile shining like light through a curtain. Relief swept him—he had made her happy—again.

"Yes! Let's get married."

Kevin hung up the phone and stared at the ceiling. It hadn't been planned. There'd been no ring, no grand speech. But it felt right—at least, it felt like something. Something better than sleeping alone. Something better than this.

But in his rarest moments of clarity, Kevin wasn't sure if they were in love—or just in love with not being alone.

Wedding planning went into overdrive, led mainly by Maritza and her mother, Dolores. Just six weeks later, on Thanksgiving Day, they were wed. Rafael, another of Maritza's uncles, offered his backyard patio in West Palm Beach for the ceremony. It was small but warm, attended mostly by relatives and family friends from South Florida. Bert and Carol were there, along with Aunt Alice, who officiated as a public notary.

After the vows were spoken and the rice thrown, Kevin and Maritza drove to the Breakers Hotel for a one-night honeymoon—Rafael's wedding gift. They were too tired to make love. They fell asleep with their clothes half-off and the television still glowing blue.

The following day, the newlyweds checked out and returned to their new apartment. It was still empty, but they were newly married and starting a life together. It felt like something. It was supposed to mean everything.

18

GIVE HER CREDIT

The first few months were lean for the young newlyweds as they began to furnish their new apartment. They started with a sectional sofa and bedroom furniture purchased from a small store in Bayview on a buy-here-pay-here credit plan. Kevin hated beginning their marriage in debt, but Dolores insisted it was normal. She knew the store's owner and happily arranged the purchases.

What could Kevin say? The apartment was mostly empty, and they needed some basics. The payments seemed manageable. He went along with it, confident they would be okay financially as soon as Maritza made her final move from Bayview and found a job. That was the story he told himself.

Still, it gnawed at him. He was working a job he hated in a city that didn't feel like home. Meanwhile, Maritza was still in Bayview, shopping for furniture—with her mother—on credit. Kevin wasn't just uneasy about the debt. He was uncomfortable about what it said. Who was steering this new life of theirs?

Kevin and Maritza traveled back and forth between Bayview and Ft. Lauderdale a few times after the wedding, especially during the holidays. On their final trip for Christmas, Kevin left Maritza in Bayview so she could formally withdraw from Jackson High and take her GED exam. He planned to return the following weekend to pick her up. That would be her last shuttle between the two cities. After a chaotic couple of months, they were both ready to settle into their apartment and new life together.

When they last spoke on the phone—once again separated by the miles—Kevin told her how much he was looking forward to seeing her. Maritza told him she had a surprise.

After getting home from work Thursday evening, Kevin rummaged through the nearly empty refrigerator, deciding what to cobble together for dinner. He was planning to drive to Bayview the next day to pick up Maritza—and after the week he'd had, he was counting the hours. But then he heard something. A familiar sound from the front of the apartment: the click of a key entering the deadbolt, followed by the lock turning, slow and deliberate.

The sound stopped him cold. For a second, he thought a neighbor had confused the units—an honest mistake. He'd once tried to unlock a car that wasn't his, parked a few rows away from where he thought he left it. But as he peered under the overhead cabinets separating the kitchen from the living room, a new worry crept in. Were the Canadian owners coming in unannounced? He was current on rent—there was no reason for a surprise visit. That's when the sound shifted in his brain.

This wasn't a mistake. It was an intrusion. *Was someone breaking in?*

Kevin's instinct kicked in. He reached for the knife drawer without thinking. *Where is it?* He could feel his pulse pounding as the deadbolt snapped open. Where was the large kitchen knife his mother packed in his starter kit?

He didn't have time to find out. The front door swung open, and two silhouettes filled the doorway.

"Hay!" the familiar voice announced as she walked through the door.

"Hello, darling," came the next voice, stretched and syrupy, dripping with accent.

A third shadow was entering the doorway, short and broad—a suitcase that Dolores rolled behind her.

"What are you doing here?" Kevin asked, stunned and still frozen behind the overhead cabinets.

"Surprised?" Maritza grinned.

"Well, yeah." Kevin stepped out to hug her, still disoriented but smiling, happy to see her.

Dolores cut in before Maritza could respond. "We have another surprise for you, darling!" She stretched out the words as if on stage, her voice thick with theatrical flair. Kevin thought of Mrs. Douglas, Eva Gabor's character in Green Acres—all glamour, exaggerated charm, and volume cranked to eleven. It always grated on him.

Kevin's gaze altered between them. Dolores was practically vibrating with eagerness. Whatever the second surprise was, it wouldn't stay secret for long.

As Dolores grabbed Kevin's hand, his first instinct was to pull it back sharply, but he didn't. *Please, not the stomach. Not the stomach,* he thought.

Dolores didn't place his hand on Maritza's belly. Instead, she grabbed it and tugged him outside, through the apartment door and onto the breezeway. She led him to the railing and pointed down toward the parking lot, still buzzing with excitement.

Kevin saw the excitement in their faces but didn't know what he was supposed to be looking at.

"There! Right there, darling—the yellow one! See it?"

Kevin followed her gesture and saw a brand-new, canary-yellow Pontiac Sunbird parked just below. It gleamed under the amber glow of the lights.

During her week in Bayview, Dolores took Maritza car shopping—without telling Kevin—and bought it from the GM dealership where Diego worked. They were proud of the employee discount he'd secured, though Maritza didn't have a driver's license yet. Dolores had driven them down, delivering both daughter and daughter's new car in one trip.

Kevin stared at the Sunbird, stunned. All bright paint and reckless optimism, it sat there like a monument to choices made without him.

"You bought a new car?" He tried to keep his voice even while his chest tightened. This wasn't a surprise. It was a warning.

It made perfect sense to mother and daughter. Maritza needed a car to job hunt, Dolores explained. Without it, how could she find work? Kevin understood the logic, but buying a new car? In a deep recession? With unemployment still climbing?

Yet Maritza hadn't even discussed it with Kevin. That part stung the most. A decision this big, this expensive—and she hadn't even thought to ask. But he swallowed his reaction. Not here. Not in front of Dolores, who undoubtedly expected gratitude. After all, they had helped. They'd found the car, secured a discount, driven it down to him—solved the problem. Kevin knew how it would look if he pushed back—ungrateful, controlling, unmanly.

So he nodded and smiled and congratulated them for the "surprise." He avoided confrontation and joined in their enthusiasm. Kevin thanked Dolores for saving him a trip to

Bayview and expressed gratitude for bringing Maritza home. But there were entirely different thoughts in his mind. They should have taught Maritza to drive and ensured she got a license. If Diego had dealership connections, why not find a used car? Something reliable and practical. Something that wouldn't saddle them with payments before she even had a job.

But Kevin had known this about them before the wedding. Dolores's flair for control. Diego's selective involvement. It wouldn't be fair to argue now—not without sounding like he was ungrateful or challenging their parenting, regretting marrying into it.

As they descended the stairwell to look at the car, more questions crowded his mind. How long was Dolores staying? How would she get back to Bayview? Was it now his job to teach Maritza how to drive? Where would they take the driving exam? Was the car even insured? And the biggest question of all—how had they paid for it?

He hoped it was a gift. Or maybe Diego cosigned a small loan. Something manageable. Being financially tethered to his in-laws was the last thing Kevin wanted. The truth, however, was far worse than he could have imagined.

Kevin lingered by the car, running a hand along the glossy hood, pretending to admire it while his mind churned. He finally asked the question that had been burning since he'd seen the keys in Maritza's hand.

"So, how did you pay for it?"

Maritza grinned, pleased with herself. "I charged it."

Kevin's stomach dipped. "Charged it?" He was sure she meant 'financed it,' but asked for clarification anyway. "How?"

Dolores piped in cheerfully, "On American Express, darling."

Kevin blinked. "You used my Amex?"

Maritza nodded like it was the most natural thing in the world. "You added me as a user after the wedding, remember? We got the employee discount, and it's a new car. Great deal!"

He opened his mouth, then closed it again. He was staring at a car he didn't choose, wanted, and couldn't afford.

Kevin forced a small smile out of nervousness, his chest tightening as numbers tumbled through his head. He had just recently opened that account when he received the promotion— his first real credit card besides the department store and gas card his mother helped him get while in high school to start establishing his credit.

This new American Express card meant something— responsibility, status, success. He was proud of it. It was his symbol of adulthood. But now, Kevin only imagined opening the next statement: $8,921.67, due in full by the next billing cycle. With one swipe, Maritza had racked up a balance of nearly half his entire year's salary.

Dolores was still talking—something about women and independence. Kevin heard her, but it was like she was speaking underwater. He tried to breathe, to smile. *Don't say anything*, he told himself. *Not yet. Not in front of her mother.*

Kevin looked at Maritza. She was beaming, excited, her hand on the driver's door like it was her golden chariot. He swallowed the lump in his throat. "We'll discuss it later."

Maritza leaned in and kissed his cheek. "You're the best, you know that?"

Kevin nodded, feeling the weight of the plastic card in his back pocket. What once felt like freedom now felt like a chain.

That night, the new Sunbird sat parked downstairs. Kevin lay awake, his name on the bill. Maritza slept beside him, peaceful and unaware, her name on the title. Delores slept on the sofa just beyond their bedroom door, her flight back to Bayview the following day.

Kevin wondered if everything he was trying to build was already falling apart.

19

Family Affair

Maritza had a few more surprises for Kevin. She explained how her parents had just decided to move from Bayview to West Palm Beach.

"They already listed the house," she said. "They got an offer. It's under contract."

Kevin blinked. "Wait—what?"

"It's a good thing," she said brightly. "They've always talked about moving here. Gabriela and I are out of high school, so there's no reason to stay in Bayview. They want to be closer to family. And Mami says she can do better with real estate here. Papi already found a job—he starts next week."

It was happening fast—almost as fast as Kevin's move had. Maybe this was how Bert and Carol felt when he dropped the news on them, Kevin thought.

Diego arrived first to start his new job, moving in with Kevin and Maritza. Dolores stayed in Bayview to pack and finalize the sale. It was an awkward arrangement, sharing a newlywed apartment with his father-in-law. He slept on the living room sofa while Kevin and his new bride slept in their bed just feet away in the next room.

Kevin tried not to resent it. He told himself it was temporary, that he owed the family after Maritza's aunt and uncle helped him through his apartment debacle in Ft. Lauderdale months before. And hadn't Diego just given Maritza's hand in marriage? Kevin told himself he owed him that much.

It was just another annoyance. One more thing stacked on a growing list—the pressures and difficulties at work and the mounting financial pressures of falling behind in payments for new furniture, a better apartment, a new car, and a wife who was unemployed and home all day. All of these things were temporary and would soon correct themselves.

Dolores quickly found a house to buy just a few miles south of their apartment. She would move down to join Diego when their house closed in Bayview, so Kevin's uncomfortable father-in-law's stay would end soon.

That's when Maritza brought up another surprise.

"Gabriela's moving down too."

Kevin raised an eyebrow. "Okay…"

"She's going to live with my parents. And they thought—well, they suggested—we move in, too. Just until we get on our feet."

"No," Kevin said flatly. "Absolutely not."

"But it's a bigger house. We'd all share expenses. It wouldn't be forever."

"Maritza, you couldn't wait to get out from under their roof. And now you want to move back in with them?"

"I know, but you know how my parents are."

Did he? Kevin wasn't so sure anymore. He told her he appreciated the offer but didn't like the idea. Everything in him screamed it was a mistake. He knew Maritza's culture celebrated close family ties, but living with in-laws was a terrible idea under the best of circumstances. It was a guaranteed disaster for newlyweds.

Still, every day at work grew worse. Kevin was getting no support from the store's management and no cooperation from the employees he was supposed to manage. He hated the situation he was in and regretted accepting the role.

Kevin tried to make it work until a heated public argument with one of his staff. The employee refused a directive by Kevin and threatened him with a physical attack. Kevin took it to the store managers and advocated for firing the employee. His managers refused, downplaying the incident to avoid further conflict.

That same day, Kevin handed in his name badge, walked out the back door, and didn't look back. The panic set in soon afterward.

Kevin's decision brought temporary relief—and immediate consequences. With no income from Maritza and mounting bills, Kevin had no choice. They accepted Dolores and Diego's offer and moved in. He smiled, nodded, and told himself it was fine. But deep down, he knew what he'd traded away: freedom, privacy—and whatever illusion of control he had.

It meant breaking his lease for a second time in less than a year.

Kevin didn't say it out loud, but the mental tally was adding up: two failed apartments, four semesters of college withdrawals, a maxed-out credit card, a faltering credit score with a worsening credit history, unpaid furniture bills, a job he couldn't handle, and now—unemployment. He was 19 years old, married, and already buried in self-doubt. Kevin didn't say it out loud, but he could feel it—his confidence was in freefall.

20

THE OUTSIDER

The franchise owner, Mr. Jackson, hired him at the end of the interview. Kevin was lucky; his unemployment had lasted only a few weeks. The job was the night manager at a Shell station, a generous title for a position that paid $4.60 an hour and came with just one employee to supervise. It was a sharp pay cut, but with the recession deepening and job prospects shrinking, Kevin felt relieved to be working again. He had no experience in this kind of work. Still, Mr. Jackson liked that Kevin had attended college and had some management experience, so he took a chance on him.

Kevin's new job was unlike anything he'd done before, but he enjoyed it. The station was small, tucked on a busy street corner, with two full-service pumps and three service bays that kept the mechanics busy. As an attendant, Kevin pumped gas, washed windshields, and checked fluid levels and tire pressure when customers asked. He and the other attendants helped with simple services like oil changes and tire repairs when business was slow. They also kept the place spotless, pressure-washing the pump islands and repainting the bumper guards once a month. It was physical, varied, and mostly outdoors—busy enough to keep his mind occupied and structured enough to give him a slight sense of control.

As the night shift manager, Kevin was responsible for closing the station and securing the day's cash and credit receipts in the floor safe. Mr. Jackson tried to schedule two attendants each night, but that wasn't always possible. On those nights, Kevin sometimes imagined how he might handle a robbery. Mr. Jackson had been clear—don't resist, hand over the money. But Kevin wasn't sure he could do that. He liked to believe he'd stand his ground. Maybe it was pride or the illusion of principle. Either way, he played out the scenarios in his head like war games, assigning himself the role of the calm, decisive hero. Fortunately, the test never came.

When few cars visited the pumps in the afternoons, and there were no tire repairs, Kevin sometimes visited Mrs. Jackson in the station's office as she ordered fuel or tallied the daily receipts. Kevin also spent time in the service bays with the mechanics, asking questions about undercarriage parts when the cars were up on the lift with their underbellies exposed. They taught him how to look up parts in the catalogs and order them for quick delivery. The whole station ran like an orchestra, with musicians playing different instruments so that, as a group, they served their patrons and made money.

Kevin found the routine strangely comforting. The hiss of the air hose, the greasy pages of the parts catalog—everything had a place. It wasn't just the rhythm of the work that calmed him. It was the illusion that, for once, he could fix something. If he followed the steps, things would run right again. He even wondered if this was the answer. Maybe he didn't need college, and working with his hands would be enough. He could study auto mechanics to have the same good-paying, secure career that the mechanics had. Perhaps he could own his own franchised business like Mr. and Mrs. Jackson.

But the fantasy never lasted. Reality always washed over to

cleanse Kevin of his daydreams of success. The truth always returned like the stench of oil and gasoline on his clothes. He was stuck, not settled.

~

At home, Kevin's already crowded household of five became six when Gabriela's boyfriend, Jimmy, moved down from Bayview to join the family. Kevin had heard the name, but they'd never met. Jimmy started dating Gabriela after Kevin left Bayview.

Kevin had once met one of Gabriela's boyfriends, a French exchange student who'd spent the night while Dolores and Diego were away. Kevin had slept over that night, too, and the two bumped into each other in the kitchen the following morning. They chatted briefly, and Kevin recalled being impressed by the French boy—thin and handsome, an intellect. Kevin imagined Jimmy would be something similar.

Kevin was anxious about the new arrival. The house would soon resemble a commune with three couples and six adults, all linked by overlapping relationships and shared space. Still, part of him hoped Jimmy might become an ally. Someone his age— someone who didn't share blood, last names, or old grudges. Even one ally in a crowded house could be worth a lot.

Jimmy rolled up in a growling '70s Dodge Challenger that looked like it belonged in a street fight. He looked nothing like the French student—nothing like what Kevin expected. He was an inch shorter, slightly leaner, but carved from hard labor. Kevin had built his body slowly—tennis, swimming, and a few rusted barbells and weights in his parents' backyard. Jimmy had built his body with labor, sweat, and struggle.

Kevin thought Jimmy looked like Matt Dillon—as if he'd stepped straight out of the pages of *The Outsiders*—a Greaser. Tough, brooding, mythic in all the ways Kevin wasn't. A dragon tattoo curled over one shoulder, visible beneath a tight, white tank top. Kevin didn't need to reread the novel—he was now about to live with one of the characters.

Jimmy shook Kevin's hand with a firm grip and a nod. He didn't smile much—just studied the room with sharp eyes like he'd already decided where he fit and everyone else didn't. Kevin tried to return the same confidence, but something in Jimmy's silence unsettled him. It wasn't rudeness. It was self-assurance. Jimmy didn't have to perform. That alone made Kevin feel smaller.

They were close in age, yet Jimmy seemed older—roughened, already carved into the man he was, while Kevin still felt like he was trying on roles that didn't fit—husband, provider, man of the house. And now this guy had arrived—muscles, tattoo, muscle car—and parked himself in the middle of the family mess.

Jimmy said he'd been a roofer, a painter, a carpenter, anything that paid. He'd grown up on the edge of Bayview, the other side of the tracks, the side Kevin only ever heard about in warnings. Dirt poor, Jimmy admitted to scraping by, sometimes stealing to get through. He'd dropped out of high school. Labor was all he knew, but he was eager for a fresh start, talking about it with a kind of hope that didn't sound naïve—just determined.

As Kevin listened, he kept glancing at Gabriela, wondering how this worked. How did she go from the French exchange student—intelligent, refined, soft-spoken, to Jimmy—rough edges, calloused hands, tattoos, and cigarettes? It didn't add up.

Then again, Kevin thought, neither did he. Not anymore. The guy who showed up to work as a manager six months ago was gone, traded in for someone who pumped gas and washed windshields, sweated through his uniform, and had to explain his rent shortfalls at dinner.

Still, Kevin and Jimmy got along surprisingly well. For all their differences—background, temperament, the way they carried themselves—they shared the quiet understanding of two guys trying to find their place in a house that didn't feel like theirs. Kevin figured the move would be a bigger adjustment for Jimmy, but if it was, it didn't show. Within a week, Jimmy landed a job with a construction crew in Delray Beach and fit himself into the rhythm of the household like he'd always been there.

Dolores and Diego seemed to accept him without much protest. Kevin had anticipated more pushback. Jimmy wasn't exactly the French exchange student type. But maybe that was the point. Maybe, like Kevin, Jimmy had learned to keep his head down, nod at the right times, and not stir the pot.

And Kevin—he tried. He kept working long hours at the station, pumping gas and fixing flats. But the job was never going to become anything more than it was. He told himself it was temporary, just a stepping stone. Still, the long evenings and weekend shifts meant missing family dinners and movie nights—things that made people feel they belonged. Jimmy, meanwhile, was there—joking with Gabriela, helping Diego with yard work, winning over Dolores with little fixes around the house.

Kevin felt himself drifting to the margins. He was putting in the hours and footing the bills, but Maritza hadn't found a job yet. The weight of their shared expenses got heavier each month. The more Jimmy settled in, the more Kevin felt like the one still unpacking.

Kevin and Jimmy searched for their place in the family food chain, usually finding it at the bottom. When they needed to escape family dynamics and drama, they went fishing or visited arcades to play video games and air hockey. That became the only recognizable activity from Kevin's previous friendships and life in Bayview. At times, they visited used car lots in search of cars to admire and dream of owning one day. It was on one of those drives that Kevin fell in love again.

She was a black 1968 Mustang GT Fastback—black leather bucket seats, thick chrome side pipes, and a high-performance 289 V-8 engine. She sat low and wide, coiled like a threat. The kind of car that made noise even when it wasn't running. Kevin had always envied the kids in high school who drove muscle cars— Camaros, Corvettes, Mustangs. This one didn't just look fast. It looked untouchable. It was strength and freedom. It was what Kevin thought he needed.

With a bit of encouragement and borrowed cash from Jimmy, Kevin traded his family's well-maintained Bronco for the object of his desire right there on the spot. No calls to Maritza. No second thoughts.

The Mustang wasn't just a car—it was a resurrection. A middle finger to compromise. Something loud, fast, and unapologetic. Something that didn't ask permission. He told himself he was trading up, but it felt more like burning a bridge. The Bronco was history—his parents, Bayview, beaches, first kisses, nights with Ricky. This Mustang? It was nothing more than anger on wheels.

Regret came fast and loud. The engine roared, and the tires smoked, but the needle climbed into the red every time. He'd traded reliability for fantasy, and the fantasy was breaking down. The Mustang looked tough. It turned heads. But it couldn't go the distance. Kevin stared at the stalled Mustang one afternoon and realized—it wasn't just the car that couldn't handle the heat. It was him.

21

A HOUSE DIVIDING

Kevin had high hopes he could turn things around. Every aspect of his life seemed off-balance since moving to South Florida. Now, he was determined to fix it, to get his life back on track—step by step, correcting mistake by mistake.

First was the Mustang. As much as he loved what it represented—freedom, strength, control—he regretted the impulsive purchase. He listed it in Auto Trader, and despite disclosing the cooling issues, it sold quickly. Kevin used the money to pay Jimmy back, and the little cash left over became a down payment on a car at the GM dealership where Diego worked.

It was a light brown subcompact hatchback. New, under warranty, and hopelessly ugly. But it was reliable, and dependability now mattered more than pride. Diego had to co-sign the loan, and while Kevin kept his mouth shut, he simmered inside. The irony didn't escape him—he was doing the same thing he criticized Maritza for having done. He had little choice, though, given his flailing credit and income.

Next came the debt. Kevin needed to repair his credit after narrowly avoiding bankruptcy the year before—a decision born of panic and poor advice from Dolores, carried out by a second-rate attorney more interested in fees than Kevin's future. Thankfully, the bankruptcy judge allowed Kevin to withdraw the petition. Thirty-five hundred dollars in credit card and furniture debt had once felt like a mountain. Now, he saw it for what it was: a test he should have climbed, not erased. The petition was dismissed, and Kevin resolved to rebuild what he'd nearly destroyed.

But the real problem was where they lived. Kevin and Maritza needed their own space. They were married, but nothing about their life felt like it. As long as they lived under Dolores and Diego's roof, Kevin didn't feel like Maritza's husband—barely even her equal.

"It's like I married them instead of her," he told Jimmy one night. Jimmy got it. He felt it, too. But Kevin had more time to resent it, more time for the pressure to build. And lately, it was building fast.

Moving wouldn't be possible, however, until Maritza found a job and they resolved their debt situation. They had no choice but to continue living with her family. Kevin hated their continuous dependency on them. He resented their grip on his relationship with his wife.

Kevin passed through the hallway on his way to the kitchen when he heard voices from the living room. Just out of sight, he paused at the corner as Gabriela's voice, sharp with irritation.

"It's not fair," she said. "Jimmy and I are paying our share. You and Kevin barely contribute."

"Kevin's working," Maritza replied defensively. "He's doing everything he can. I'm still looking—"

"Looking?" Gabriela cut her off. "It's been months. A year!"

"You know it's not that simple," Maritza said. "We moved

down here, started over. We didn't have—"

"Everyone else figured it out," Gabriela snapped. "Maybe it's time you do the same."

Kevin stood frozen, his reaction caught between anger and shame.

"Gabriela's not wrong, mi amor," Delores weighted in, Kevin realizing she was also part of the sibling rivalry. "This house is not made of rubber—it can only stretch so far."

"So, what am I supposed to do?" Maritza asked, her voice frustrated, smaller now.

"Get your real estate license," Delores replied as if she had been waiting to suggest it again. "Come work at the office with us. You're pretty, Maritza. You're good with people. You smile, they listen."

"I'm not like you, Mami."

"Then be better," Dolores shouted, no mistaking the steel behind it.

Kevin didn't hear another word and quietly stepped back, retreating to the bedroom. He sat on the edge of the bed, staring at the wall. The voices from the other room faded into a hum, like background static.

They hadn't known he was listening, but the message couldn't have been clearer. He wasn't just struggling. He was being discussed. He was being judged.

~

When Maritza couldn't find work, she set her sights on getting her real estate license and joining her mother's new office. Kevin agreed to take the course with her—not just to help her but as an opportunity to do something together that might help the couple repair some of the divides forming between them.

Kevin helped Maritza study for the four-hour professional licensing exam, and they took it together. It was an all-out effort to support her, but when they received the results in the mail, he had passed the exam while she didn't.

Maritza stared at the envelope in silence, her fingers still resting on the edge of the dining table.

"I'll just study and retake it," she said without looking up.

Kevin tried to smile. "You'll pass next time. I'm sure of it."

But the words felt thin. Kevin could already feel the shift between them—like the distance wasn't in miles but in confidence. She wanted this win. Maritza needed it. And now, even as he stood there ready to reassure her, he wondered if she blamed him for passing when she didn't.

Maritza continued studying to retake the exam while Kevin put his new license to work. He joined Delores's agency as a part-time associate. It was a help to her—answering phone calls, staffing the office on the weekends, placing listings in the local paper—but Kevin had no genuine interest in selling real estate. The country was in a deep recession, and home mortgage rates were at sixteen percent, an all-time high. It was a tough market for a young and inexperienced new associate to break into.

Kevin worked sixty hours a week at the gas station, then clocked weekends at the real estate office. He was burning the candle at both ends and, in the process, burning himself down. Still, it wasn't enough. The money wasn't enough. His effort wasn't enough. The walls were closing in—debts, obligations, strained silences. His marriage. The household—a complicated web of commitments, disappointment, blame, and guilt. It took a toll, and he bore it—until the morning he couldn't.

Kevin couldn't get out of bed. Not because he didn't want to—because he couldn't. The sheets felt heavier than his own body. Kevin was immobile, unable to cope with the simplest of tasks. He called in sick, barely recognizing his own voice on the line, and spent the entire day in bed.

The same thing happened the next day. The sheets felt safer than sunlight. He couldn't move, couldn't think beyond the weight in his chest. The silence in the bedroom was louder than any argument—and for two days, he listened to it swallow him. He couldn't eat, and as the family worried about his hiding behind closed doors, he, too, wondered what was wrong with him.

He told the others he felt under the weather, but it wasn't a fever or a cold. It was something he couldn't name, something foreign he hadn't experienced before.

The phone rang on the evening of the third day of his irrational and uncharacteristic behavior. Mrs. Jackson's voice was polite but clipped. "We're just checking to see if you plan to return."

Kevin knew the answer. He knew he was past the point of return. She probably did, too.

That one phone call ended it. The job. The trying. The illusion of control. Kevin didn't quit—he just stopped showing up. And with that single call, Kevin was unemployed again. Another crack in the foundation. Another quiet failure folding into the weight of the others.

On the fourth day, Kevin got out of bed and stepped back into the world of sunlight and noise. He wasn't okay, but he was out of bed, which felt like a victory. He needed to find a new job, but for now, he threw himself into real estate, scraping by on a few small commissions from rentals and co-listings. It wasn't enough. With Maritza still unemployed, their spiral into debt only deepened.

One afternoon, with bills on the table and no solutions left, Kevin called his mother. He told Carol he needed four hundred dollars for dental work. It was a lie—shame disguised as a necessity. The words caught in his throat, but he pushed them out anyway. It felt like stealing. Not quite—but close enough to make his skin crawl.

Kevin hated himself for asking, hated himself more for lying. But he couldn't tell his parents the truth—not about the debts, the broken jobs, the mistakes piling behind him. Kevin was always the son who made them proud. How could he tell them what he had become? So, instead, he drifted. The more he struggled, the more silence filled the gap between him and his parents. They couldn't help because they didn't even know. Kevin had made sure of that.

Carol's check arrived in the mail a few days later. Kevin held it in his hand before cashing it, the relief short-lived. He handed the money to Dolores to cover a portion of what they owed the household. By the end of the week, the money was gone—and so was the brief moment of respite.

Every time Kevin clawed a few inches out of the hole, the ground gave way beneath him. And each time, he fell harder and deeper. The fall was always a lonely one.

~

While Kevin struggled, Jimmy thrived. He'd gone from employee of a construction company to small business owner in months—selling the Challenger, buying a truck, and bidding on jobs directly as a subcontractor. With each paycheck, Jimmy handed the money to Gabriela, who kept the books, paid the bills, and doled out his allowance, just like Dolores did with Diego. Gabriela was the firstborn—her mother's mirror, her father's favorite. Kevin and Maritza, meanwhile, kept slipping lower in the household's invisible ranking of productive couples.

Kevin watched it happen. Gabriela stepped into Dolores's shoes with practiced ease—balancing the checkbook in the dining room, giving orders in the kitchen, and even reminding Dolores when bills were due. Maritza, once her mother's shadow, had become just that—a shadow. Less involved and less relevant.

Kevin saw it in how Dolores looked at her daughters—one with pride, the other with mounting disappointment. And he saw the effect on his wife. Maritza's smile tightened during dinner conversations. Delores and Gabriela dismissed her when she offered to help manage the office. Gabriela had become the one their mother turned to for decisions, the one with the answers.

One afternoon, Maritza slammed a drawer shut.

"What's wrong?" Kevin asked.

"Nothing," she muttered. Then, quieter: "She's just Mom's golden girl. She always has been."

Kevin reached for her hand, but she was already walking away. He stayed where he was, letting the silence settle between them. He didn't know how to respond. He was used to feeling invisible in that house, but now Maritza felt it, too.

As Jimmy's business grew, he needed help. Kevin needed income. When Jimmy asked if he'd assist part-time, Kevin agreed immediately. The same reflex led him to move to South Florida, propose to Maritza, and trade the Bronco for the Mustang. Say yes first. Regret later.

Jimmy taught him the construction basics—how to shingle a roof, frame, drywall, install windows and doors, and weld. They dug fence posts and worked long days in the blistering Florida heat. Kevin cut his hands on razor wire and let the rain soak his shirtless shoulders without complaint. He hoped the soreness in his body might rebuild something inside him. He'd grown soft—physically and otherwise—and the labor gave him the illusion of strength again. It was a type of penance.

The work was grueling. Kevin dug holes in the hard shell-like Florida soil manually with post-hole diggers. He laid asphalt tiles on hot roofs in the tropical sun. He toiled inside buildings under construction that were not yet air-conditioned. Although demanding, Kevin enjoyed the manual labor. He hoped it would harden his muscles and restore the fitness he had lost over the previous two years without tennis, swimming, or soccer.

Still, Kevin knew it couldn't last. He couldn't make a long-term career out of it. He had seen what construction did to a man's body, how it leathered his skin, ruined his joints, and aged him before his time.

Kevin needed more than labor. He needed a career—benefits, stability, dignity—a future that could support a family.

Kevin needed something more—something worthy of his potential. He needed a career with benefits, something stable, a job with dignity, and a path to retirement. He wanted to find what his father Bert had found—structure, respect, and a future.

Kevin didn't want to live like this, but he didn't yet know how to live any other way.

22

HEAT OF THE MOMENT

L ike most construction work, Jimmy's subcontracting jobs were feast or famine—cycling between long stretches of urgent demand and days of frustrating downtime. Some days, they worked from sunrise to sunset. Others ended by lunch. When the weather stalled or jobs dried up, they didn't work at all.

During those slow stretches, Kevin searched for something better. He applied for jobs that promised a real future—steady income, benefits, and a career with a path forward. He sent applications to the Florida Highway Patrol, but his poor credit history became a roadblock. Then he applied to the Palm Beach Fire Department, confident that his father's impressive career as a paramedic and fire station chief would give him an edge. But openings were rare, so no call for an interview came.

Next was the Riviera Beach Police Department. Kevin passed the written exams and physical endurance trials easily. He advanced to the final round of interviews, and with each step forward, hope and anticipation soared. Near the end of the final panel interview, they posed one last hypothetical.

"If your wife ever demanded that you quit," one of them asked, "would you choose your marriage or your career as a police officer?" It was a delicate question—possibly a trap. But Kevin understood the intent. He'd grown up watching his father leave the house every third day for a 24-hour shift. He knew the toll these jobs took on families—how easily duty could erode a marriage. He also knew officer attrition rates were high, especially in smaller departments still tense after the Liberty City riots.

He paused for a few seconds, then answered.

"I could honestly be devoted to both," he said. "But if I had to choose one, I would choose my marriage."

Kevin believed it was the correct response. To say otherwise, claiming he'd leave his wife for a badge, felt cold and dishonest. Undoubtedly, the panel would see his devotion to family as a strength. It meant commitment and loyalty—the kind of man who wouldn't quit on the job either.

When the interview ended, they told him he was wrong. They expected complete, unwavering devotion to the job. Nothing less. Kevin left the building unsure if there even was a correct answer.

The rejection stung—but Kevin was getting used to rejection in increasing doses. The silence at home hurt more. Sex with Maritza had waned not long after their wedding. Then, it vanished entirely after moving in with her parents and sister. Now, it was nonexistent—and intimacy had disappeared with it.

There was always an excuse: something else to do, another family dynamic interrupting privacy, or simply fatigue. It didn't seem normal for a young couple less than two years married. Not in Kevin's eyes.

Maritza had been different when they dated—playful, flirtatious, magnetic. Kevin had tried to be patient. Maybe it was the stress of unemployment or living under her parent's roof again. Perhaps it was her real estate exam failure or her weight gain. But more than anything, it felt like something in her had changed. Maybe it had changed in both of them.

The girl in the red dress seemed like a memory now. And Kevin wasn't sure if she—or the version of himself who once chased her—would ever return.

~

When Maritza's job offer for a secretarial role came, they were ecstatic. Kevin couldn't have been prouder of her for finally landing a job.

After a three-day training session in nearby Jupiter Beach, she would begin her new position the following Monday. As they spoke on the phone the two nights she was away, Kevin thought about the first time apart, talking for hours at night, expressing their longing to be together. This job was the critical break they had been waiting so long for.

Kevin left for work with Jimmy early that morning, kissing Maritza on the forehead and wishing her luck on her first day. She smiled and thanked him. When he came home that evening, he couldn't wait to hear how Maritza's first day on the job had gone.

There had been no first day, though. When pressed for an explanation, Maritza said the training over the weekend had not gone well, and she didn't get the job after all. It made no sense— they had already hired her—she had already spent a weekend away in training. What could have happened for them to rescind their job offer?

Kevin was tired from a long, physically challenging day in the field. Still, it didn't compare to the mental exhaustion of hope slipping through his fingers once again. It felt like thin twine pulled through his tightly clenched hands. Like Santiago in Hemmingway's *The Old Man and the Sea* trying to land the great marlin after an extended run of bad luck and no catches— desperately clenching that rope of hope as it burns and cuts through the flesh of his palms. The harder Kevin pushed for answers, the more agitated Maritza became, pacing around the bedroom until finally breaking into tears.

"What's wrong?" he asked, reaching out to touch her arms, trying to stop her nervous tempo and comfort her. She didn't want to be comforted, though, pulling away from him each time he tried. Kevin was about to feel the irony of his answer to the police department's interview panel and their subsequent rejection of him.

"I'm sorry," she replied, her eyes reddening as the tears began to flow.

"Hey, it's all right. Don't cry. You'll find another job soon."

"It's not the job," she snapped, pulling away from his touch. "There never was a job!"

Kevin stared at her, stunned. "What are you talking about?"

"I needed a break. I lied. I just—needed to get away."

But Kevin wasn't buying it. Not the way she avoided his eyes. Not the way she flinched.

Maritza admitted there was no job offer and no weekend spent training. She had spent the weekend in Jupiter Beach but at a small beach motel, not a business training center. The pressure to find a job after being unemployed was overwhelming. Fabricated out of desperation, Maritza knew the story would fall apart when she didn't start an actual job. She was willing to pay the price for the lie in exchange for the few days of isolation it bought her. She asserted she needed to get away, to have some time alone to think, and to rejuvenate her spirit.

Kevin listened, wondering what exactly she needed to rejuvenate from. It was her employment status that needed revitalization. It was her figure that needed restoring. It was her interest in intimacy that needed reviving. None of this made sense, and his intuition told him there was more that she was not revealing.

Hemmingway's Santiago eventually landed the great marlin, lashing it to his tiny boat, only to have it ripped apart and stolen by sharks. Santiago was left feeling drained, emotionless, and exhausted. The plot revolves around a man's attempt to win a battle against nature.

"You lied to everyone and took a weekend vacation at the beach? Are you fucking crazy? Kevin found it hard to stand still and began shadowing Maritza in her nervous pacing, turning to follow her each time she turned to avoid eye contact with him.

"Don't you realize how strapped we are for money?" He continued, feeling his chest tighten.

"That's the most selfish and irresponsible thing I've ever heard." His attempt at consoling her faded, replaced instead with frustration and anger.

"I'd like to take a fucking beach vacation, too," he added, "but I'm too busy working two fucking jobs for that."

Internally, Kevin urged himself to calm down and relax, but a long list of disappointments filled his mind instead. The surprise car purchase without consultation, charging it to his credit card without permission. Kevin thought about her real estate exam failure despite all the help he gave her. The rage within grew over her laziness, inability to find a job, the resulting pressure on him to pay the bills, and the indebtedness to so many people it had all caused.

"How did you pay for it?" he pressed.

"I charged it," she replied, shaking and pacing and sobbing.

Kevin knew she was lying now. He continued pressing for details, asking her to produce the receipt and questioning everything she said. He dug deeper into the root of the infectious lie she was weaving, aware that his voice was growing louder as hers grew more panicked and avoiding.

When Gabriela lightly knocked to ask if everything was okay, Kevin shouted at the closed door. "Leave us alone!" He stood between Maritza and the bedroom's exit. No one was entering or exiting until he had the truth. Kevin was weary of her laziness, her selfishness, and her irresponsibility. He wanted the truth—Kevin deserved the truth—he demanded the truth. Kevin continued to press her with his questions, like an attorney pressing a hostile witness on the stand.

"I wasn't alone," she finally shouted back. "I was with a guy, okay? Please, Kevin, please," she begged, "Please stop."

Then, Maritza confessed she had spent the weekend with someone else. The lie insulted his intelligence. The truth shattered his heart. As she wept and reached out to him for forgiveness, Kevin stepped backward in anguish and disgust.

Kevin was Santiago. Success was the marlin. And Maritza? She was the shark.

"Don't touch me," he snapped, throwing up a hand like a stop sign between them, warning her to keep her distance. Maritza stopped, and Kevin stared at her in contemptuous silence. She had disrespected him, giving someone else the affection he desperately wanted and patiently waited for. That the attention that *he* earned and deserved. Kevin's frustration, born as concern and for console, now tasted like disgust as he maintained his distance and disdain.

The room fell silent, the air heavy. Like two gladiators in the lull of battle, burdened by the weight of their armor, both weary and wounded, their breathing labored by the swings and strikes of their verbal barrages upon the other, the young husband and wife stared at one another as enemies, waiting for the next round of oral attacks to begin.

Maritza's crying subsided, and she slowly regained her composure. She told Kevin about meeting one of Jimmy's friends when she, Gabriela, and Jimmy were out one evening. It had been right before their marriage, while she was still in Bayview and he was already in West Palm. They had sex then and somehow kept in touch. The weekend was a reconnection for the two. She claimed it had no meaning, that she had no feelings for him, and that it was only physical. She claimed her unemployment and depression made her feel like a failure, and she craved attention from someone outside of those closest to her weaknesses. She said she had made a mistake and realized it now. She promised it would never happen again.

She cheated on me before our wedding, for fuck's sake.

Kevin wanted to lash out at her for her betrayal. He yearned to demand an explanation of how she could sleep with someone else while denying him. He also wanted to hug and comfort her, to appreciate her confession, to hope she would keep her new promise and that he could forgive her. But again, hope is the last thing lost. Kevin could do none of those things. Instead, he slammed the bedroom door shut as he left the house, blinded with anger and dying from sadness.

Kevin ended up at the subdivision's lake—the one he and Jimmy sometimes fished. He wanted to be alone with his pain, his guilt, and his regret. He sat quietly on the bank until the sun fell below the horizon across the water's still surface, disturbed only by the quick zigzag skimming movements of the water bugs.

-

In the past, pleasing his parents and earning their approval was most important. Kevin knew they were proud of him, but he couldn't help but focus on the times he thought he had been a disappointment.

During his elementary school years, for instance, his father enrolled him in Little League in West Bayview. The neighborhood was known for developing excellent baseball players, many of whom played professional ball in minor and major leagues, but not Kevin, who only participated in one season and was an awful player. He couldn't bat the ball, even when it sat stationary on a tee. He couldn't catch the ball either, even in the outfield. When someone hit a ball in his direction, Kevin was busy studying his shoelaces or the blades of grass as dozens of players and parents shouted at him to get his attention. Kevin was fortunate that a fly ball descending upon his inattentiveness never knocked him unconscious. He was just as bad at choosing a wife and being a husband as he had been playing baseball.

When it was clear that baseball wouldn't work, Bert took him to the West Bayview Boys Club next. Still, Kevin's trepidation over being left there alone sent a clear message of fear and disinterest. Boy Scouting was the only activity that held his interest and that he enjoyed. It was also the only group activity Kevin stuck with. After a handful of years, though, he lost interest in that too, falling short of achieving scouting's highest rank of Eagle Scout.

Kevin tried guitar and piano lessons, but his lack of natural musical talent and apathy toward practicing ended those activities before wasting too much of his parent's money.

Kevin had been just as poor at maintaining childhood and teenage friendships as he had been at sticking to organized group activities. It takes effort, especially when it does not come naturally. He had not seen or spoken to Ricky, Jeff, Daniel, or Mike for two years. It had been even longer for Steve, Miguel, or Keith. Jennifer and Rachael were distant memories. After his move to South Florida, he had little contact with his true family, grandparents, sisters, and aunts. Because of his laziness then, he had no one to turn to now.

Earning his teacher's approval had become Kevin's top focus in school. Whether volunteering as a Safety Patrol in elementary school, working as an office assistant in junior high, or being a teacher's assistant to his eleventh-grade English teacher, Kevin wanted to be the student who could be trusted and counted upon to fulfill his responsibilities. Kevin wanted to be helpful, and he wanted to be recognized. In many ways, his relationship with teachers was more important than with his fellow students, just as his quest for parental approval took priority over allegiance to his siblings. Kevin had become a college dropout, unable to pay his bills, and helpful to no one. His only recognition now was depending on others for the food on the table and the roof over his head.

Kevin's need for approval from parents and teachers changed when he began working. It transitioned to a pursuit of peer approval from friends and coworkers instead. Ricky, Jeff, Daniel, and Mike all influenced his actions, or more accurately, his desire to please them motivated his behavior. Kevin was always happy to drive, eager to pick up the next round of drinks, and willing to go to whatever movies, bars, or events everyone else wanted. He considered himself a great friend because he was the great enabler, making everything they did easier and, in some cases, possible.

But what about what Kevin wanted? Was all that approval he sought over the years worth the cost of understanding what he truly wanted and who he genuinely was? It had always been about pleasing others, but now, who was pleasing him?

-

The sun fell entirely, and the darkness came fully. Kevin wanted to be gone for a long time, long enough for Maritza to suffer in contemplation over her deception. He wanted her to miss him and to wonder if he would ever return. Kevin wanted her family to shame her—to say the words he didn't have the strength to speak himself. Kevin now felt like pleasing no one as he sat on the bank of the lake in the dark, hearing only nature's collective sounds of anger, fear, and despair.

Several weeks passed, and a quiet tension prevailed over the household. Dolores and Diego learned about their daughter's lie over the job and training, but not about her infidelity. Gabriela and Jimmy had known about Maritza's original affair with his friend but not about their recent rendezvous. That's what they claimed, anyway. It hurt that they had kept it from him all this time. As their defense, they claimed it was not their business or place to tell him. Everyone felt slighted by everyone else over one element of the betrayal or another. They coexisted out of necessity while keeping an extra distance from one another. No one openly discussed what had happened. Multiple secrets and untold truths are difficult to keep track of over time. Maybe they were all feeling guilty as sinners, accomplices, and victims. Everyone lived in quiet tension—a house full of ghosts, none brave enough to speak the dead's name.

23

ALL MIXED UP

Kevin continued working with Jimmy to finish several large projects in Miami. He welcomed the long hours and grueling labor—not just for the paycheck but for the escape. The less time spent at home, the better.

Driving to and from job sites, they vented about life in the house and how little of it felt like theirs. Both were frustrated in their relationships with the sisters. They admitted sex had become rare, nearly nonexistent, and the closeness they once felt had eroded into something colder, transactional. They agreed on one thing without hesitation: moving in with the girl's parents had been a colossal mistake, and something had to change.

During one of their long commutes, Jimmy brought it up.

"Hey," he said, eyes fixed on the road. "I never told you, but I'm sorry about what happened—with Maritza and my old friend."

Kevin said nothing.

"I didn't know she was engaged," Jimmy added. "We all just went out to dinner and had a few drinks. I had just met her that night."

Kevin stared out the window, jaw tight.

"I didn't even know they hooked up until after," Jimmy continued. "The guy bragged to me about it the next day. Asshole thought it was funny." He paused, then shook his head. "I should've said something back then, but I didn't think it was my place. And once you two got married…"

Kevin finally spoke. "So you knew?"

"Not when it happened. Not until later. And I haven't talked to the jerk since," Jimmy said. "That's part of why I left Bayview. I was done with all that crap. I wanted to start over—with Gabriela, but also away from that mess."

Kevin nodded slowly, unsure if he believed him. But at this point, Jimmy was his only real ally in the house, which counted for something. Although they were from different backgrounds, they shared the same reality—they would always be outsiders within the sister's family.

~

It was hot for October as Jimmy and Kevin wrapped up the Miami project earlier than expected. By mid-morning, they'd returned the leftover materials to the shop, and Jimmy had collected payment. With the rest of the day free, they agreed they'd earned a break.

"We deserve it," Jimmy said, tossing his work gloves on the dash. "I know just the place."

Instead of heading home, they picked up two six-packs and drove to a remote pond off a U.S. Forestry Service road used as a firebreak. Jimmy said he'd stumbled on it months ago—tucked deep in the woods, a pond ringed by limestone, the water transparent and greenish blue.

"No signs, no fences," Jimmy said as they bounced along the dirt road. "I think it's federal land. Never seen a soul out here."

The idea of disappearing for half a day sounded perfect. As Jimmy drove, Kevin stared out the window, his thoughts drifting back to Bayview.

He thought about the guys at Joni's Pub—cold beer, darts, pool tables scarred from years of use. He remembered Mike and Ricky, their fishing trips from canoes in the lakes and rivers or casting lines off the Gandy Bridge at night, watching headlights blur across the water as they debated UFO sightings. Then he thought of Steve—hours spent swimming, racing, diving, daring each other to go deeper for longer.

Those were simpler times. Better times. And right now, Kevin would've given anything to go back.

When Jimmy veered off the dirt road, the thick forest gave way to a small clearing beside the pond. They parked beneath the vast canopy of a sprawling oak. The tree reminded Kevin of the Ear Tree back home—of childhood afternoons spent climbing to its highest branches to watch the world from above. A peacefulness here pulled him back to that simpler world—not so long ago—and he welcomed the thought of spending the afternoon in it.

"This place is perfect," Kevin said, handing Jimmy a cold bottle from the small cooler behind the pickup's bench seat.

"Yeah, it's cool," Jimmy replied. "Too bad we didn't bring rods."

"True. Here's to a break well earned," Kevin said. They clinked bottlenecks and drained them in silence. Kevin doubted any bass were in an artificial retention pond like this. It probably just had turtles, maybe a gator, likely snakes. They rolled the windows down and let the breeze drift through the cab as they opened a second round.

Staring through the windshield at the glassy green water, Jimmy was the first to break the silence. "What Maritza did to you," he paused, "that was shitty."

Kevin nodded slowly. "Yeah. It was." He didn't look at Jimmy. He wasn't sure what Jimmy meant—whether he was offering sympathy or trying to distance himself from the mess. Did he think Kevin blamed him? Was this an unspoken plea for absolution because his friend hooked up with Maritza?

Kevin thought about asking what the guy looked like. How old he was. Was he good-looking? But he stopped himself and didn't. Kevin knew it would only make things worse if he obsessed over details like that—just more to measure himself against. In the end, it didn't matter. Her betrayal was hers to own.

"So…" Jimmy exhaled slowly. "What are you gonna do?"

Kevin let the question hang; he had no answer for it. What could he do? Keep avoiding her? Keep pretending everything was fine in front of her parents? Was this the only incident or the only one she admitted to? Had she cheated on him at their first apartment before her parents moved down, during the daytime when he was working long hours in Ft. Lauderdale? What about when he worked nights at the gas station?

He hated how his mind filled with images of her taking her clothes off in some cheap motel—him at work, exhausted and faithful. Her, not.

"If it were me," Jimmy said, taking a long drag on his cigarette and flicking the ashes through the pickup's open window, "I'd want to kill her."

Kevin didn't reply. He just took another sip of beer and stared straight ahead.

Kevin opened the door and climbed out, sliding the bench seat forward to reach the cooler. "Come on," he said, grabbing two more bottles. As Jimmy rounded the front of the truck, Kevin tossed him one. "Chug race. No choking or spitting—and no spraying it out your nose."

Jimmy chuckled, already raising his bottle. "Three, two, one—go!" he called. They drained the beers in sync, slamming the empties to the ground and each claiming victory.

"I won, and you know it," Kevin grinned. "Let's go in."

"Don't have suits."

"We don't need fucking swimsuits," Kevin said, crossing his arms and peeling off his shirt like one of those Body by Soloflex guys in the advertisements. It was a purposeful move.

Jimmy smirked. "What if someone sees us?"

"Who the fuck is going to see us?" Kevin exclaimed, unlacing his boots to kick them off. "Look around. We're in the middle of the woods." Kevin raised his hand to his eyebrows and made a 360-degree sweep of the woods and pond as if looking through binoculars to mock Jimmy. He shoved his socks inside the boots and laid them on the hood. His shorts landed on top. "Swim in your underwear if you're a pussy."

Jimmy grabbed the back of his shirt behind his neck and pulled it forward over his head one-handed in a single swift motion, still holding his lit cigarette with the other. "Nah, I'm good. You go in if you want."

Jimmy pulled two more beers from the cooler and handed one to Kevin. Then he hoisted himself onto the truck's hood, planting a boot on the bumper before swinging back into a casual sprawl beneath the oak's shade. His knees poked through the frayed slits in his faded jeans—tight-fitting, worn from work. He leaned back on one hand, the other lifting his beer for a long, slow gulp.

Kevin tried not to stare, but how Jimmy's abs caught the light, exposing every cut and separation in his abdominal muscles and chest, was hard to ignore. The fluid flowed into Jimmy's mouth, his lips wrapped around the bottle's long neck while his bicep constricted into an orange-sized knot of round, hard muscle. Kevin looked away, heat rising to his face.

Jimmy let out a deep, guttural belch and laughed like it was the funniest thing he'd done all week. Then, with a flick of his wrist, he dropped the dead cigarette into the empty bottle.

"Fucking pig!" Kevin yelled, grinning with amusement despite himself.

"Hey," Jimmy shot back, raising both arms in mock defense. "Who the fuck's gonna hear us? We're in the middle of the woods, remember?"

"Smartass," Kevin replied, tipping back his beer. He tried to force out a competing belch but failed. The two boys killed the fourth round and cracked open a fifth, trying to one-up each other like middle schoolers on a sugar rush.

Jimmy took another swig and leaned his head back. "Why are they such bitches, man?" His words began to take on a noticeable slur.

Kevin glanced over.

"I mean, seriously. We never fuck. Ever. I bust my ass all day in this goddamn heat, and *she's* the one who's too tired. Fuck that."

Kevin grabbed the last two bottles, popped the caps, and handed one over. "Here. Drown your sorrows, Romeo."

"Thanks, man."

"Anything for the Big Boss Man," Kevin said with mock solemnity.

"Oh yeah? Anything?"

Kevin paused, pretending to consider it. "Well, yeah. You're my sugar daddy boss-man, right?" He kept a straight face for a beat—then burst into laughter.

Jimmy laughed, too. "Good. Wash this dirty piece of shit when we get home."

"The truck or your dick?" Kevin shot back, pointing to both, his laughter rolling now. "Maybe that's why she doesn't have sex with you anymore."

"You prick!" Jimmy barked, sliding off the hood and lunging—only to trip and stumble onto the ground, landing in the grass with a grunt.

Kevin lost it, doubled over laughing as Jimmy scrambled to his feet and charged again. He backed up, darted around the open truck door, and dove headfirst into the pickup. Kevin scrambled across the bench seat to the driver's side of the cab, giggling like a kid playing tag, his ribs hurting from all the laughter.

Jimmy caught up fast. His chest slammed into Kevin's back, pinning him halfway across the seat with his legs dangling out the door. The impact knocked what little breath Kevin had left out of him as his hands flailed, grasping for anything he could grab as leverage inside the cab. Jimmy snatched Kevin's right wrist and twisted it around his back, holding Kevin in an armlock from behind, like a wrestler pinning his opponent or a cop about to cuff a suspect he had just chased and brought down to the ground.

"Say, uncle!" Jimmy yelled.

Kevin gasped for air, trying to squirm free, still half-laughing and half-panicked. "Okay! Okay, man—" He tried to tell Jimmy he gave up, but there was no referee to hear Kevin concede or see him tapping out.

"Stop fighting me," Jimmy growled, his breath hot against Kevin's neck.

All Kevin could see was the gritty and worn cloth material of the truck's seat as his head pressed into it. It stank of work sweat and sunbaked cloth and vinyl. His breath caught in his throat, the beer rising.

"What, now you're done playing around?" Jimmy sneered. "Who's the pussy now, bitch?" Jimmy kept his weight on top of Kevin and the restraint on Kevin's wrist.

Kevin's left arm remained wedged in the gap between the backrest and seat. He had no leverage. Jimmy had all of it—feet planted, weight centered.

Jimmy eased up, lifting his bare chest off Kevin's back, and for a second, Kevin thought the horseplay was over. It wasn't. It was only a repositioning by Jimmy, increasing the pressure on Kevin's wrists to twist them higher into the space between Kevin's shoulder blades. The move drove Kevin deeper into the seat, his arm numbing as he struggled to catch his breath, trying to tell Jimmy to stop. The rough play was going too far. Jimmy had already won the game of power.

"Jimmy! Stop it!" Kevin yelled. There was no humor left in his voice now. The laughter was gone—all that remained was confusion and fear.

"Bitch," Jimmy snarled, his teeth grit, his movements honed to a single purpose.

Instead of stopping, though, Kevin felt Jimmy's grip on the waistband of his underwear as Jimmy yanked it down with his free hand. He heard Jimmy spit, and then unexpectedly and abruptly, Kevin felt the pain.

"Be still!" Jimmy commanded.

Kevin stopped struggling. He could hear Jimmy grunting, urging himself on, and the rest was incoherent. It wasn't clear if Jimmy was proving his dominance in retribution for Kevin's jeering and laughing at him or indirectly showing his frustration toward Gabriela for not satisfying him when he wanted to be satisfied.

"Please," Kevin implored, unsure if Jimmy even heard his plea. Probably not.

Kevin saw only darkness behind his tightly shut eyelids as he squeezed them closed. He heard only Jimmy's rhythmic and rapid panting and gasping. Kevin tasted the sweat of his own tears as they rolled down his nose and across his lips, wetting the dirty cloth seat as the side of his face pressed into it. Kevin felt the pause and then the shudder behind and within him. Then, as quickly and fiercely as it started, it was over.

When Jimmy released Kevin's wrist, the numb arm dropped to the floorboard. Kevin didn't move at first. He lay there—his face pressed into the scratchy seat—his skin damp with hushed tears and Jimmy's sweat. The air in the cab felt thick. He was stone-cold sober now, trying to steady his breath and make sense of what had just happened.

Eventually, he slowly pushed himself upright off the truck's bench seat, his body stiff. His head turned just enough to catch a glimpse of Jimmy—still behind him—but Kevin looked away just as fast, out toward the small pond's greenish-blue surface.

"You okay, dude?" Jimmy's voice was flat and dispassionate—satisfied and distant.

Kevin gave a slight nod. He wiped his face, smearing away the tears, the sweat, the fear. Then he backed out of the truck, his bare feet hitting the dirt. The sunlight felt disorienting, too bright and sudden, as smoke from Jimmy's freshly lit cigarette drifted past him.

"You're not gonna weird out now, are you?"

"No. I'm good." Kevin replied, his voice empty. Not angry, not shaken—just not there.

He ran a hand through his hair as if he'd just woken from a nightmare, then rolled his shoulders, trying to work the stiffness and ache from confinement out of his chest, back, and arms.

"Cool. Let's go, dude." Jimmy said 'dude' like they were strangers. Maybe now, they were.

After wiping himself clean with his briefs, Kevin balled them in his fist and hurled them deep into the brush. He thought of the time he threw his tee shirt out the window of his Bronco after dropping Rachael off at the pub. There was something about first encounters—of the sexual kind. You could toss the evidence, but the memory always stuck.

The semen-stained fabric would rot, disintegrating slowly like everything else in life: confidence, lust, love, relationships. Hope itself.

Yes, hope is the last thing lost.

The long ride home was silent. Jimmy drove with the window down, his left arm resting on the door, cigarette in hand, flicking ashes into the blur of the road. Kevin stared out the passenger window, watching the world smear past—cars, trees, signage, memories—each disappearing like a flash, gone before it registered.

The wind curled around Kevin, brushing his cheeks and lifting his hair. It circled through the cab like a cleansing current, trying to carry away the scent of the afternoon's transgression. He sat with his arms crossed, shoulder pressed into the door, head tilted back against the cab's corner—angled as far from Jimmy as possible. He let the breeze wash over him, hoping it could scrub his thoughts clean, rinse away his guilt, and absolve him of whatever he had just become.

Kevin's mind drifted into his childhood, thinking about Sandy, the youngest of the Fernandez kids who lived across the street when he was a boy. She was stout, built like a Sherman tank, and took pleasure in taunting him. At her house or his, it was the same: Sandy would reduce him to tears, sending him running home for cover.

Getting beat up by a little girl wasn't exactly an ego booster for a kid wearing a cowboy hat with plastic six-shooters strapped to his hips. It was embarrassing, and he worried his patient father was quietly disappointed in him.

But one day, Kevin took his dad's advice and stood his ground. It happened in front of their parents, outside the Fernandez house, during some she-said-he-said spat. Sandy's chubby cheeks puffed as she pointed her finger in Kevin's face, nearly poking him in the eye as she spouted her awful little lies.

That's when Kevin snapped. In front of their parents and God himself, he lunged, shoving her with both hands as hard as he could squarely into her chest.

Sandy stumbled like she'd stepped on a banana peel, arms flailing and cheeks wobbling until she landed on her backside with a thunderous thud. The world paused. Then came the scream— sharp, startled, and high-pitched—as tears burst from her eyes like lawn sprinklers on a hot summer day.

Kevin strutted home like a real cowboy, chest out, head high. He had toppled the giant. For the first time in his young life, Kevin believed he would never be tormented or bullied by anyone again. It was one of life's first lessons: Stand up for yourself early and hard before the world walks over you.

But today, Kevin hadn't stood up for himself. Not hard enough. He sat with that thought, cold and silent. In his mind, what had just happened was his fault. Maybe he'd encouraged it— or at least allowed it to happen.

Jimmy, like Sandy, had imposed his will, solidifying his dominance over Kevin—and Kevin had let him. It was like the Bee Hunts back in Bayview. The illusion of control. It's always an illusion.

24

BOILING THE FROG

The sun was well up, but Kevin hadn't slept. He lay still in bed, listening as the house emptied—doors closing, footsteps fading. Jimmy had left before dawn without saying whether he needed Kevin for the new project he'd be starting. Even Maritza was gone, though she had no job to go to. Just as well. Kevin didn't want to see or speak to anyone.

He had nowhere to be, no one to turn to. He stayed under the covers, motionless, staring out the window at the driveway, where only his car remained—a reminder that he was still here though everything else had moved on.

Last night, things erupted the way they did when silence became unbearable. After returning from the pond with Jimmy, Kevin showered, skipped dinner, and went straight to bed. Maritza snapped. She accused him of slipping into another depression—just like after he lost his job—and of letting Jimmy rub off on him, becoming moody and distant.

Kevin said nothing initially, but there was no pulling back once it began. Everything spilled out—her joblessness, the infidelity, the lack of sex, the simmering resentment that poisoned the air between them. The truth about her cheating had been bad enough, but now they'd crossed another line. They'd said things that couldn't be unsaid.

And her timing. God, if she only knew what had happened at the lake—what Jimmy had done—and how much he was *not* like Jimmy. Kevin was assaulted for the second time on the same day, but this time, he fought back.

Maritza stormed out, slamming the door behind her. This time, it was her turn to make the dramatic exit. Kevin locked it and buried himself in the sheets, unsure where she spent the night, only knowing it wasn't beside him.

The morning had come and gone now, and as he lay there staring out the window, his gaze landed on his car in the driveway. The sight almost made him chuckle. He didn't know why. Maybe it was because it was proof he hadn't disappeared entirely. Not yet.

Kevin stared at the ceiling, his mind drifting back to college and his psychology course, one of the only classes he finished and passed. One lesson had stuck: the Boiling Frog Syndrome. A frog dropped into boiling water will jump out. But if you warm the water slowly, it won't notice the danger until it's too late. By then, it's exhausted. Cooked. Dead.

That was how Kevin felt. Like the frog, he had spent the past few years living for others and adapting to situations and relationships as he encountered them. He had allowed himself to get stuck in those deteriorating circumstances and didn't think about it. Little by little and without realizing it, the heat kept rising, and his life kept spiraling out of control. He had become a victim of his adaptation to harmful situations, silently disconnecting and abandoning his needs, desires, and emotions. It was passive submission and consistent resignation to fear, low self-esteem, and uncertainty. Now, he was cooked, emotionally spent, and spiritually numb.

He'd felt this way before—paralyzed, waiting, afraid to move. Once in second grade, he needed to use the restroom. He raised his hand and patiently waited for permission from his teacher to do what was necessary and inevitable. Kevin sat in agony, waiting and hoping, afraid to move, until finally, it was too late. He wet himself in front of the whole class. The shame never left him. And the worst part? He could've avoided it. He should have listened to his internal voice of reason. He could've saved himself. Kevin suffered while having the power to prevent it all.

He was doing it again—waiting, hoping, enduring—when he should be running.

Today was the last chance for Kevin to save himself, and he had to move quickly now that the house was empty. Maritza was gone too, which suited him fine—the last thing he needed was a repeat of last night's clash with her, especially if it allowed time for others to return home and derail his escape. There was little room in the small car, so he grabbed his clothes and what small personal possessions meant the most to him and filled the space. His last moments at the house were brief and rushed.

Before he left, Kevin grabbed the biggest pot he could find, filled it halfway with cold water, and left it on an unlit stovetop burner. Let them puzzle over it. Kevin doubted any of them would understand his message, but he did, and that was all that mattered.

25

THE RADIO'S LIGHT

Maritza and Kevin spoke only once by phone in the months after he left. There were no apologies, no explanations—nothing to salvage. There was no need for blame and no room for more pain. The divorce was inevitable. She only needed his address for the county sheriff to serve the papers.

Kevin suspected it gave her a sense of control to be the one to file, and that was fine by him. The fact was, he preferred it. She would have to hire an attorney, appear before the judge, and pay the court fees. He had already done all that—endured the shame of filing for bankruptcy the year before, mainly because of her reckless spending and her mother's constant meddling. It was her turn now.

Maritza also needed his address so her father, Diego, could retrieve the car he had co-signed for. Kevin, unemployed and unable to make payments, agreed to release it. Diego planned to sell it back to the dealership, freeing them from the loan's obligation. That seemed fair, and Kevin was grateful. He regretted that two people would have to make the round trip from West Palm to Bayview and back, but he had no plans to return himself. He knew he never would.

The day they arranged the pickup, Kevin left the keys outside and made sure to be gone. He didn't want to see anyone. By the time he returned, the car was gone—and sitting in its place on the carport were a few of his possessions: his yearbook, a few pieces of clothing, and a handful of photos from their short life together. The items were balled up inside his high school graduation gown, its corners tied into a knot, like a red bag of garbage left on the concrete floor by the front door. It was her pot of cold water left for him.

Aunt Alice arranged for Kevin to buy a used car from her dealership's lot. It was a dog of a car—like most American-made models from the mid-seventies—but it ran well and came with payment terms he couldn't refuse. Without Alice's help, he would've had no roof over his head and no money in his pocket. Her timing came near his darkest hour.

Kevin could have returned to his childhood home, as many do after college or hard times, but the optics of that kind of failure were too much. Bert and Carol would have welcomed him without judgment, and they had the space to do it. But what little pride Kevin had left wouldn't allow it.

Despite being aunt and nephew, Alice and Kevin made good roommates. Their differences complemented each other, and unlike marriage—something both had failed at—this arrangement came without expectations or insecurity. Within weeks, they settled into an easy, mutually beneficial rhythm.

Without obligation, Alice left Kevin a little spending money on the dinette table each week—a quiet gesture to help bridge the gap until he could find a job. It covered gas, food, car insurance, and the basics. Just enough to stay afloat.

In return for her generosity, Kevin did minor repairs around the house. He resurfaced the driveway, remodeled parts of the bathroom, cleaned up the yard, and freshened the walls with a new coat of paint. He also took on the tasks Alice avoided—organizing paperwork, sorting the towering stacks of unopened mail, and balancing her checkbook.

Alice was the classic case of the cobbler's children going barefoot. She managed the accounting office at a large car dealership but couldn't bring herself to handle her own mail and bills. Before long, she was handing Kevin her paycheck each week. He paid the utilities, tracked the expenses, and even left her a set allowance for groceries and "mad money."

Kevin couldn't control what he didn't have—but Alice relinquished some control over what she had to him. Whether she intended it or not, she offered him something far more critical than cash: the chance to rebuild his confidence. In her house, at least, he could feel like the man again.

Kevin began job hunting when he returned to Bayview, but there wasn't much to find. Unemployment had been climbing all year, and by December, it peaked near eleven percent—a postwar record. The country was deep in a recession, paralyzed by what economists called stagflation: high inflation, high interest rates, and high unemployment all at once.

It was an apt metaphor for how Kevin felt—stagnant, inflated with worry, and failing to thrive. The irony wasn't lost on him. When stagflation first took hold, he was fresh out of high school and thought he was beating the system. He had a full-time job, a promotion, a girlfriend-turned-wife. He thought he was building something, but he couldn't have been more wrong.

Now, even in the best of times, the end of the year was a slow season for hiring. But these weren't the best of times. The economy had stalled, and so had he.

Thanksgiving and Christmas passed without fanfare. Kevin

spent New Year's Eve alone. Alice was out with friends, and he had no interest in joining the celebration at his parent's house with relatives.

He hadn't reached out to any former coworkers or friends—not because he didn't miss them, but because he didn't know how to explain the last two years. Too much had unraveled. He was still too ashamed to try. Better to wait, he told himself—better to get resettled, regain his footing, maybe find a job—then reconnect. Until then, he didn't have the energy to revisit the past or the will to start anything new. Explaining himself felt like a task he couldn't yet tackle.

By eleven o'clock, Kevin was in bed. The room was dark, lit only by the soft orange glow of the stereo receiver's tuner dial. It was one of the few things he'd packed in the car before leaving—something familiar, something his.

Across the room, the radio played a live broadcast from a local nightclub. Music and laughter drifted through the speakers as if the party were in the room with him. But it wasn't. Except for the radio, the room was dark and silent.

A cold drizzle fell outside, and a dense fog wrapped around the night. Kevin lay on the air mattress in the corner, his sleeping bag pressed against the dampness seeping through the exterior wall. Every few minutes, a bottle rocket shrieked, or a firecracker popped—small, random bursts that reminded him the world was still turning, still celebrating without him.

He had chosen solitude that night, but the choice didn't make it easier. He felt disconnected, sealed off from the noise and joy, tethered to it only by the radio's faint, persistent light.

Tradition said New Year's Eve was a time for reflection—but Kevin had no interest in looking back. As for accomplishments, there were none.

He hadn't made any resolutions either. The thought amused him. Still, people needed goals, or at least the illusion of change. New Year's was when everyone got to forget what they wanted to forget and promise to fix what they couldn't. Reinvention, however fleeting, belonged to anyone willing to write it down. Kevin didn't want midnight to pass without his chance.

He reached for a notebook and pen on the makeshift shelf beside him. Sitting up against the damp wall, he opened it to a blank page and balanced it on his knees.

He stared at the blank page for a long time. The paper glowed faintly in the radio's amber light. He could hear the world outside—under the fog, beneath the moon—and the world inside the dial. Celebrating, laughing, moving forward. Still, Kevin had no resolutions. Not yet. There would be plenty of time tomorrow to focus on the practical. But his hand moved anyway, and the pen began to write:

It's eleven o'clock as I lie on the floor,

alone in my room and behind the locked door.

The radio's light illuminates the dark room,

as I contemplate life inside my sealed tomb.

Kevin thought of Maritza—what had happened a few months ago and everything that had unraveled in the two-and-a-half years since they met. Was she out celebrating tonight? If so, with whom?

He wondered what had gone so wrong between them. Would they have even been together if a thousand small decisions hadn't lined up just so? Of course not. This moment would be very different if any of those thousand events had played out differently.

Did she feel the same quiet shame he carried now? Or had she already rewritten it in her mind, filing it away as a bad mistake she never had to revisit? What promises had she made for the new year? Kevin leaned forward and kept writing:

It's eleven-fifteen, the whole world has fun,

my silent walls ask me what I have done.

Where are my family and my friends now,

I know where I am, but I still wonder how.

Kevin glanced again at the glowing dial. He wondered if he knew anyone in the crowd at the nightclub broadcasting the program. He might've been there any other year—dancing, drinking, shouting the countdown with strangers. But not this year. This year, he was alone.

It's eleven-thirty as the radio plays on,

all that I once loved is now somehow gone.

My loneliness surrounds me like the cold darkness of night,

while the pain in my heart I cannot fight.

Outside, the fireworks had grown louder. The occasional burst gave way to a steady rhythm—crackling flares and bottle rockets whistling through the fog. When they burst, faint flashes of red, green, and yellow shimmered against the dark walls, like the world's joy trying to seep into his room. Kevin kept writing:

It's eleven forty-five as the fireworks are heard,

thoughts seem to flood me, yet I can't speak a word.

What cruel punishment has been inflicted upon me,

while the rest of the world celebrates with such glee.

Midnight struck. Cheers erupted from the radio. Horns blared, bells rang, and voices shouted with delight. The new year had arrived, full of promise for everyone—except him.

Kevin stared at the dial's soft light. He imagined a room packed with people, confetti falling from the ceiling, strangers kissing and hugging as the countdown ended. He still felt the same. With blurred vision, Kevin picked up the pen one last time:

It's twelve o'clock as the magic hour tolls,

from eighty-two to eighty-three, the calendar rolls.

With tears in my eyes, I succumb to the night,

turning off the radio and bidding farewell to its light.

He was a ship that had struck a reef—taking on water below the surface, drifting far from shore on a cold, foggy night. The radio's glow flickered across the room, like a lighthouse barely visible in the distance. Kevin could hear the world on the shoreline, alive and celebrating, while he remained adrift and unseen.

Kevin didn't just mourn the distance as he lay in the dark. He used that solitude to consider whether he should use that distant and dim light to find his way—to navigate what lay ahead.

26

Holiday Spirit

Most people looked forward to holidays, but the next few months were draining for Kevin—quietly exhausting in ways he couldn't have expected.

Soon after moving into Alice's house, Halloween arrived. Each time the doorbell rang, Kevin forced a smile and handed out candy to cheerful little trick-or-treaters.

He remembered the excitement of his childhood costumes: a firefighter, a cowboy, an astronaut, a mummy, a hippy. The streets had been full of kids in plastic masks, guided by parents and flashlight beams. He and his younger sisters would go house to house, bags bulging with candy, and later dump them into piles on the living room floor—trading for their favorites. Candy Corn, Milky Ways, Almond Joys, and powdery Pixy Sticks were worth bargaining for. Kevin gladly traded away any chewy, sticky sweets that clung to his teeth.

He also recalled a house a few doors down where the cranky old man lived. The man sat in his living room watching TV every Halloween with the door open. He was just eight feet from the screen door, in plain sight. And every year, Kevin and his sisters walked up, knocked, and were told to go away. Kevin never understood why the man left his porch light on if he didn't want visitors—or why they kept returning each year. Maybe they hoped, irrationally, that he'd change.

Kevin didn't want to become a newer version of that grouch. So this year, he made the effort. Every time Alice's doorbell rang, Kevin opened it. He acted surprised or scared—whatever the costume called for—and dropped candy into the waiting bags with a cheer he didn't entirely feel.

The following month, Kevin joined his sisters, aunts, uncles, and grandparents for Thanksgiving dinner at his parent's home. In the spirit of the holiday, he expressed gratitude for everything they had done for him over the years. But it was hard to feel thankful for the last two. Too much had unraveled.

There was no easy way to explain the scattered jobs or events of the past two years. The questions were too layered, the answers too exhausting. Discussing why he left West Palm and was back in Bayview was especially difficult. Pressed for time and filled with shame, Kevin kept things vague. He smiled and said he was glad to be home and to see everyone again. That much was true.

Christmas came next—the most commercial and cheerfully phony holiday of them all. It brought the usual pressures: sending cards, making gift lists, shopping in crowded stores to purchase items people didn't ask for, decorating trees, hanging lights, planning dinners, and attending Midnight Mass as a once-a-year gesture toward faith.

It was overwhelming—and nearly impossible without a job or money. Still, Kevin went through the motions. He smiled, expressed regret that he couldn't afford gifts this year, and thanked everyone for theirs.

He knew they meant well. But each time a relative pulled him aside to ask what had happened or if he was okay, something inside him recoiled. The questions reopened wounds he was still trying to heal from.

Christmas was hard. Hard enough to justify his decision to spend New Year's Eve alone.

Too often, it takes a crisis to realize what you still have—and on New Year's Day, Kevin let that truth sink in.

Despite his missteps and failures, he was incredibly privileged and had much to appreciate. His fitness may have slipped over the past few years, but he was still young and healthy. He had experienced no tragic accidents or lasting injuries. His marriage had ended, but it was a blessing they had no children. No one Kevin truly loved had died.

He had failed a few classes, but he was only twenty. College would still be there when he was ready. An ex-father-in-law may have repossessed his car, but a reliable replacement had landed in his lap. The job market was brutal, but it was also cyclical. Opportunities would come back, and Kevin was optimistic he'd find work again.

He withdrew the bankruptcy filing—one of his most embarrassing failures—before it could leave a permanent mark. His credit was damaged, yes, but not destroyed. That, too, could be rebuilt.

It was all a matter of perspective. From where Kevin stood now, he believed he had landed on his feet.

He had spent New Year's Eve alone and despondent, haunted by his failure. But today, literally and figuratively, was a new year. It was time to hope again, move forward, and even tentatively believe he could shape a better reality.

Kevin had just one lingering uncertainty to reconcile.

27

False Start

(1983)

After Alice left for work each morning, Kevin sat at the kitchen table with a cup of coffee and the classifieds spread before him. Most days, he circled job listings with a pen, folded the page neatly, and took it with him to apply in person. Occasionally, the paper just sat there—marked but ignored—as he stared through the glass doors into the backyard, waiting for the motivation to return.

While flipping through the newspaper one morning, a different article caught his eye—a full-column piece on the homosexual lifestyle in Florida's larger cities, namely Fort Lauderdale, Miami, and Bayview. It covered gay hotlines, the counselors who answered the phones, and the people who called in. It even referenced a handful of Bayview's gay bars, primarily tucked in Ybor City or beyond the downtown fringe.

Kevin had noticed the increased frequency of articles reporting on the mysterious virus spreading across the country, mostly among gay men. AIDS, they called it. It was terrifying, uncharted territory. The papers described young men with weakened immune systems and rare cancers—their bodies wasting away. The disease had first surfaced in New York and San Francisco but was now spreading rapidly across the country, creeping closer, case by case.

The coverage made it sound like a death sentence—a punishment, almost—for gay men with multiple partners. That was the phrase used: "promiscuous homosexuals." The papers offered a few caveats, mentioning drug users and hemophiliacs, but the underlying message was clear. It was a gay disease with horrifying symptoms and a very short life expectancy for those diagnosed with it. Shameful. Contagious. Fatal.

Kevin read it with growing dread. It was a frightful time to assess one's sexual orientation and one more reason to be who he was supposed to be—to follow the rules and act the part.

Before this, Kevin had barely read about homosexuality at all. He'd never picked up a gay magazine or watched a gay movie. His only exposure had come in the form of news clips: pride marches filled with men in leather vests or drag queens in rainbow wigs. It all looked theatrical, radical—another world entirely.

What did gay men even do? Where did they live and work? All he knew were the caricatures—the flamboyant, the perverse, the broken. Gays were the ones who couldn't get a girlfriend, who must've been abused, neglected, or lacked something essential.

He'd read about them as a thirteen-year-old in his parent's sex book during those secret hallway readings. That book confirmed everything he thought he knew: that gay men were deviant, desperate, and damaged. It was proof enough that he was not gay.

And yet, Kevin had always appreciated the beauty of the male form—he told himself that it was intellectual, like the Greeks or the Romans. It wasn't attraction. It was appreciation and admiration, self-validating the notion of his artistic sophistication. He reminded himself often that he supported people's rights to express love in whatever way felt true to them. He was open-minded and progressive. All of that was rubbish, of course.

One article struck a different tone. It profiled the people behind a gay hotline—volunteers who took late-night calls from scared, isolated men. Calls from men worried they might be infected, afraid to tell anyone. They were callers looking for someone who wouldn't hang up. The piece didn't mock or sensationalize—it humanized the suffering of AIDS patients. Kevin appreciated the article's portrayal of these gay patients as ordinary people. It also unsettled him.

The article also listed several gay clubs in Bayview, most near Ybor City. Kevin knew the area by name but had never been to that side of town. He didn't even know precisely where the clubs were, just vague coordinates in his mind. The gay disease he read about frightened Kevin, and his Catholic upbringing denounced the lifestyle. Yet something about their mention in the article—their existence acknowledged without judgment—stuck with him.

He folded the paper and sat back, restless.

Kevin didn't know what he was looking for, not exactly. He wasn't even sure he was looking. All he knew was that something in him stirred when he read about those places. It wasn't longing, and it wasn't lust. Perhaps it was curiosity or a sense that part of himself might already be there, waiting to be discovered. Whatever it was, Kevin was both drawn and fearful all at once.

The idea of actually going into one of those clubs felt absurd. Impossible. Kevin had never gone into a bar alone, and certainly not one like that. Before Maritza, he had only walked into bars with friends, and there were none now to ask. Kevin would have to go alone if he went at all, which he had no intention of doing. At least, that's what he told himself.

Kevin left the house a little after ten. The streets felt quieter than usual, heavy with indecision.

Halfway downtown, he stopped for gas and pumped half a tank, just enough to feel safe. He placed a pack of gum and a roll of breath mints on the counter as the attendant rang him up. Kevin avoided eye contact with the clerk as the thought crept in. *Does he know where I'm going?* Of course not. No one knew. That was the point.

Back in the car, Kevin drove slowly, glancing at signs while looking for the names and street numbers from the article. He passed the city's police headquarters, then block after block of liquor stores, shuttered pawn shops, and glowing neon signs of bail bond agencies.

What if I broke down? Who would I call? What was my reason for being in this area on a Tuesday night?

The deeper into the district Kevin drove, the more nervous he became. The area wasn't just unfamiliar—it felt exposed, as if every turn left him vulnerable, the streetlights casting sharp shadows that seemed to scrutinize his every move.

South on Palm. The streets here ran like a grid—avenues east to west, streets north to south. Kevin traced his way block by block, watching the street numbers tick upward.

At the intersection of Palm and Seventh, he hesitated at the light. Right or left?

He turned right, which had always been Kevin's instinct, just like he always chose heads over tails when flipping a coin. He wondered if he were someone else—a girl instead of a boy, a college grad instead of a dropout, wealthy instead of working-class—would he still choose right? Or would he go left? Would he even be here at all?

Kevin drove slowly, letting the car crawl through the dark, unfamiliar streets. The buildings leaned in close—century-old brick and plaster with Spanish and French detailing. Wrought iron balconies sagged over narrow sidewalks like tired shoulders. It reminded him of New Orleans, or at least the postcards he'd seen.

Some storefronts were gutted and vacant, boarded up and plastered with playbills. Others revived into edgy offices or urban art galleries, likely part of a slow neighborhood comeback. Still, the street was mostly empty—just a few figures drifting aimlessly on foot, hunched in jackets, eyes downcast.

Here and there, signs flickered above dim doorways: El Goya, The Eagle, The Carousel. Kevin didn't see anyone going in or out, but the packed street parking told its story. It was proof there was life behind those doors—hidden, throbbing, sealed behind steel and neon.

This must be it, he thought, his pulse quickening.

Kevin circled the block and made a second drive-by, slower this time. Every window, every darkened doorway seemed to watch him. What if someone he knew saw him—a sucker about to be entrapped in a sting operation while cruising the streets looking to score drugs or pick up a prostitute? *This is how it happens*, he thought. *This is how people get caught.* He imagined his father having to come downtown after an accident or robbery, asking, "What the hell were you doing here?"

Kevin's heart pounded as countless combinations of tragic events leading to his discovery filled his head. His palms were slick against the wheel. He wasn't one of them, for Christ's sake, not any of those deviants and perverts described in his parent's sex book. He wasn't like the men on the evening news. He was just a young, regular guy. Just curious. Just driving. Just—

He kept going, past the clubs, past the lights, past the fear. He didn't stop until the roads became familiar again—until the hum of suburban silence embraced him.

Kevin pulled into the driveway and killed the engine. The dashboard light dimmed, and the car fell silent, leaving only the thrum of his pulse and a hollowness in his chest. He'd gone out looking for something but didn't know what—or maybe he did—but the fear that had followed him home was louder than any answer he might have found out there. He felt five again, beaten up by Sandy, the little girl from across the street, running home to escape her torment like it was the only safe place on Earth. He was older now but no braver.

Kevin was no closer to understanding himself—but for the first time, he realized how much he wanted to. One day soon, something would have to give.

28

THE MIDNIGHT SWIM

Kevin knew what the envelope contained when it arrived from the Circuit Court of the Fifteenth Judicial Circuit. The judge had signed the final Judgment of Dissolution of Marriage, and the court had officially recorded it on February 14th. His first marriage had ended formally on Valentine's Day, five days earlier.

The day dedicated to lovers had come and gone like any other—no cards, roses, or dinner plans—just another Monday. And just like that, Kevin was a divorced man. He would never have to speak to Maritza or deal with her family again.

Later that evening, after telling Alice about the signed paperwork, she nestled into her usual corner of the sofa to watch television. After a brief chat, Kevin stepped out for a drive to the causeway. He parked at the water's edge and stared southward toward the Howard Franklin and Gandy bridges, their slow, silvery line of headlights crawling across the Bay.

He and his friends used to fish there at night just a few years earlier. Back then, they'd sit on the bridge looking north, toward the very causeway where Kevin now sat. He was on the opposite side of the bay now, gazing back at where he used to be.

Alone with his thoughts, Kevin realized that was why he went there. The view was a complete reversal. Looking back was easy. Figuring out where he was going was much harder.

On the way home, Kevin stopped to get gas. After paying inside, he lingered in the convenience store, scanning the snack aisle without knowing what he wanted. He wasn't hungry but knew he was craving something.

As his eyes skimmed the racks, he caught a flicker of movement—a head on the other side of the shelf, mirroring his path down the aisle. Kevin focused on the swath of wavy black hair hung lazily over a familiar forehead.

"Daniel?" Kevin asked, the name tumbling out with surprise. "I don't believe it."

After a brief pause, the figure looked up and offered that same lazy, half-cocked smile Kevin remembered so well. "Hey, bud!" he replied in a deep and raspy tone.

Kevin stepped around the endcap, hand extended. *Yep, that's Daniel*, he thought. Just as he remembered—casual and carefree, wearing sandals and a half-buttoned shirt hanging untucked below his waist. His hair looked like he'd just rolled out of bed. Sloppy, maybe, but not unkempt. It was a look, and Daniel wore it well, a nonchalance that never quite faded.

"So, what's new?" Kevin asked, shaking Daniel's hand and patting his shoulder with the other.

Daniel shrugged and shoved both hands into his loose-fitting jeans. "Not much. You know, same old stuff."

"You working? Not in school, right?"

Daniel scoffed. "Hell no. You know how much I loved school. I'm working at my dad's restaurant. Got married, too."

Kevin blinked. "No shit. Married to who?"

"You remember Stacy? I was seeing her a while back. We got married last year. We've got an apartment a few blocks away."

Kevin nodded, though the name didn't ring a bell. She must've come along after Daniel's dad made him quit work for summer school or after Kevin's transfer to Fort Lauderdale.

"Well, congratulations," Kevin said. He wanted to say something else entirely.

Daniel barely graduated high school, was married, worked for his dad, and lived in some Drew Park dump. It didn't add up. Daniel had always struck Kevin as someone who moved through life allergic to structure—careless, untamed energy—more about barefoot afternoons and half-buttoned shirts than rent payments and grocery lists. Still, Kevin wasn't sure if he was feeling judgment or envy. Maybe it was a little of both.

"Thanks, man," Daniel replied, but his face clouded. "She's a bitch, though. Big mistake. We fight all the fucking time. That's why I'm here now. Just taking a breather."

Killing time at a gas station because of a fight at home sounded sad and a little pathetic. And yet, it also sounded familiar.

"Sorry," Kevin said quietly. He could have said more. He could have told Daniel he understood and knew what that felt like. Kevin wanted to be there for Daniel, as Daniel had once been there for him after the pool party when they scrambled to clean the house before Bert and Carol returned from their out-of-town vacation. He wanted to confide, to say me too. But Kevin didn't. He stopped himself—too raw, too soon. His last heart-to-heart with Jimmy still echoed in his mind, leaving a trail of discomfort and raising his defenses.

Instead, Kevin said, "Listen, I was grabbing some chips for a movie night with Alice. You remember her, my aunt? She's the one who stopped by at the pool party and told us to shut it down. I'm staying at her place these days. She's cool. Want to chill with us for a bit?"

Kevin saw the flicker of hesitation in Daniel's expression. But then came the smile, slow and lopsided.

"Sure, why not? Got anything to drink there? Want me to grab some cold brewskies, dude?"

"Yeah, sure, get something for yourself. I'm good." Kevin rolled his eyes at the "dude" speak but felt a warmth he hadn't felt in weeks. He looked forward to catching up with Daniel. He picked out chips while Daniel grabbed a six-pack, and they met in the parking lot.

"It's just a few blocks away," Kevin said. "Not far from my parents' place."

"Yeah, cool. I'll follow," Daniel said, slipping into his car.

As Kevin turned the key in the ignition, he wasn't just driving home with snacks. He was chasing something he hadn't felt in a long time—a connection, maybe, or the chance to feel seen again.

~

Kevin turned the key and stepped into the dim living room, the flicker of the television casting shifting shadows across the walls. Alice was already out cold on the sofa, curled into a fetal position beneath a handmade throw blanket she'd knitted during one of her many hobby phases. She had her hands tucked under her cheek, her mouth slightly open, and she was snoring with the television static. Motioning Daniel to follow, Kevin quietly laid the bag of chips on top of the coffee table and walked into the kitchen.

"She's out for the count," Kevin whispered. "A nuclear bomb couldn't wake her. I swear, the woman sleeps with two alarm clocks and still does not hear them in the morning. I usually go into her bedroom to shake her by her feet while one alarm is ringing and the other is blaring music. Seriously, It's a whole system."

"No kidding," Daniel said, leaning against the kitchen counter. "Guess she wasn't in the mood for a movie after all."

Kevin smiled. "She probably prefers it this way."

"You going to leave her there all night?"

"That's where she sleeps half the time. We can still watch TV if you want. We won't bother her."

"Is she going to snore like that the whole time?"

Kevin grinned and answered, "If we're lucky, it won't get louder."

Daniel winced as Alice caught her breath and let out a louder snort. "Yeah… I'll pass. How's the water out there?"

"Still pretty warm," Kevin said, motioning toward the back patio. "Come feel."

Even in early February, the daytime temperatures lingered in the low eighties, and with no trees to shade the backyard, the pool soaked in sunlight all day. Daniel slid the glass door open and stepped outside. Kevin followed, barefoot now.

"That's the one thing I miss from high school," Daniel said, dipping his hand in the water.

"You want to go in?"

"Hell yeah!" Daniel replied. "Let's get smashed and see who can do the best jack-knife."

Kevin laughed. "Pass on the smashing. And we both know who'd win, swim team boy." He glanced at Daniel's form, noting how his old T-shirt clung to his broad shoulders and lean, tightly built frame. A swimmer's body, even now.

"You're no fun, old man," the nineteen-year-old muttered.

"That's right, dive boy," Kevin replied. "My room's through the kitchen, first door on the right. Swim trunks are on the shelf in the closet. Grab a pair while I get some towels."

As Daniel slipped inside, Kevin's mind flashed back to Jimmy. The lake. That afternoon. The suggestion to swim. The alcohol. The joking turned, suddenly, into something else. No, this wasn't the same. Still, the air held that same quiet hum like something unspoken was about to stir.

Shaking it off, Kevin grabbed a large Tupperware bowl, filled it with ice, and buried Daniel's beer inside. He snagged two towels from the laundry room, dropped them on the patio chair, and peeled off his shoes and tee. The soccer shorts he already had on would do just fine.

The screen door slid open, and Daniel stepped outside barefoot in a black Speedo, tugging at the waistband as he crossed the patio.

Kevin was already sliding into the shallow end, letting the water swallow him up to the neck. "Watch your head," he called out.

Daniel didn't slow down. He sprinted toward the edge and leaped clean over Kevin's head, slicing through the water in a smooth, horizontal dive. When he surfaced, Daniel jolted his head violently to the right, sending streams of water flying from the ends of his wet hair.

"Wow, that feels fantastic!"

"Didn't your mother ever warn you about diving into the shallow end?" Kevin asked.

"My mother warned me about many things," Daniel replied, grinning. "Never listened to any of it. So, where's my beer, dude?"

Kevin twisted off the cap and passed him a bottle. "She probably warned you about drinking and swimming, too."

Daniel shrugged and leaned back, floating on his back as he took a sip, the bottle balanced on his stomach like an otter with a shell. His body glided with ease, muscles taut beneath the surface.

"So, one minute you're creeping around a convenience store," Kevin said, "the next you're in someone's pool drinking beer. You need to check in with the little lady?"

"Hell no," Daniel replied. "She's probably at her mom's house complaining about what a bastard I am. I'm good right here."

Kevin laughed and rolled his eyes. "What possessed you to get married, anyway?" He paused. Maybe Daniel didn't even know he had married, too. That happened after Daniel left the warehouse and Kevin transferred to Fort Lauderdale. It was entirely possible they'd never spoken about it.

"Beats me," Daniel said. "She was the one pushing for it." He cracked open a second beer and, with practiced ease, slipped underwater with the bottle. Kevin remembered that trick— Daniel's signature pool party move. Sit on the bottom of the pool and drink the whole thing underwater, replacing beer with exhaled air, and then release the bottle to float up and break the surface like a missile launched from a submarine.

Kevin leaned against the pool's wall, watching the beer rocket to the surface. Daniel broke the water after it, brushing a slick hand through his wet hair. He said nothing more. Whatever led Daniel to marry, it wasn't his place to ask. Still, his mind raced, wondering if she'd been pregnant, if there had been pressure, or if Daniel didn't know what else to do after high school. He had always hated working in his dad's restaurant. Had he chosen that life?

Kevin caught himself. He was overanalyzing again, projecting his need for control onto Daniel's wandering, impulsive nature.

"Dude, let's see who's got the best dive," Daniel called out from the deep end, grinning.

Kevin smirked. "Let's go. But no head injuries allowed this time."

They splashed, raced, dove, and wrestled like kids in the water for the next hour. Daniel polished off a few beers while Kevin switched to rum and Coke but paced himself. They argued over flip turns and fought for sunken quarters—all the things Kevin enjoyed with Steve in junior high.

By the time they returned to the shallow end, both were out of breath, floating shoulder to shoulder with their heads resting on the bullnose tile, staring at the stars overhead—quiet now, the space between them calm again. Their bodies were weightless in the warm, tranquil water. The stars above them flickered dimly in the haze, soft and distant, like they were underwater, too.

Daniel broke the silence first. "I'm so fucked up." His voice sounded tired, almost apologetic. It carried across the surface between them, suspended like their drifting limbs.

Kevin turned his head. "You shouldn't drink so much, then. Remember what your mother told you."

"Not the beer, man. My life. My life is fucked up."

"Your life isn't fucked up, Daniel." Kevin imagined responding differently by telling his friend how fucked up *his* life was, but he didn't. He felt lightheaded but knew he had not drunk enough to be inebriated. Not even close to drunkenness. "You're still a baby, for Christ's sake," Kevin said instead.

"Yeah, I know," Daniel said, staring at the sky again. "But it's still fucked up."

"So, what's so fucked up about it?"

"Everything," Daniel muttered. "I hate my job. I wish I never got married. I already feel like I'm at a dead end. I'm bored. Trapped. I should've done what you did and gone to college. You don't make mistakes, dude. You're always perfect at everything."

Kevin chuckled while his gut howled with irony, not at the compliment but at its absurdity.

"Oh, I make plenty of mistakes," he said. "I just don't let other people find out about them." Kevin turned to face Daniel as he spoke, holding onto the pool's edge with his left hand. The warm water swirled around him, and he kneeled low enough to bring the waterline up to his jawline while bouncing up and down on his toes on the pool's bottom. Kevin concealed himself beneath the dark water as if cloaking his true self from the world, whatever that true self was. He revealed only enough above the surface to breathe and to speak. Nothing more.

The sight of Daniel in a speedo was not unfamiliar. Kevin had seen it in his parents' pool and at the beach. He had seen Daniel at the school's pool during swim meets. Kevin couldn't recall ever having seen what Daniel looked like without the Speedo, though. He didn't remember Daniel's bulge being that pronounced. Not like it was now. He had never noticed or focused on it before—he was concentrating on it now, however, as it pressed against the wet suit, outlined, hanging to the right, and pointing towards him.

He blinked, catching himself staring, his gaze on Daniel lingering too long. Kevin was relaxed and had let his guard down as those past but familiar feelings, thoughts, and questions retriggered. They flooded back unexpectedly. Panic surged internally in that instant of awareness. Kevin quickly glanced at Daniel's face, relieved to see him still looking toward the night sky. *Thank God*, Kevin thought. He assumed Daniel was oblivious to his momentary loss of control and drew in a deep breath to recenter his focus.

"You know," Kevin said to break the silence, "you can change anything you're unhappy with."

"Yeah, I know," Daniel replied, his voice softer now as if awakened from a deep, peaceful rest. "I just don't know what to change or how. All I know is that life is shitty, buddy."

Kevin raised one leg beneath the water and kicked Daniel's butt gently. "Listen to you. Where's the carefree, happy-go-lucky guy I knew? When did you turn so glum?"

Daniel didn't answer immediately, but a slow grin crept across his face, even with his eyes still closed.

"People make mistakes," Kevin said. "That's what life's about. You live, you learn. Try things. Screw up. Succeed. That's the whole deal." He paused. Was he consoling Daniel or himself? Probably both.

Daniel floated in silence for another few seconds before speaking again. "Hey. Can I tell you something?"

"Yeah, of course."

"If I tell you, you promise not to think I'm a freak?" Daniel's brown eyes were open again, staring upward into the night sky.

"I promise. Besides, I already think you're a freak. What's the big secret?"

Daniel opened his eyes, still looking upward. "Last year, before we got married, one of the waiters at the restaurant came on to me."

Kevin straightened slightly. "Came on to you? As in, propositioned you?"

"Yep. Older guy. Well, not old, just older than me. Like, mid-twenties, maybe. He's not there anymore."

"Well damn, he must be ancient," Kevin teased lightly, trying to keep the tone neutral, even as his curiosity sharpened. "So what happened?"

"Nothing happened," he said, turning to look at Kevin. "I just said 'no thanks,' that's all. I told him I was engaged. I was nervous as hell, too. I thought my heart was going to explode."

"What'd he say?"

"Not much. The dude apologized, and it never came up again."

"No," Kevin said. "I meant, what did he say to proposition you?"

Daniel shrugged. "Oh, yeah. I don't remember exactly."

Kevin suspected he did. You don't forget that kind of thing when it comes out of nowhere. But he let it go. "You tell your dad?"

Daniel barked a laugh. "Hell no! Are you kidding? He'd have shot us both."

Kevin let the silence fall for a moment before asking, "So, why does it bother you now?"

Daniel floated still again, arms stretched out like a cross. "I don't know. I guess—I keep wondering why I didn't get mad. Like, I didn't hit the guy or even get upset. I just got nervous. And the reason I gave was 'I'm engaged.' Why didn't I say because I'm straight?"

The water lapped softly between them, warm but humming with electricity. Kevin's heart thudded beneath the surface.

"So, if you weren't mad, you think maybe you wanted to?"

"No," Daniel said, glancing over at him. "I didn't want to have sex with him."

Kevin heard the emphasis land hard and clear. It was not a blanket 'no,' just not with that guy. Was Daniel trying to say something, or just the beer talking?

They both turned and let their crossed arms support themselves on the pool's edge, resting their chins atop their wrists as their bodies hung relaxed and limp under the water's surface. Closer to one another now, their elbows touched briefly as they both stared through the glass door at the flashing reflection of the television against the dark living room walls. They spoke softly, afraid that someone might overhear their words.

"So," Kevin said slowly. "Have you ever thought about being with another guy?"

"I don't know," Daniel answered. "I mean, I've wondered. You know, not like wanted to, or tried to, or anything. But yeah. I've wondered. You think that's creepy?"

"Of course not," Kevin replied. "I think most people have wondered. It's part of figuring yourself out. Besides, I don't think humans are any different from other species—no one is one hundred percent anything. We all fall somewhere on the sexual spectrum, like with other traits. People who say they haven't thought about it are lying."

Daniel turned his head, grinning smugly. "So you've thought about having sex with a guy?"

Kevin smirked. "Are you trying to entrap me in my own logic?"

"You said everyone, didn't you?"

"Okay, fine," Kevin answered. "If you must know, I've thought about it. Yeah, sure I have." Finally, like Neil Armstrong's first step on the moon in 1960, one small truth from his mouth, one giant leap for his authenticity.

"With anyone in particular?" Daniel pressed.

"No, not really. Just in general."

That was a lie, of course. Over the years, Kevin had secretly thought about it with plenty of guys. It had surfaced first as envy in junior high—envy over the boys who were stronger, better looking, and more popular. That envy sometimes morphed into desire. Sometimes, that desire wasn't about being them; it was about being with them.

He'd imagined what it might feel like to kiss his sophomore lab partner, Adam. He'd wanted to see Ricky naked. When he used to sleep over at Steve's house, he sometimes imagined crawling into the other twin bed and laying next to him, wrapping his arm around Steve's warm body in the dark, spooning him under the covers. Had Kevin sensed any indication that Steve felt the same way or had the same desires, he undoubtedly would have acted upon those urges. Kevin dared not tell Daniel any of this, though.

"Did you ever?" Daniel asked. "I mean, for real?"

Kevin hesitated. "No. But I don't think I'd feel bad or guilty about it if I had."

Another half-lie. Kevin had been with another boy but didn't consider what happened between him and Jimmy as having had sex. But what happened with Jimmy didn't feel like a choice. It didn't feel like sex, but it wasn't abuse, either—at least, not in Kevin's mind. It wasn't even something he wanted to label. It was just one of those things that suddenly and unexpectedly went off-script—horseplay gone too far. Yet somehow, Kevin still felt more responsible than victimized. He shouldn't have brought up skinny-dipping. Kevin shouldn't have teased. He shouldn't have drunk so much. Jimmy would never have initiated intimacy with another guy, so whatever happened was his fault. But guys do that sort of thing. It only lasted a few minutes anyway, so no harm was done, right? Kevin had already put it out of his mind. Until now, that is.

"Why not?" Daniel asked gently.

"Why not, what?" Kevin asked, having momentarily lost track of what they were discussing.

"Why wouldn't you feel bad about it if you had?" Daniel repeated.

Kevin paused again, thinking carefully.

"I guess because I think people should be allowed to do what they want if it doesn't hurt anyone. If two people have feelings for each other, a guy or girl, they should be allowed to express that. Guys are conditioned to be tough and suppress their emotions."

In his worst John Wayne imitation, Daniel grinned and said, "Yepper. That's a big affirmative."

Kevin laughed. "Besides, sex is sex, and sex is supposed to be fun. What's the big deal?"

He didn't believe that entirely. Or rather, he wished he did. He wanted to be the guy who could live that truth and act on desire freely and without fear. But Kevin was too used to being the good boy: the one who didn't cheat on tests, who followed the rules, and who fed the parking meter, even on the weekends. He lived a clean life—a straight-and-narrow boy scout, the responsible first-born son, a safety patrol captain, and a teacher's assistant. And still, his life had fallen apart.

"Yeah," Daniel said, "I guess I can go along with that. So, you think you ever will?"

"Will what?"

"D-U-D-E! Stay on the planet," Daniel replied.

"What, have sex with a guy? I don't know. Sure. Maybe. I don't know." Kevin paused and turned his head away from Daniel, resting it on his crossed forearms again. He gazed into the darkness of the yard's corner, where the pool lights didn't shine. Kevin didn't want Daniel to see his vulnerability.

"If I did, Kevin added, "it would have to be with someone I know, someone I trusted and felt comfortable with. Like I said, if two people have feelings for one another, they should be able to express those feelings physically if that's what they want to do. Don't get me wrong. I'm not sure I could duck into a dark alley or a dirty bathroom stall with a guy I didn't know just to get off. That's a completely different thing."

There was a long pause between them. The water was still warm, but Kevin felt a ripple of cold bloom under his skin, not from the temperature but from how the conversation suddenly shifted.

"So," Daniel said, voice barely above a whisper, "do you have feelings for me?"

Kevin turned his head. "Why, Daniel! Are you propositioning me?" he said in his worst Southern drawl.

"I don't know," Daniel replied. "Do you want to be

propositioned?"

Kevin's heart was racing. He couldn't tell if Daniel was teasing or testing him—or maybe both. Neither one wanted to go first. It was like a silent dare. Say the unsayable, and the spell might break. Or it might not.

Was Daniel baiting him? It was now a dangerous game of cat-and-mouse—the same game Kevin had played with Maritza. Kevin sensed no one wanted to admit anything first or tip their hand too far for fear of being unable to recover their dignity by pretending to have been kidding or teasing.

For a moment, Kevin thought of all the times he'd hesitated. All the chances he'd let pass because he was too afraid of the fallout. He wasn't going to do that again.

"Yes," Kevin said. "I like you. I've always enjoyed your company. I'm glad as hell we ran into one another tonight."

"Thanks," Daniel said with a crooked grin, "but that's not what I asked, is it?"

Kevin inhaled, and this time he didn't dodge it.

"You want me to say it?" he asked. "Fine. Yes. I would have sex with you." He said it plainly. Calmly. Like it was just the truth—because it was. If Daniel was only playing—if this was all some game to test boundaries—then so be it. Kevin had said what he meant. For once, there was no calculus, no escape hatch built into the words. Kevin then upped the ante.

"In fact," he added, feeling the shift inside himself, "I think we should." His tone shifted from carefree to confident. There, he said it. The horse was out of the barn, and Kevin was relieved. Yes, he was now out on a limb and vulnerable, but he was taking control of his desire and taking a chance. Kevin's boldness didn't feel competitive, like his truth-or-dare comparison with Michael or his streaking adventure with Miguel and Keith. His statement felt honest and genuine—as close to touching and tasting authenticity as Kevin had ever been.

Daniel looked at him, not surprised, not shocked, just searching. A subtle smile crept in, disbelieving but not dismissive. "You really want to?" he asked.

"Yeah, why not?" Kevin said. "We're both curious. We're alone. We're friends. I trust you. I feel comfortable with you. And I know this stays between us, right?"

"You can trust me," Daniel said. His smile lingered. "And yeah, why not? I want to."

Kevin dissected the words. *Daniel said 'want.'* Not maybe, not would, not sure. He said he wanted to.

Kevin's anxiety eased with Daniel's admission. What had felt like panic now shifted into something quieter—anticipation. His chest loosened, his breath deepened, and the tunnel vision that had narrowed everything to the reaction on Daniel's face began to fade. They'd both said it now. Both wanted it. And for the first time, neither stood alone on the edge; neither was left at an inescapable disadvantage waiting for the other to decide.

Kevin began to sense his surroundings again. The night air was warm, the water warmer. The pool light glowed softly beneath them, casting luminous shapes on their legs, torsos, and swimsuits. The space between them pulsed with quiet energy.

Kevin stood slowly in the water, gliding toward the edge. "Hold on a second," he said, stepping out of the pool. Water sluiced down his legs and padded across the concrete. Reaching through the sliding glass door, he found the switch and flipped it. The backyard went dark. Only the moonlight remained, soft and silvery, shimmering over the surface.

"There," Kevin said, lowering himself back into the water. "That's better." He swam toward Daniel and stopped just a few feet in front of him. Daniel's back leaned against the pool wall, his feet planted, the water's surface slicing across his chest. Kevin faced him squarely, placing his hands on the pool's edge, one on either side of Daniel. Close, but not touching. It was dark, late, and quiet. Kevin knew they had privacy.

"Don't freak out on me now," Kevin whispered. He froze as soon as he said it, realizing those were Jimmy's words that afternoon at the lake. But this wasn't that. Kevin wasn't taking anything. He was asking—and offering.

Kevin shook the thought and leaned forward.

Daniel didn't move—not away, not toward—until Kevin's lips brushed his. It was soft. Barely anything at all. A whisper of a kiss. Kevin backed away an inch to read Daniel's face. Their lips tasted like pool water—and an intense longing. Daniel smirked and closed his eyes again. He wasn't pulling away.

Kevin leaned in again, and this time, the kiss held. He let his hands drift from the pool wall to Daniel's back, slow and cautious, settling on his hips to draw him closer. The pool no longer held Daniel in place—Kevin did.

Daniel responded, resting his arms on Kevin's shoulders, letting his body float into Kevin's embrace as they sank into the cover of the warm, dark water. Kevin bent his knees beneath the surface, settling into a chair of muscle as Daniel followed— straddling him, wrapping his legs around Kevin's waist as they continued their kiss. Their bodies pressed together, chests touching, arms enclosing. The water surrounded the two boys, rocking them gently as the heat and yearning between them swelled.

"Are we going to do this here?" Daniel asked, his voice

quivering slightly.

Kevin's nerves lit up again. It wasn't fear, exactly, but caution. His legs trembled under the water when they first kissed, and now he felt a chill he shouldn't be feeling in the water's warmth. It was dark, and Kevin knew they were alone, yet he felt uneasy about being out in the open, as exposed as they were, just like he had been with Jimmy at the lake.

"No," Kevin said. "Let's go inside."

The water splashed onto the concrete deck as they lifted themselves out of the water and grabbed towels from the patio chair. Daniel bent to dry his legs, and Kevin's eyes followed—the graceful pull of towel over muscle, the moon catching the curve of his back, the smooth line of his spine. The Speedo clung tight. Daniel gave it a light pat dry, then rubbed the towel over his head to dry the youthful face and messy dark hair.

They wrapped the damp towels around their waists. Kevin opened the sliding glass door and stepped inside, bare feet silent on the tile. Daniel followed him in just as quietly. The television's light flickered across the room, pulsing against the walls like a heartbeat. Alice was still curled on the sofa, fast asleep, her breathing slow and steady beneath the blanket.

Neither of them said a word as Kevin led Daniel toward his bedroom. That was the moment either of them could stop, but neither did. The door softly closed behind them, and Kevin turned the lock.

Daniel hadn't said anything since they left the pool. He stood in the center of the room, back still to Kevin, surveying the space in silence. It was sparse: a makeshift bookcase, a receiver with speakers, a turntable with a few albums, and a sleeping bag stretched out over an air mattress on the floor. Light from the streetlamp spilled through the open blinds, casting faint shadows across the terrazzo floor and walls.

"Well," Daniel said, finally turning, "it's not the Ritz, buddy."

Kevin looked at him, and the breath caught in his throat. The same light that had illuminated Daniel's back now moved across his chest and abdominals, casting sensuous shadows into the firm crevasses that defined his hairless torso—smooth, lean, and cut. His hair was damp and messy, falling into his face. Beads of water still clung to his skin.

Kevin took a slow step forward, wanting to reach out—to touch Daniel's chest and run his fingers across his warmth—but he hesitated. He wasn't sure what came next. The talking had stopped—this was the space between words, where everything felt fragile and unfamiliar.

"It may not be much," Kevin said, gesturing toward the makeshift bed, "but it's comfortable."

Without saying a word, Daniel turned toward the corner of the room. He released his towel and let it drop to the floor. His hands slid down his sides, peeling the black Speedo down his legs in one slow, fluid motion, stepping out of them toward the sleeping bag with unhurried grace.

Kevin stood frozen, watching the curve of Daniel's body as he walked—the play of muscle across his back, the motion of bare legs and buttocks in the low light, the pale skin framed by sharp tan lines.

Kneeling forward, Daniel laid himself flat on his stomach and stretched his arms above him, wrapping them around the pillow to form a ball to tuck under his head. He didn't speak. He didn't move.

Kevin watched him in silence, studying the nude figure lying on his bed. His pulse drummed in his ears, and he could feel the heat rising beneath his skin from desire and awe. This was something he had only imagined, privately and painfully, for years. And now, here it was, real and terrifying in its simplicity.

He didn't know what Daniel was expecting as he watched his friend lay motionless and quiet. Maybe Daniel didn't know either. Kevin thought he might be content to watch him lie there all night, but tonight, he wanted more than simple contentment.

Kevin's heart raced as he took a step forward. He wasn't sure what would happen next, only that it was happening.

Kevin stepped toward the bed and discarded his towel and shorts, letting them fall next to where Daniel's towel and Speedos lay. Following Daniel's path to the sleeping bag, Kevin hovered above his body, supporting his weight with his knees on each side of Daniel's legs and his hands on each side of Daniel's back. He slowly lowered himself without making contact, lightly kissing the back of Daniel's right shoulder, then his left. Kevin moved to the middle of Daniel's back, planting small kisses down his spine, eventually reaching the tan line that separated the sun-soaked back from the baby-white softness of his cheeks. Kevin continued, venturing downward, brushing his lips lightly against the soft flesh below his waist.

He returned to Daniel's shoulders, gently running his tongue up along the same route he had taken downward. As he did, Kevin bent his elbows to lower himself onto Daniel, stopping when his skin lightly brushed the skin of the object of his attention. Kissing Daniel's neck and the backs of his ears, Kevin's body tingled from the contact his chest made against Daniel's back and from his own arousal, now sliding forward and backward, upward and downward in the furrow of Daniel's two muscular cheeks.

The sensation at that very moment—the sensitive skin of Kevin's tip grazing the warm, welcoming divide of Daniel's body—was indescribable. Kevin slid his hands underneath Daniel's arms under the pillow, squeezing his hands. He slowly allowed the full weight of his body to pause and rest motionless atop Daniel's exposed willingness.

"Mmmm. Feels good," Daniel murmured.

They lay together for a few minutes without moving as Kevin cycled through sensations of desire, fear, excitement, and anxiety. He had read books on the art of foreplay and lovemaking. He had practiced each move on the women he had been intimate with, but this was very different. What was happening now was uncharted territory without a guide. They were both guys, and although Kevin had taken the lead thus far, he was unsure what would happen next or who should initiate it. What Kevin had fantasized about for so long was finally happening, and it was simultaneously arousing and frightening.

Holding Daniel's back firmly against his chest, Kevin rolled onto his left side, rolling Daniel with him. Kevin's right hand, next to Daniel's under the pillow, now held Daniel's chest, and the two intertwined their fingers. Kevin slowly explored Daniel's chest with his fingertips as Daniel's hand guided Kevin to where he wanted to be touched. With each circular motion, their hands moved lower and lower across each nipple and every ribcage bone.

Each time Kevin traced the cuts between Daniel's abdominal muscles with his fingertips, he trailed closer and closer to his waistline, where the top of his Speedo had left a low-cut impression around his hips. As Kevin lay behind him and did this, he could feel Daniel's breathing shallow and his heartbeat quickening, hammering against his bare chest.

The experience was raw for both of them, but there was also a tenderness to it, a rhythm Kevin did not want to rush.

Daniel continued to guide Kevin's fingertips lower. As he did, Kevin felt the outer part of his hand and wrist brush against the top of Daniel's rigidness, now moistened with anticipation.

The prolonged buildup was practically unbearable, and Kevin could hear his own heart pounding in his eardrums like the sexual drumbeat of a man about to go mad. His rapid and deep breathing matched Daniel's—it felt like they shared a set of lungs—Kevin's torso and Daniel's back contracting and expanding in unison, meshing as one and running the same race together.

Kevin's senses were becoming overwhelmed, and he could only focus on bits and pieces of the touch, smell, taste, and sounds of what was happening. Exhaling into Daniel's ear, Kevin kissed his neck, and as he inhaled the scent of Daniel's shampoo from his hair, he could taste the sweetness of his skin.

Daniel's panting quickened, and as it did, Kevin felt his hardness press against the back of Daniel's legs and tightened cheek muscles. Kevin couldn't help but make slow rotating and grinding motions against Daniel with his hips. They were involuntary and natural, and each time his hips gyrated, he could hear the faint exhales of Daniel's approval escape his lips.

Daniel finally guided Kevin's fingertips onto his erect cock, and Kevin cradled it in the palm of his hand. Daniel pressed Kevin's hand hard into himself, pulling it closer to his lower abdomen, tightening his grip on their interwoven fingers. Kevin followed Daniel's lead and tightened his grip around him. Daniel was larger than he had appeared as a bulge in the Speedo earlier that evening, now that he was fully aroused and unconstrained.

With Kevin's grip now established, Daniel removed his fingers around Kevin's hand as an act of trust and consent, making his desire and intent known. Kevin hadn't expected it to feel this intimate—more than a kiss—and it surprised him in the best possible way.

Kevin stroked him slowly. His grip was firm but gentle as if handling his own—lightly squeezing the shaft, brushing the head with his thumb on each upward stroke, swirling the fluid there as a natural lubricant. Daniel moaned, and Kevin took it as confirmation of his desire, his permission, and his yearning for Kevin to continue.

Kevin didn't want to stop. He wasn't ready for it to end. But after a few minutes, he let go, allowing Daniel's body to roll back and settle into the warm space Kevin had just vacated. Daniel was now on his back, and Kevin hovered above him again, his weight supported by hands and knees.

This time, he planted soft kisses on Daniel's chest, alternating between lightly licking his nipples and gently sucking on them. Daniel arched his back with each touch, quiet sounds of pleasure slipping from his parted lips. Kevin continued downward, running his tongue along the center of Daniel's chest and stomach, pausing regularly to press exploratory kisses and slow, deliberate licks along the way.

As Kevin floated above his friend, his arousal brushed softly along Daniel's legs, tracing his inner thighs and occasionally grazing his testicles. Each time Kevin neared the engorged length with his mouth, Daniel's back arched with anticipation, his hips rising in quiet urgency, wordlessly inviting him to take it.

But Kevin didn't—not yet. He paused each time instead, bypassing it deliberately, painfully extending the pleasure by kissing Daniel's inner thighs and hips. He wanted Daniel to feel every second of it—to remember this not for speed but for every breath, every inch, every ache of wanting, and the slow burn of being desired without hesitation.

Each time Kevin got close, he could see drops of Daniel's gleaming need drip down to form small, moist pools on his taut lower abdomen. Each time Kevin approached, the strangely intoxicating musk of Daniel's body became more overwhelming and inviting than the last.

Finally, instead of evading it, Kevin surrendered to the desire building between them. He ran his tongue slowly from the base of Daniel's length up to the tip, tracing each side with purpose, his hand steady at the base. Kevin did it repeatedly, letting each pass linger, feeling Daniel tense beneath him. Then, with a breathless pause, Kevin took him into his warm mouth, licking the head of Daniel's cock as he slowly slid his lips over it.

Each time he did, Daniel moaned—soft, broken sounds rising from his throat. With every moan, Kevin took a little more, swallowing him deeper. The taste was subtle, warm, slightly sweet, and unmistakably him. Daniel was long and lean, like the rest of his body—at least seven or eight inches—and while Kevin couldn't take all of him at once, he took what he could, which was most of it. And what he couldn't take, he delighted with his hands and breath.

Kevin understood the pleasure Daniel was experiencing. He had often felt it with Jennifer, Rachael, and most other girls he'd dated. But this felt different. Kevin knew the pleasure of receiving, but now, he was learning the deeper power of giving. It wasn't just about sensation anymore. It was about agency—about choice. For the first time in a long while, Kevin was the one in control.

His rhythm increased, taking in its wholeness more intensely than the last. It seemed Daniel continued to grow harder than he already was—degrees of hardness Kevin didn't think possible. He presumed Daniel responded not just to touch but to the sheer intensity of desire, the thrill of surrender, and the unrelenting pleasure of being consumed by someone else's need—without question or restraint.

Daniel's moans grew louder, his hips trembling with unspoken urgency. Kevin no longer needed to move. He held his head still as Daniel's hips instinctively bucked, driving himself in and out of Kevin's warm mouth. His breathing broke into fragments, scattered and uneven, as his body searched—hungrily, helplessly—for a kind of pleasure it had never known until now.

When Kevin sensed Daniel edging toward the point of no return, he pulled his mouth away. Still, he continued stroking the long, thick shaft with his hand, drawing out the final ascent.

Daniel soared to a shuddering release. His body arched as his breath caught, and then, with a helpless moan, he let go. Thin ribbons of pleasure arced through the air and across his chest, pulsing in waves that seemed to come from somewhere deeper than just his body.

Kevin slowed his hand and let go, watching in quiet awe as Daniel surrendered to it, completely, entirely, without concern. There was something raw about it, something almost beautiful, the way Daniel's body trembled with each wave, his muscles tightening, releasing, again and again.

The first burst landed high across his torso, followed by another, then another—painting his chest, the pillow, and even his hair. One stream reached as far as the wall above his head. Kevin had never seen anything quite like it.

"Fuck," Daniel moaned. "Fuck, fuck, fuck."

Daniel clenched the sheets that covered Kevin's sleeping bag, gripping them tightly in his fists. It took a while before he slowly eased his grip, his fingers uncurling with the aftershocks of release.

It wasn't just about the climax. It was about being there, witnessing it, having caused it. That was the part that made Kevin's breath catch. The trust. The need. The response.

Daniel's body slowly relaxed, his chest rising and falling as he stared at the ceiling. "Damn."

Kevin smiled faintly, unsure whether Daniel's words were shock, approval, or both. "Don't move," he whispered.

Kevin stood, his legs unsteady beneath him, and walked to the bathroom—his erection still engorged with unmet needs of his own. He returned a moment later with a warm, damp washcloth.

Kneeling beside him, Kevin gently cleaned Daniel's chest and stomach, wiping the release from his skin and the sheets with care and without a word.

Then, quietly, Kevin disappeared into the bathroom and tossed the cloth into the corner. When he stepped back into the room, Daniel was already getting dressed.

"I gotta go, man. It's late."

"You can stay if you want," Kevin said. "You don't have to go." He suddenly felt awkward, standing there naked with only his hard-on separating them.

"Thanks, but I really gotta go," Daniel replied, slipping his shirt over his head. He still hadn't made eye contact. Kevin realized that Daniel hadn't made eye contact since dropping his wet towel to the floor and lying face down on the bed.

"Hey, are you okay?" Kevin asked, stepping into Daniel's space and touching his waist.

"Yeah, I'm fine," he said. "It's just late."

"Okay, that's cool," Kevin said as he leaned in for a kiss, but Daniel looked down and turned away as he did.

Daniel walked to the door, unlocked it, and glanced back at Kevin with a tight, almost apologetic smile. "I'll call you later, buddy, okay?"

He slipped into the hall. Alice was still snoring. He turned back one last time and whispered, "See ya."

"See ya," Kevin whispered, watching the door close behind him. He heard the car start and back out of the driveway a moment later.

Kevin stood alone in his bedroom, naked, the damp towels at his feet, the sheets still warm. He was alone again. Naturally.

29

HUMAN NATURE

Kevin hadn't slept. He stared at the ceiling, with the towels still damp on the floor and Daniel's scent lingering on the sheets. The room was quiet, but his thoughts weren't. He could still feel Daniel's body, the press of skin against skin, and the way their breathing had synced for a few electric minutes as if they were sharing one set of lungs. It had finally happened—all of it—and now Daniel was gone.

A week passed, then two. The anticipation of Daniel calling or stopping by eventually dulled into disappointment. Kevin considered swinging by his dad's restaurant but knew better. Whatever happened between them hadn't earned him the right to show up uninvited, looking for someone who might not want to be found.

Still, he thought about Daniel constantly—especially at night, as he lay in the same bed where it happened. He wondered where Daniel was, whether he was still with his wife, whether that night had changed anything. Had Daniel already rewritten it in his mind? Had he filed it away as a drunken mistake or brief curiosity? Kevin knew how easily people did that; he had done it more than once. But this time was different. This time, he hadn't lied about what he wanted. Not to himself.

Kevin also thought about what he didn't say—what he withheld from Daniel in the pool. The classes he dropped, the jobs he lost, and his failed marriage. Kevin didn't talk about how far his life had fallen. He let Daniel believe he was still on the path to success. He could've said, 'Me too.' He could've told the truth. Instead, he let Daniel carry the weight of honesty alone. And maybe, Kevin thought, things would be different now if he hadn't.

At night, when Kevin replayed the hours they spent together— the electricity in the water, the vulnerability in the dark, the way Daniel's voice faltered when he said, 'I want to'—it all came flooding back. But so did the final moments. The part that didn't linger but ran out of the room and disappeared.

'I gotta go, man. It's late.'

'You can stay if you want.'

'Thanks, but I really gotta go.'

No eye contact. Just the quiet shuffle of clothes, a nervous smile, a front door shutting softly behind him.

Kevin had stood there naked, the towels still damp, the room still warm with what had just happened.

Kevin hadn't told Daniel about the past. Still, he'd shown him something else—his present—a piece of himself, unfiltered and unguarded. It wasn't the whole truth, but it was truth enough.

Kevin knew what they shared was real. He knew he wanted Daniel, not just physically, but emotionally. Or maybe he wanted the feeling of wanting someone again and being wanted in return.

And now, in the silence that followed, Kevin was left with that truth—raw and undeniable—another layer of complexity in his already complicated situation.

30

Hello Old Friend

It was a Tuesday, and the nightclub was slow. Kevin hadn't set foot in a bar since coming home four months earlier—he usually just drove past them. Most nights, his aimless drives led to quiet spots overlooking the bay. But tonight, he wanted a drink—and to be around people, even if not with them.

It was a large straight club with three levels, one he had been to once with some of the Darksiders after his eighteenth birthday. Kevin looked down at the dance floor two stories below from the third level's railing. From what he remembered, the dance club was popular with young people on the weekends. It was sparsely attended tonight with music that thumped faintly, like a heartbeat only he could feel.

Kevin thought about Daniel again—their swim, the physical intimacy, Daniel's abrupt leaving, and the emotional aftermath. Alone in the darkness of the nightclub with his drink and the low thump of blurred music in the background, Kevin sat with the truth he couldn't escape.

"Hey!"

The sound was faint, barely loud enough to pull him from his thoughts of Daniel.

"Kevin?"

The second time, he heard it. A voice he hadn't heard in years, familiar enough to disarm him. Kevin turned, the images of Daniel in his mind dissolving like mirages of bliss sometimes do.

It took several seconds for Kevin's eyes to adjust to the tall figure behind him—clean-cut, like a Polo ad, all-American in the most Midwestern way.

"Steve?"

"Hey, buddy," Steve grinned, flashing white teeth and that same broad smile Kevin used to envy during his own brace-faced junior high years. His hair was neat and clean-cut, like a Polo ad—classic and untouched by passing trends.

Kevin reached out to shake his hand, only half registering the moment. They hugged and patted one another on the back, a jointly simultaneous and unconscious signal to end their enthusiastic embrace. Shaking hands, they agreed on the surprise of running into each other in a bar neither frequented, let alone on a weekday night, in the south part of town where neither lived.

"Fancy meeting you here, mate," Kevin said. "What's it been—five, six years?"

"I know. We were just kids with learner's permits!" Steve's laugh had not changed. It was loud and unabashed. Sometimes when he laughed and sucked in the air simultaneously, he made snorting sounds through his nose. It was a confident and fearless laugh.

"What brings you here?"

"Same thing you're here for," Steve replied. "Trying to get drunk and pick up women."

Nothing could have been further from the truth.

"No, seriously," Steve continued. "Just down visiting my mom. Needed some fresh air, you know?"

"Down from where?"

"Oh, Florida State. I have one more semester left. What about you?"

"Wow, Tallahassee," Kevin replied without stopping to answer Steve's question. He was finishing college after what, only three years? "And after graduation?"

"Law school. Maybe Penn State or Northwestern. Maybe stay in Tallahassee. Still deciding. What about you?"

"USF," Kevin replied automatically. It wasn't a lie exactly—just an unfinished truth. He still needed to retake classes, raise his GPA, and find work. USF was a hope, not a plan.

"Nice," Steve said. "So you stayed local?"

"Sort of. I was in South Florida for a bit. Just moved back."

The conversation, once easy, began to wobble. Kevin could feel where it might lead—college, work, relationships. So he steered it backward instead.

"Hey, do you remember when…?" he asked, cycling through old memories: tennis, camping, rockets, comedy records, swimming. Moments that still shimmered with teenage warmth.

Steve remembered some. Others barely rang a bell.

Then came talk of girlfriends—Steve's in Tallahassee, others from high school. It hit Kevin slowly but clearly. They had chosen different paths. Steve had moved away, planned for a future, built toward something. He had a girlfriend but no obligations. He was home visiting because he wanted to.

Kevin had already lived a whole other life—work, marriage,

deceit, unemployment, divorce. He had no idea what came next, what he wanted, or even what he could do. He was back because he had nowhere else to go.

Steve's voice faded into the background. The music merged with memory. Kevin's mind cataloged it all—sex in its many degrees, some Steve might never know. Marriage. Losses. Failures. Longing. His old crush on Steve now felt as distant as the green flash he and Ricky had once waited to see on Daytona Beach—fleeting, untouchable, maybe never there. Kevin didn't want to be Steven James Mason anymore. He couldn't be.

After an hour of small talk and half-hearted laughter, they shook hands again and wished each other luck. They promised to keep in touch, though neither asked for a number.

Steve left the club to become a lawyer.

Kevin left to become himself.

31

DARK WORLDS, WHITE KNIGHTS

Kevin had spent weeks regretting that first failed attempt—driving past the gay bars but never going in. Then he ran into Daniel and learned that old friendships could become something more. Only days ago, after running into Steve, he learned they could also become something much less. Fear, desire, intimacy, expectations, and disappointment—he was starting to understand how strangely inseparable they all were.

By Saturday night, he was ready to try again. This time, however, he did his homework. Kevin called the local gay hotline listed in the newspaper article he'd read and asked for advice on where to go. No leather bars or cowboy hangouts. Nothing dark or seedy. A dance club would be nice—a clean, friendly place with young, regular guys like him. He preferred a place in a decent area, not downtown, and nowhere near where he lived.

The volunteer thanked "Jack" for calling and wished him a pleasant stay while visiting Bayview on his work trip. Kevin's anonymity held, though not convincingly.

He chose Rene's on Kennedy Boulevard. It was in a mixed-use district just outside downtown—half residential, half commercial. The parking lot was well-lit and full of cars. Kevin found a spot up front, far from the street and well away from the darker back lot, which, in his mind, was probably swarming with hookers, muggers, and undercover cops.

As he locked the car door and approached the building, the bass thumped through the concrete walls like a second beating heart. It felt like opposing punches of shock waves—the club's heartbeat and the one in Kevin's chest—would shake him apart. Both were loud, and both were uncontrollable.

Inside, Kevin pressed his back against the first empty section of wall he found, exhaling as he leaned into its comfort and relief set in. He was in. There was no bouncer, no ID check, and no public reading of his name beneath bright entrance lights for everyone to see. He was safe in the dark.

Guys walked past Kevin in both directions. As his eyes adjusted to the darkness, he scanned most of the club's interior from his vantage point against the wall's safety. The room occupied almost half the building with a large bar and tables. Toward the back were pool tables, elevated above the main floor. Through doorways, Kevin glimpsed a stage and dance floor in the next room—the source of the bass that still reverberated through him.

The club was more crowded than he'd expected. Mostly men. A few women. Kevin guessed most were in their twenties or thirties, a few younger—the older ones clustered at the bar.

He found himself in a sort of hallway with only one wall. Guys stood like sentries along it, backs pressed flat. Everyone watched everyone else: rapid glances, half-smiles, sidelong looks. The scanning efficiency was remarkable, with assessments made in fractions of seconds. Sometimes, a wall guardian pulled a streamer aside. Sometimes, streamers stopped and blocked the flow. It was a complicated dance in a beehive of activity between queens and drones and workers following their own naturally programmed tasks within the larger community with purpose.

After ten minutes, Kevin peeled himself off the wall and made for the bar. He needed something to hold, so he bought a beer and wandered toward the music. The dance floor pulsed with colored lights that strobed against the bodies of men dancing together. Some kissed. Kevin lingered at the perimeter, slowly acclimating to an entirely new world.

It struck him how normal everyone looked. No drag queens. No leather chaps. No protests. It was just a crowd of people having fun—a loud bar full of men.

"Want to dance?" The voice came from behind, close and clear above the music. Kevin startled, then straightened.

"Oh—no thanks," he said automatically before seeing who had spoken. The man was about Kevin's age, maybe a few years older, with dark hair and a mustache.

"Sorry," the stranger said, smiling gently. "Didn't mean to startle you." He touched Kevin's bicep lightly.

"Oh, no, that's fine. I mean, you didn't."

"So, no dance then?" the stranger asked, still smiling, gesturing toward the dance floor. Kevin thought about what Daniel had said in the pool about the older waiter who made a pass at him at his father's restaurant.

"I just got here," Kevin said. "Taking it all in."

"Maybe later," the man replied and walked off.

Kevin watched him disappear into the crowd, unsure why his nerves had spiked again. The man had been polite—just asking to dance. Still, as soon as he left, Kevin retreated to the first room and ordered a vodka tonic.

Perched on a barstool, Kevin sipped the cocktail. He studied his surroundings, waiting for the adrenaline to ease. Like any other busy bar, the room was heavy with a blend of smoke and liquor. The thumping bass of the dance music and the sound of a hundred different conversations saturated the crowd.

Some guys were attractive despite their aloofness, and he wondered what drove these handsome men to be gay. They could have their pick of beautiful women if they wanted. Maybe some of them did and came here after dropping their girlfriends off at home for the night. How perfectly deceptive that might be for them, taking their girlfriends to a movie or dinner to fulfill the illusion, only to hit a gay bar later in the night to satisfy the secret and persistent desires that lived within them. That was speculation and projection, of course.

Some guys sat around the bar or stood in darker corners, wearing sweatshirts, tennis shoes, and baseball caps. They were casual, drinking beer by holding the bottles by the neck. Some stared at the floor, contemplating their shoelaces while looking shy. *What was their story? Were they ashamed of being here? If so, why come into this club?* Maybe they fought with their girlfriends, boyfriends, or someone else. A conversation with one of these guys was a possibility. Unlike the man who boldly asked Kevin to dance earlier, they seemed harmless. He would reserve that decision for later. Still, as shy as they looked, the first move would have to be from Kevin, which was unlikely.

Other guys looked aggressive. They sported tight tee shirts or tank tops and wore wide black belts as they cruised around the bar or hung out by the restroom in the hallway. Many had their hands on their hips or leaned against the wall with a ready-for-action look. They undoubtedly all knew one another and were there for one thing and one thing only. *Too fast and tough-looking for me*, Kevin thought. Thanks, but no thanks.

Some boys appeared flamboyant, each looking for their stage or spotlight. Most smoked and had too much motion in their wrists and hips as they bounced between conversations with a cigarette in one hand and a cocktail in the other. These guys knew everyone. *It's too feminine for me.* Thanks, but no, again.

A few men looked like they had been there too long or had started too early. Some slumped against the bar or cigarette machine, alone and sometimes conversing with themselves. Others stumbled through the crowd; the focus and quick eye movement necessary to be a successful streamer were gone. No, these guys had passed the point of cruising and were now trying to stay afloat. *No conversations with sloppy drunks for me tonight.* Thanks, but no thanks once again.

Some appeared to be just like Kevin—clean-cut with a lucid and strait-laced presence about themselves. His group was young and normal looking, some attractive but without the snobbish behavior. They looked like the casual sweatshirt types, only dressed better and not as shy. Kevin thought them likely better lovers than the fast and rough types. His mother always told him, 'Still water runs deep.' This group didn't smoke or seem to know everyone in the bar like the flamboyant types. *A pretty good group to be associated with*, he believed. Then he caught himself.

Kevin was doing precisely what he'd come here to undo— judging, projecting, and assigning people to categories based on their appearance, dress, and mannerisms—social typecasting.

Wasn't judgment just a byproduct of naivety and fear?

But fear has a way of sneaking in through the cracks.

Some guys looked his way, trying to make eye contact. Kevin glanced away each time, pretending to be waiting for a friend to return from the bathroom.

He thought he wanted to meet someone—to talk to or maybe see a movie with. Someone to pal around with that could, perhaps, develop into something more. He wanted to meet someone handsome, athletic, and even sexy—someone he might even consider having sex with. But how? The risks were enormous.

It all seemed impossible, given what he read in the newspapers about the new gay disease. What about what had happened with Daniel? That was different. Kevin had known Daniel. He was straight and posed no threat. Sex with a stranger, however, would be something entirely different and a risk much too hazardous to take.

Kevin was most afraid of discovery, though. He was terrified of disappointing his parents and being judged by them. He feared getting rolled during a one-night stand or, worse, being blackmailed for it afterward. Kevin sat and endlessly analyzed the possibilities, churning his inner emotions until his stomach felt like the paper napkin he was nervously rolling and shredding in his hands.

The paranoia grew like an evil green genie released from its bottle, filling the surrounding air in gigantic proportions. Kevin felt every eye in the bar watching him—seeing right through him. They all knew his name and true identity. They all knew this was his first time in a place like this. They all knew he knew nothing about who he was, why he was there, or what he was doing. They understood more about him than he did of himself. They could smell his fear as he basted in his sweat, the walls closing in, and the oxygen leaving the room.

Kevin shoved the exit door open, and the night air hit him like a wall of fresh and spacious comfort. He could breathe again. The pounding of the dance music faded, replaced by the crunch of tiny pebbles of asphalt under his shoes as he made for his car.

"Leaving already?"

The asphalt stones ground beneath his heel as he pivoted. He was Kevin's age, with neatly combed blond hair that shined under the parking lot lights. He wore a white tee under an untucked button-down, jeans, and hiking boots. He had a clean, collegiate look—Gap ad meets small-town farm boy.

"I saw you inside," he said, taking a few steps closer. "Are you sure you're leaving?"

Kevin shrugged before looking into the stranger's blue eyes. "Don't have to," he said, his hands nervously sliding into his pockets as he moved a few small steps closer to the conversation.

"I'm Josh."

Kevin took Josh's extended hand and shook it. "Kevin," he replied.

"No, I'm Josh," Josh repeated with a grin, pointing at himself.

Kevin laughed, easing. "Right. Sorry. I meant, my name's Kevin." It dawned on him Josh was being cute with his response, trying to break the ice and ease Kevin's apprehension.

Josh chuckled at Kevin's response, his honest laugh helping to soothe Kevin's anxiety. "Want to go back inside for a bit, Kevin?"

Kevin wanted to. Josh appeared charming and wholesome— he looked safe. Kevin had a hundred questions—about his story, why he was here, and what he was looking for. Was he gay? Straight? Bi? Curious? Had Josh been here before, or was he a regular? What about this specific place brought him here tonight, and what were the other bars in town like? Kevin was especially curious why Josh followed him out and chose him to stop and talk to. Why was he asking Kevin back in? Was it to chat, dance, or make out like some of the other men were doing?

"Thanks," Kevin said, "but I've had my fill of smoke and noise for one night."

"Yeah, I get it. It's loud. And the smoke's a killer." Josh paused. "How about coffee? There's a 24-hour diner down the street."

The offer was tempting. Kevin could ask Josh all the questions he had for him, and they could sit quietly and chat without crowds of guys watching or bumping into them. They might get to know one another and become friends. An actual connection might even spark between them. Getting coffee in a public place sounded innocent and safe, but it could also be a huge mistake.

Kevin's thoughts ran wild. What if someone saw them, recognizing Kevin sitting at a table chatting flirtatiously with a guy late on a Saturday night? Worse, what if Josh asked about him? Would he be honest and tell Josh he was already divorced—from a woman? That he was unemployed, crashing at his aunt's house, sleeping on the floor in a sleeping bag? A college drop-out? Would he tell Josh about Jimmy? What about Daniel—the boy who left, the one right before him? It all felt messy and pathetic.

Kevin wasn't ready to start something new built on old, unsorted truths—even over coffee with a stranger. Kevin wouldn't do it.

"It's just a cup of coffee," Josh added before Kevin could respond.

Kevin smiled. "I know. And I do love coffee. But I'm going to call it a night. I appreciate the offer, and I hope you're not offended."

Josh smiled and looked straight at Kevin with his bright blue eyes. He stepped closer and extended his right hand, gently placing his left on Kevin's forearm. "I'm not offended at all," he replied, adding, "I understand, and I'm tired myself." His tone was kind, and Kevin knew Josh said that so he wouldn't feel bad or guilty for not taking him up on his offer. "I'm this way," Josh added, still smiling and pointing behind Kevin in the same general direction where Kevin was parked.

The two walked a couple of rows through the parking lot until they came to Kevin's car first. He thought about changing his mind and asking Josh to follow him, just as he had asked Daniel to do when he ran into him at the convenience store. Kevin wanted to, but he didn't. He knew he shouldn't. Instead, Kevin opened his car door and grabbed the ballpoint pen from the center console. Reaching for Josh's hand, he turned Josh's palm upward and wrote his phone number on the underside of Josh's smooth forearm.

"Less likely to smudge than the palm," Kevin said. He was sure he had seen that in a movie once.

Then, without overthinking it, Kevin stepped forward and hugged Josh in an innocent and friendly embrace, one arm across his back and the other at his waist. He held Josh firmly while he whispered, "Call me," through the silky golden hair that cradled the white knight's ear.

Call me. It was the title song in *American Gigolo* at the drive-in as Maritza whispered into Kevin's ears and made his will hers. It was also what Daniel had promised to do after making Kevin's desires his. This time, however, Kevin was whispering the words, doing it without fear and with authenticity.

32

Both Sides Now

Life gave Kevin a do-over, and the rest was ahead of him. The family fabric, torn and frayed, was slowly and naturally mending itself now that Kevin was back. He visited his mother several times a week in the evenings, sometimes with Alice and at other times alone, chatting over freshly brewed coffee and a slice of cake or pie. On other nights, the three met for happy hour at TGI Fridays, where the sisters introduced Kevin to sangria and silly cocktails like Fuzzy Navels and Sex on the Beach.

He was reconnecting with his father, too. Bert used to take his son to a driving range and a nine-hole executive course when he was a boy, but the clubs had collected dust in the closet for over a decade. When Kevin asked to learn the game, Bert didn't hesitate. Before long, Kevin was joining him and his buddies for rounds of golf on Saturday or Sunday mornings. They didn't talk about anything deep—never about feelings or fears. That was reserved for coffee with Carol or drinks with Alice. With Bert, it was yardage, club selection, and the last swing. And maybe that was enough. When it came to who Kevin was—or wasn't—his father couldn't be ashamed of what he didn't know. Still, Kevin sometimes wondered about everything else. He knew his father loved him and assumed their silence was how father-son relationships worked.

Kevin also stayed busy helping Bert build an addition to the house: a new family room full of windows constructed over the patch of yard where the Ear Tree once stood. The project was practical but bittersweet. Kevin missed the tree's massive presence, canopy of shade, and quiet companionship. As they finished the structure, Kevin felt what they were doing on that sacred patch of his boyhood freedom insulted the tree's once-mighty dignity. When Kevin left town, the tree was still standing. When he returned, it was already gone. Kevin understood the logic of the tree's age and why it needed removal. He also appreciated how functional the new room would be. Still, he didn't like it.

The Ear Tree had been Kevin's best friend. As it grew taller, so did he. As it stretched its limbs, so did Kevin. Both had been cut back—one by time, the other by consequence. The Ear Tree, like his childhood, would never return. It was time to let go of hiding in branches too thin or pretending the leaves could shield him from the truth. It was time to grow something new on solid ground. The tree had given its space to something useful. Kevin could, too.

~

Kevin got a call two days after writing his number on Josh's forearm. Their chat was light and promising. Kevin told Josh about recently enrolling in the upcoming summer session. Josh expressed how much he enjoyed meeting Kevin, even if briefly. Kevin explained how he had just moved back to town and was getting resettled. He didn't go into details over the phone. Still, he did mention that someone once told him about a twenty-four-hour diner that was pretty good, suggesting they grab a cup of coffee sometime.

When Josh and Kevin met, they took a booth and talked for five hours—starting with breakfast and staying through lunch. They had much to discuss, and the conversation flowed easily without agenda. It was uncharacteristic for Kevin to be so open, especially with a stranger, yet talking to Josh now seemed effortless.

Kevin told Josh everything: his girlfriends, his marriage, the divorce, the fallout. For once, the words came naturally, without hesitation. Kevin even told him about Jimmy—about the encounter at the pond, the confusion, the self-blame, the shame. That's when Josh stood, walked around the booth, and sat beside him, wrapping an arm around his shoulder.

"It's called assault," Josh said compassionately. "And it wasn't your fault."

Josh shared, too. He'd always known he was gay—never kissed a girl, always dated boys. He'd come out at fourteen; by seventeen, his parents finally believed him. Josh was unapologetic and honest about his sexuality, yet not hardened by the world. He hadn't been in a serious relationship yet. Josh hadn't found someone he trusted enough to try. He was waiting for someone sincere and genuine—something honest and meaningful—and was unwilling to settle for less, even if it meant being alone and sometimes uncomfortable.

Kevin took it all in, moved by how effortlessly the truth flowed between them. Something unfamiliar stirred in him—new, not quite nameable. Not desire. Not yet, love. Something deeper than comfort. Something rooted.

They eventually ordered lunch, not because they were hungry but because they didn't want the conversation to end. Kevin told

Josh about running into Daniel—about the midnight swim, their connection, and the abrupt end that followed. Kevin described the rush of it all, the fear and thrill, the sudden absence—the rejection and disappointment—that left him hollow.

Josh listened. Then, again, he stood and sat beside Kevin.

"That's called living," he said. "And it's nobody's fault."

When they finally left the diner, the day was warm, and the sky was open. They stepped into the sunlight, their secrets shared and stories told, walking side by side into whatever might come next.

33

Love and Happiness

(6 months later)

Garlic sizzled in the pan, Al Green's "Love and Happiness" played in the background, and laughter filled the apartment until a series of firm knocks at the door cut through the music.

"You mind getting that?"

"Yeah, of course," Josh replied.

"Well, hello there, honey," Alice said with pleasant surprise as her outstretched arms reached to hug him. "So you beat me here? Good to see you again."

Josh relieved Alice of the dessert and returned her hug. "Only by a few minutes. Come in, come in. Fresh baked?"

"Fresh from the grocery store, thank you very much!" she quipped. "Where's the kid?"

"I'm here in the kitchen," Kevin called out.

"Well, good, I'm starving. Say, this place is pretty nice."

Kevin chuckled. "Thanks. Better than that last dump I was in."

"Watch it, buster," she shot back. "It was better than sleeping on the street, don't ya think? You landed at my door looking like you were 'rode hard and put away wet!' You're lucky I took you in."

"Well, I suppose that's half true," Kevin replied, focusing on dinner while his two guests chatted beside him.

"Anything we can do to help?" Josh asked, passing behind Kevin to retrieve the chilled bottle from the fridge.

"No, I think we're good, thanks. Just open the wine, please."

"None for me," Alice shouted from the living room. "I'll just have coffee later."

Kevin glanced over as she roamed the room, inspecting his clean, functional furnishings. The apartment was spare but intentional—a calm space Kevin had shaped on his own terms. It didn't carry the traditional feel of his parent's home or the oppressive weight of his former wife and mother-in-law's décor. It was minimalist and honest.

"It's called Scandinavian," he shouted back. "I'm bringing the '60s back."

"Yeah, well, good for you. It looks better than my crap. Maybe I'll come live with you for a while. Smells good. What are we having?"

"Chicken scallopini with mushrooms and oven-roasted asparagus with parmesan," Kevin replied. "And I'm not taking any boarders at the moment, thank you."

"Well, so much for gratitude," Alice huffed, mock-offended. She walked back into the kitchen and looked at Josh. "After all I've done. No appreciation, right?"

Josh shrugged and chuckled. "Well," he replied, "he has been selfish with his time lately—"

"Not selfish," Kevin interjected, "just focused on work and school, that's all."

During dinner, Kevin filled Alice in on how things were going. He liked his job and was relieved to have a steady schedule that allowed time for night classes. He'd passed three CLEP exams for course credit and was enrolled in two evening classes and one full-day Saturday course. He was focused and committed—determined to finish this time.

"It's never too late to reset," he said. "What happened before was just a lesson I don't need to repeat."

"So, Alice asked, raising an eyebrow, "anyone special these days?" She itched for a cigarette but knew better than to light up indoors.

"Of course," Kevin replied, glancing at Josh with a crooked smile before turning back to her. "The two of you are special: my special aunt and my special best friend. Honestly, I don't know where I'd be without the two of you. I mean it."

"I'm just glad you gave me your phone number that night," Josh said.

"And I'm just glad you called before the ink washed off your forearm," Kevin replied.

"Yeah, okay," Alice cut in. "Let's not turn this into a lovefest." "How about you, honey?" she asked Josh.

Josh mirrored Kevin's smirk. "A few possibilities in the works," he said. "We'll see."

"Fuck you both," Alice said as she pushed away from the table. "I'm going outside to smoke before I suffocate from all the bullshit. Put some coffee on, would ya?"

Kevin grinned at Josh, "She's fully pronouncing her cuss words now."

"F'ing jerks," Alice muttered as she walked away, grabbing her cigarettes. Just make my damn coffee."

"No Sweet'n'Low crap," Kevin called out to her.

"Love ya too!"

As Josh cleared the table, Kevin started the coffee and thought about that first night back in Bayview at Alice's house. She'd told him to relax—that he had just made a mistake—that life wasn't perfect. She told him to get over it, to figure himself out, and to move on. Within an hour of arriving, Alice had been right about everything.

He had made mistakes. He should've gone straight to college. He should've stayed the course. He might have made lifelong friends or started his career by now. Instead, he took a shortcut he wasn't ready for. A promotion. A new city. A marriage built on loneliness. But that was the past, and the past was no longer in charge.

Now, Kevin was back in school. He was working, building a space where he could be himself. He was alone—but not lonely.

"Is that coffee done yet?" Alice shouted from the balcony, lighting a second cigarette.

The stainless steel percolator gurgled and hissed on the stovetop. Kevin watched the coffee bubble and swirl inside the glass bulb in the lid. It was the same coffee maker his parents used when he was a kid. The nostalgia was comforting. It had a lifetime of brewed memories, both good and bad. It was original, authentic, and had weathered life's challenges. The liquid popping and swirling inside the bulb was reminiscent of his own turbulent times churning within him. It could be bitter, sweet, or both. He accepted the nuances—he now understood identity was fluid and multifaceted.

When Alice told him to figure it out and move on, he thought she meant his failures or the job. Now he knew better.

"All right, boys!" she called. "Pour that coffee. Let's get this party started!"

The path ahead required patience, introspection, courage, and unyielding hope. Kevin knew it was a journey he needed to take on his own—at least initially. He would grow to love himself first, just like another would grow to love him. And when that time came, with truth and freedom, Kevin would love him back.

END

Thank You!

I appreciate you reading my debut novel and hope you enjoyed the story! You are making a difference in my journey as a writer.

Please consider leaving your honest feedback on Amazon. It helps me and other potential readers. You can still leave reviews on Amazon even if you obtained the book elsewhere. If you are a member of Goodreads, you can leave feedback there too. Reader feedback does wonders for a book, and I genuinely want to hear about your reading experience. Just scan the QR code below to leave a review on Amazon:

Thank You Again!

ACKNOWLEDGMENTS

I want to express my deepest appreciation to my beta readers: **Michael Casisi**, **Nancy Cimino**, **Megan Middleton**, **Juan Delgado**, and **David Singleton**. Thank you for the long hours spent reading those early drafts and your invaluable feedback.

Completing this novel wouldn't have been possible without the support and nurturing of my best friend, **David Singleton**. A lifelong reader, library system administrator, and book collector extraordinaire, David never faltered in his encouragement to continue putting words on the page while enjoying the process.

I am deeply indebted to my partner and husband, **Juan Delgado**, for his expert proofreading and patience as I searched for and debated that exact word to make the sentence perfect.

I cannot begin to express my thanks to **Kristin McTiernan** of The Nonsense-Free Editor for her partnership in guiding me through the editing, production, and publishing processes. Your reviews and critiques helped me make my voice and tone consistent and my story structure sound. You coordinated excellent cover design, file formatting, and publishing services. Your professionalism, friendliness, skills, and experience made the enormous undertaking of getting my story to market possible with limited anxiety and heartache.

LET'S STAY CONNECTED

I have many stories in the works to offer you in the future. Please visit my website for a complete list of past and upcoming works. For exclusive updates and announcements, please use the QR code below to subscribe. Thank You!

https://www.djciccarello.com/

Thank you again for your support!